Doubt Will Come

I0589968

THE LAST
STRANGE KINGS
Book Two

Doubt Will Come

Carla Fraga

Quills & Pixels

The Last Strange Kings, Book Two

Doubt Will Come

Learn more about The Last Strange Kings series and download a full-color map:
laststrangekings.com

Published by Quills and Pixels
Seattle, WA
quillsandpixels.com

ISBN   978-0-9860686-3-8

Copyright © 2017 by Carla Fraga
First Edition

Notice of Rights

All rights reserved. No part of this publication may be reproduced, distributed, or transmitted in any form or by any means, including photocopying, recording, or other electronic or mechanical methods, without the prior written permission of the publisher, except in the case of brief quotations embodied in critical reviews and certain other noncommercial uses permitted by copyright law. For permission requests, email the publisher at publishing@quillsandpixels.com

Copyeditor:	Kyra Freestar, Bridge Creek Editing
Design, map, and layout:	Steve Laskevitch, Quills and Pixels

Per i cugini Steccati

Contents

*A multitude of thanks to my beta readers
Jennifer Laba, Diana Lull and KLH, to
my sounding board SML3, and to the
wonderful copyeditor Kyra Freestar of
Bridge Creek Editing in Seattle.*

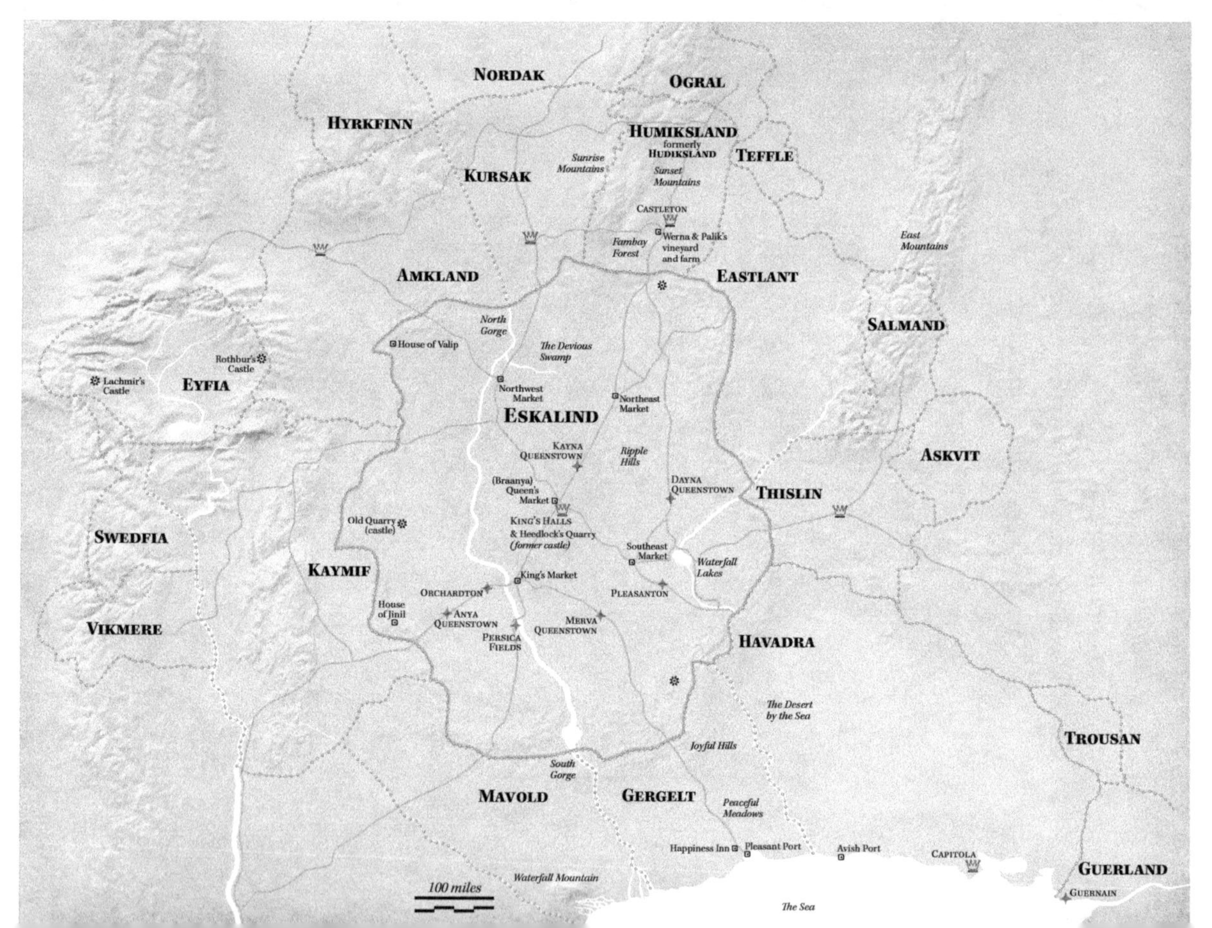

View and download a high-resolution, full-color map at laststrangekings.com

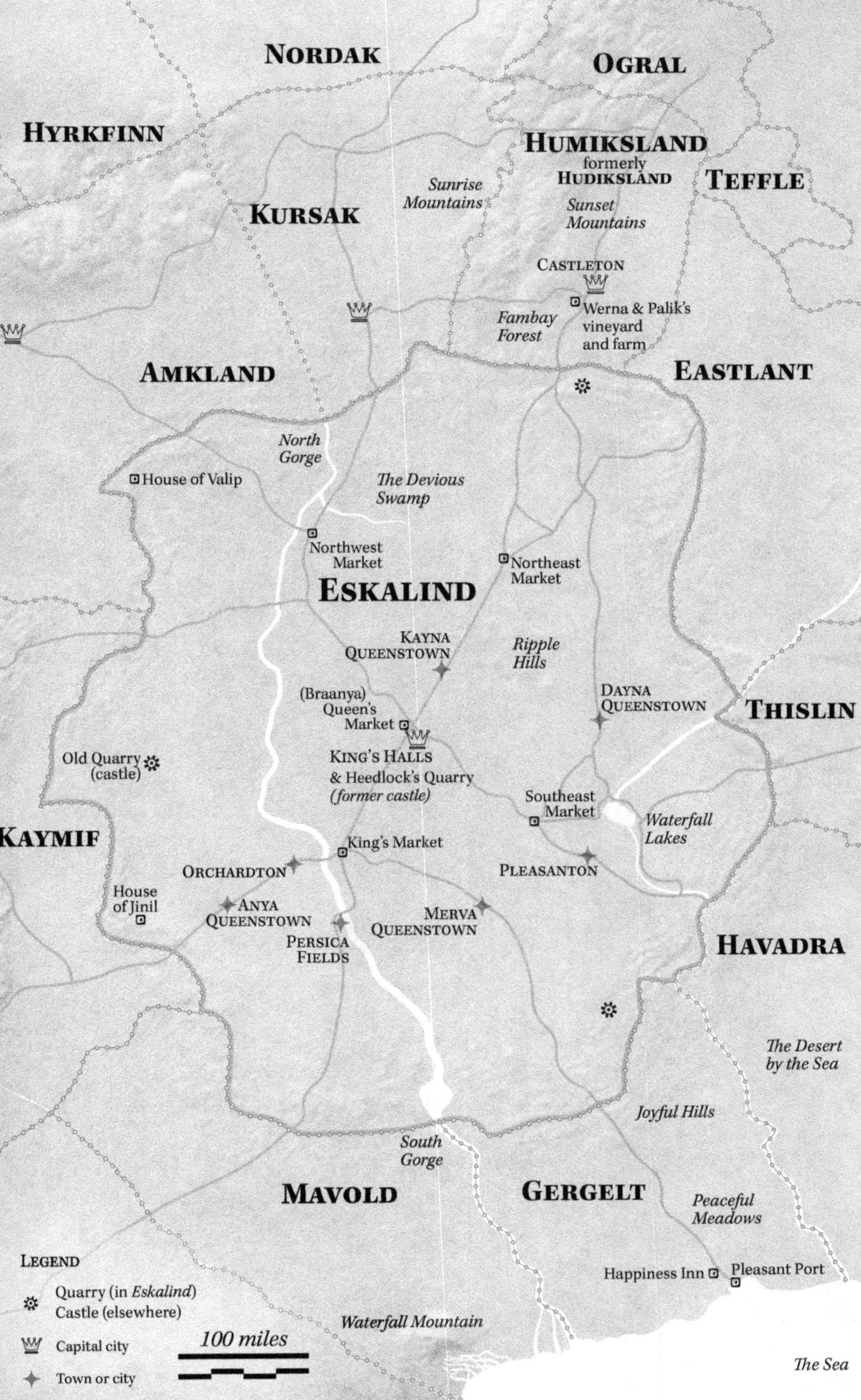

NORDAK
OGRAL
HYRKFINN
HUMIKSLAND
formerly
HUDIKSLAND
TEFFLE
KURSAK
Sunrise
Mountains
Sunset
Mountains
CASTLETON
Werna & Palik's
vineyard
and farm
AMKLAND
Fambay
Forest
EASTLANT
North
Gorge
The Devious
Swamp
House of Valip
Northwest
Market
Northeast
Market
ESKALIND
KAYNA
QUEENSTOWN
Ripple
Hills
DAYNA
QUEENSTOWN
THISLIN
(Braanya)
Queen's
Market
KING'S HALLS
& Heedlock's Quarry
(former castle)
Southeast
Market
Waterfall
Lakes
Old Quarry
(castle)
KAYMIF
King's Market
ORCHARDTON
PLEASANTON
House
of Jinil
ANYA
QUEENSTOWN
MERVA
QUEENSTOWN
HAVADRA
PERSICA
FIELDS
The Desert
by the Sea
Joyful Hills
South
Gorge
MAVOLD
GERGELT
Peaceful
Meadows
LEGEND
Happiness Inn
Pleasant Port
Quarry (in Eskalind)
Castle (elsewhere)
Capital city
100 miles
Town or city
Waterfall Mountain
The Sea

THE LAST STRANGE KINGS
BOOK TWO

Doubt Will Come

There are moments in which one senses that one's world is on the threshold of an irrevocable change.

On his thirteenth Naming Day, as he chewed a crispy wing of roasted chicken, peering through half-closed eyes at the meager portion remaining of his meal, Dalich King's Son had no such awareness.

His thoughts rested on which part of the chicken to devour next and, thinking farther ahead than usual, on whether or not he might be granted a second serving, were he to ask. A quick glance at his mother, sitting alone on the far side of the crimson cloth covered table, revealed the Queen directing her attention to the open book beside her empty bronze plate, rather than monitoring her sole child's progress with his tasty lunch.

Hoping to gain her notice, the Heir of Eskalind sighed hoarsely, but she merely thumbed to the next page, heedless of his needs. At that moment a trio of red-cloaked Apprentice Ambassadors entered through a side door, passing through the Great Hall. Dalich rose slightly in his seat, hoping his closest companion, Saril, might be amongst them. Then he noticed that each bore a scabbarded sword on his waist, marking them as men—a status for which he and Saril must wait at least three more years. In other words, forever.

Sighing again, louder then before, he licked his long fingers and reached for a morsel of meat. Mindful to face his mother and chew with his mouth open, King's Son crunched into his meal.

This was the precise moment The Powers chose to forever alter him, for in his mind he heard a girl's voice, clear as though she sat by his elbow. *"Who are you?"*

Dalich stopped midbite and hastily glanced about. "What?" he mumbled through a mouthful of lunch. His mother shifted in her seat but did not glance in his direction.

"I don't know who you are or why I can hear you," said the voice.

Swallowing, the lad cautiously peeked under the table, discovering nothing but a fork embedded in the wood, which normally would have been quite a discovery but did nothing to aid his search for the source of the voice. "Who are you? Where are you hiding?" he ventured, quietly as he could.

"I'm not hiding, I'm just lying here in the grass looking at the sky, and then I could taste that wonderful chicken, and—oh!"

"What?" King's Son whispered, raising his head to scan his father's Great Hall, certain she hid behind a stout column or thick tapestry.

"Your house is so big!" The surprise in her voice sounded genuine.

"You can see what I see?"

"I . . . I just closed my eyes, and I see long tables and a big woman. Who are you?"

"King's Son."

"Kingson! Your name is strange. My sisters are calling me, I must go."

"Go where? Wait! Who are you?" He did not care that he spoke in a normal tone of voice. But she did not reply.

"Are you talking to me, Dalich?" His mother fixed him with the stern expression that usually meant he was in some sort of trouble.

"No." The lad puzzled at his thoughts, wondering who the girl was, and how it was he could hear but not see her. Not thinking, he wiped his greasy fingers on the stiff bronze threads of the embroidered *D* on his tunic.

"Dalich." The Lady of Eskalind raised an eyebrow, pointedly brushing a linen napkin over her fingers. "Lady Dara labored for weeks embroidering your Naming Day fancy clothes. Please treat her labor with respect." Her pronouncement complete, the Queen rose from the table and, with a swish of her smock, left the room, clutching her book tight to her bosom as though concerned he might touch it with his soiled hands.

The lad slumped forward in his seat, hands upon the table and dark locks sliding across his forehead, curtaining the view of the room. He felt as he had once felt as a young child, confused by his parents' unusual bickering and fearful that they no longer loved each other. He gazed at the metal-threaded embroidery encircling his red cuffs. It sparkled with his parents' interlocking initials—*D* for Dalock King and *M* for Marna Queen—a reminder of their shared reign. A stabbing loneliness shot through him. He leapt to his feet and chased after his mother.

"Mother?"

She turned toward him, the folds of her deep brown smock lit by warm sunlight streaming through the corridor's diamond-paned windows.

"How will I know when I have found my wife?" He tried to hide the worry and embarrassment that crept into his voice.

"You are but thirteen," she said, her tone instantly soft and patient. "Why does this trouble you now?"

"I would have my future settled," he pronounced, his voice tinged with the firm will one would expect of the sole heir of a powerful Lord.

Dalich's mother smiled, perhaps discerning his underlying distress. "Some Kings of the Strange Kingdom had the Gift of foresight, but perhaps it is not your Gift. Tell me, why are you thinking of this?"

"I cannot be certain..." Now that he had begun telling her, he might as well finish. He flicked his fingers on the edge of his belt. There would be no stopping her queries till he began, and the idea formed as he spoke. "A girl came into my thoughts and talked to me, but I am not certain who she is?" He hated that it came out as a question.

Again the Lady of Eskalind raised an eyebrow. "Do you know her name, or where she is from?"

"Um, no." The lad thought a moment, recalling the girl's words. "I think she sounded like a Strange Kingdomer, maybe? And she said 'I'm' instead of 'I am,' so she did not use Noble Speech." He felt a flicker of pride for noticing that.

"I see. Well, that is a strange and unusual Gift, indeed." The Queen gazed steadily at her boy. "Dalich, my son, I know I say this to you often: spend more time in my Library. The whole history of Eskalind, of every Strange King and Queen, is recorded there, especially in the royals' personal chronicles in the cabinet of Trelich King. They are a powerful guide." She leaned toward him with a smile. "You never know what The Powers will show you there."

He groaned. Yet again she had found a way to suggest that scrolls and books would solve all the world's problems. "I thank you, Mother." King's Son spoke as politely as if she were a visiting queen from one of the borderlands. "For the chicken." He turned and left.

———

Marna Queen chose not to acknowledge her son's rudeness. Unlike her husband, who would have called the boy back and delivered a stern lecture on respecting his parents, she found it more effective to let attention-seeking behavior—such as the lad's loud chicken chomping earlier—go unrewarded.

Still, when her son stomped back toward the Great Hall, she felt a bit slighted that he did not heed her advice. "Would that I could have read at his age," she murmured, tracing the pair of bronze closures on the tome she carried. One bore her husband's initial, with delicately carved swords bent to form the *D*. The other shiny clasp was comprised of miniature books, some open, some closed, to create an *M*. "I was more than twice Dalich's years when I learned letters. So much lost time, but I will not waste the remaining decades granted me."

Marna's sole child's odd behavior and questions demanded an immediate conference with her husband. His return from a long diplomatic journey to Eastlant but a day ago meant there were two places he was most likely to be: in her bed, or overseeing his horses. As roasting her son's favorite meal had called her away from her chamber earlier, she made for the stables. Spying Dalock's young Page Bafnil in the main doorway, she bade the boy deposit her book in her quarters.

"Yes, my Lady! Have you come to see the newborn foal?" Bafnil's brown eyes sparkled with the innocent delight of an enraptured nine-year-old. The Page hugged her book to his chest like it was a fond toy.

Marna smiled, pleased to see the lad's joyful enthusiasm. "If the King is with the youngling, then yes."

"He is, my Lady."

Lifting the hem of her smock, she stepped into the airy stables, breathing in the deep scent of horses and fresh straw. She brushed past groomsmen with lovestruck expressions, pleased as new fathers. They pointed her toward the quiet corner where the King stood peering, captivated, into the dim light of the foaling stall.

She moved slowly and quietly to his side. Dalock glanced at her, grinned, and drew her tenderly to his side, placing a firm arm around her shoulders. "Marna, watch," he whispered. Inside the shuttered stall, the determined foal stood on wobbly legs, dark mane still wet and clinging while his mother nudged the chestnut fur of his belly as though she might bolster his stance.

Marna's heart skipped a beat as the wee one wavered on uncertain hooves, but he gained his balance, raised his head high, and stepped toward the royals.

"I named him Haanip; he will be a fine gelding for our son when he earns his sword," murmured Dalock, his voice warm with pride as he massaged her shoulder tenderly.

"A fine old Eskalinder name." Marna reluctantly broke from his embrace. "I too am thinking of Dalich's future," and she drew her husband away, murmuring of King's Son's questions, but omitting his rude behavior.

"A girl has spoken with him in thought?" Dalock smoothed his long brown hair behind his protrusive ears. A year past his fortieth Naming Day, the King's beard was pervaded with gray that contradicted the solid shade of his mane; he would lose ten years were he to shave clean. "Does that mean this girl can read his thoughts?"

"I wish I knew."

"If she could, it would be dangerous, should he reveal a hidden strategem or secret plan to her. Though he is still years from involvement in such matters." A corner of his lopsided mouth turned downward, his forehead wrinkled in thought. "Is she a Strange Kingdomer?"

"Dalich believes so, but was uncertain. He said she did not use Noble Speech."

Her husband's expression softened. "Well, perhaps she is a Bladesmith's daughter, like his mother, aye?" Dalock touched her cheek with his fingertips.

Marna laughed lightly but continued speaking in a serious vein, leaning closer to him. "Perhaps, but we know very little at this time. Let us be cautious in our speech near him, and hope The Powers will reveal more soon."

The King nodded slightly, his brown eyes narrowed as though he assessed a foe. His voice was tinged with a gruff tone. "I hope They do not let this girl distract him at any inopportune time." Marna shook her head, wanting him to spell out what he was thinking.

"I mean if he were in battle."

Her thoughts froze at this mention of a mother's worst fear. Despite all her husband's past reassurances that as King's Son without an heir, their child was protected by The Powers from harm, a cold fear seized her shoulders and breath.

Perhaps he sensed her concern, for her husband changed his tack and ran his beloved warm fingers down her arms, gathering her hands in his. "Marna, I cannot recall any King or Queen of Eskalind with such a Gift. Can you?"

She swallowed hard but answered steadily. "No, but I suggested he study the histories in our Library to see what he might learn."

"You and your books!" Dalock said with a gentle laugh. "If I were a jealous man I would be envious of your love for them." He brought their clasped hands to his broad chest, their eyes level with one another.

"But you are pleased with my progress," she teased, leaning against him, glad for the press of his weight against her after his months-long absence.

"In the first two years we were joined, you learned to read and developed a new way to bind parchment." He lifted a stray hair away from her nose. "Marna, my Queen, I have never been anything but delighted with you."

"Bound books are much easier to store and use than scrolls. I still cannot believe no one before me thought to thread loose parchment pages together."

"You are a remarkable woman, Marna: organizing my once chaotic Library, founding the Scriptorium…" She enjoyed his praise, but fifteen years of being joined to Dalock King had taught her that a request usually followed such a lengthy compliment. "I would not have my Marna any other way," he said. "Well, I might change one thing." He glanced quickly at her chest.

"Oh?"

"These smocks you wear. I enjoy seeing more of you, and your shape. Why do you hide it?" The King's hands drifted to her waist.

"Would you have me ruin fine clothing with ink? You know I am clumsy with my quill. Besides, I have no taste for rich cloth, unless it is to bind books." The Queen hoped the firm smile on her lips conveyed that they were finished with that topic. "Dalock, I say we wait and see if this girl comes into our son's thoughts again. The Outer Peace holds steady for now; Dalich is but thirteen. Let us be cautious of our speech in his presence, observe him closely, and hope we learn more about this girl before he earns his sword."

"Very well." His eyes glinted mischievously. "Just one more request."

Dalock reached for her hand, lightly kissing her ink-stained digits. "Marna Queen," he whispered, brown eyebrows raised in a mock plea, "do not wear smocks to our bed."

She laughed. "As you wish," she said, tilting her head, her gray eyes sparkling.

———

Peering around one of the smooth marble columns that lined the Scriptorium, Dalich hoped his mother would not catch him spying. She sat at her broad desk as a trio of red-cloaked Apprentice Scriptors approached her. His cousin Palika, a Scriptor, led the group. The four stood with their backs to him; one of the Apprentices fidgeted under her cloak, sending cascading ripples through the fabric.

Palika walked to her Lady's side carrying a stack of three books, which she passed to the Queen, who motioned the Apprentices to stop before her desk and await her pronouncements. Convinced that he witnessed the beginning of a lengthy meeting, King's Son dashed away to visit the Library without his mother's eyes upon him.

What he did not consider was that the Queen enjoyed the confidence of the Librarians, their numerous Apprentices, and most of the patrons of the Library. Thus, when Dalich approached the towering cabinet that housed the confidential chronicles of the Kings and their Queens, several pairs of eyes followed his progress. Amongst them, a visiting scholar from Mavold, his shoulders draped in the tightly woven linen fabric of his homeland. Near the Mavoldian, a scroll merchant from Ghemif lifted her eyes from the ancient texts before her—texts that in her lands a woman would never have been allowed to touch—to watch King's Son as well. Lastly among the intent observers, blond Favik, Eskalind's most recently returned Ambassador to Havadra, home for the first time in two years, sat in a comfortable upholstered chair holding a recently acquired scroll of love poems in his thick hands. Out of long habit of following his Lady's interests, he made it his business to study and note King's Son's movements, whilst the others did so on specific instructions from Marna Queen.

Dalich quietly detached the lock with his bare hands, oblivious to the people around him who seemingly gave their full attention to the books or scrolls before their faces. Reaching into the cabinet, he hastily grabbed several scrolls, stuffing them into an empty reading basket by his feet. Around him, a silent inventory was kept: orange and green from the years of Palock, 116th King; black-and-gold scrolls from the reign of Farlock King, grandfather to Dalich; faded blue and red from the time of Salich, 107th King, over 500 years ago.

The Queen would receive a full report, while her men and women inwardly thrilled at witnessing a legend come to life: a member of the house of the Strange Kings unlocking the cabinet of Trelich King, which housed the secret scrolls of the Kings, and their Queens, of Eskalind. For the lock would unlatch only for the descendants of Trelich and their wives, and each of the watchers carried a guilty secret: attempting to separate the lock from its latch when they thought no one watched. Generations of visitors to the King's Library had tugged, pried, coaxed, and cursed the conjoined steel leaves that formed the lock. For none of them had it separated, save for one girl, later known as Bravna Queen.

For Dalich, the lock held no allure. It opened for him. It always had; it always would. That was all he needed. He was thirteen, and that was all he cared to know.

Later, in the solitary, cloistered confines of his own quarters, the boy read the hidden chronicles of the Kings, these secret volumes reserved for the King's immediate family. King's Son relived the lives of his ancestors in his imagination. He pictured the battles, both small and great, fought by his forefathers against alliance breakers and armies invading the borderland nations. But this time Dalich found himself most drawn to the tales of how each King found his wife. He wondered what his own tale would be like, and half longed to be an old man who knew the course of his days and had solved their mysteries.

"Dearest Favik!" Marna Queen rose from her desk, beaming at the blond-bearded man, her arms open and beckoning. "You are returned."

"My Lady." He smiled and bowed, lowering the letter sack over his arm to the floor of her chamber and leaving it behind as he stepped forward. She met him midway across the crimson carpets, in a firm and lasting embrace.

"Thank The Powers you are safe! Let me see my former Page, all grown up." She squeezed him harder. "I can scarcely believe it, our youngest ever Ambassador to Havadra. Only twenty-three." They released each other and she gazed at him, gray eyes light and euphoric. "You appear unscarred."

He wished that were true, but did not want to share the tale with her. Too much was at risk. Instead he smiled, replying, "Well, the sojourn in Mavold after Havadra was a welcome break. But truly, my Lady, my training served me well."

"Oh, you flatter me. Was that something you learned in Havadra? Ha! Come sit with me by the window and tell me all." He retrieved the letter sack, and the Queen lightly guided him by the elbow to the red cushions, their coppery threads glimmering in the sunlight. Just as the pair sat, the door that adjoined the royals' private chambers opened. The King stepped into the room.

Favik rose, bowing, as his Lady said, "Dalock, look! Favik is freshly returned from his postings."

"I see." The Lord of Eskalind entered the room, long locks wet and tied behind his head, a few fresh silver strands glistening at the temple that had not been there when Favik last saw his Lord, two years ago. Dalock King paced past the fireplace to stand before them. "Yet I wonder why you were delayed?"

Favik raised his head. "My Lord, my apologies that I did not present myself immediately upon my return. Your Guardsmen told me you were with the Queen in private quarters, so I detoured to the Library. When I came back to inquire, the Hall Guard told me my Lady was available, while you were indisposed."

"Yes, my husband, it seems you recently had a much-needed bath," the Queen noted, a teasing lightness in her voice.

Dalock King reached for her vacant desk seat and with little effort lifted and rotated the heavy chair to sit facing them, arms crossed across his broad chest. "I was inquiring about why you delayed in *transferring* the Ambassadorship in Havadra. My order for Ambassador Kinakil to assume your position in Havadra, and the orders for you to journey to the Mavold and temporarily relieve Ambassador Savsa were sent in the Ninth Month. That was eight months ago."

"Eight months? My Lord, I received the transfer order six months ago, in Eleventh Month, from the very hands of the Havadran general Yirlofts." As he spoke, Favik reached for his letter sack. "I suspect the general knew the content of your letter prior to giving it to me. His departing words to me were 'Thank you for your service.'" He searched for the missal. "I also wondered at the odd size of the parchment." Finding the sought-after message, he passed it to his Lord. "Though I suspect we will come to the same conclusion."

Favik returned to the Queen, who motioned for him to sit as the

King flipped the letter open.

"Gah, the top of the page, where I wrote the date, has been cut off. The Powers curse the Havadrans, interfering with my correspondence!" Dalock King glanced at the cleanly cloven seal on the envelope, then easily peeled it off. He shook his head. "We must use more-brittle wax." His brown eyes darted to his wife. "Marna, what do you think they are playing at? Why delay my Ambassador's departure from Havadra?"

The Queen placed a hand on Favik's arm. "Can you think of a reason they would want to keep you there?"

He hoped he gave nothing away as he said, "None that I can imagine, my Lady." Favik pondered. "Perhaps they thought I enjoyed myself too much there." He smiled ruefully, but both royals watched him keenly, and he opened his palms to them both, shaking his head. "My Lord, the Havadrans are a fascinating people. Nothing is as it appears there. A man who impresses kindness upon another is looked upon with suspicion, enemies are secretly allied, watchful eyes and ears are everywhere, mouths are as full of rumor as they are of teeth. I observed much while I was there." The young man gazed at his Queen, his protectress. "I am thankful to be an Eskalinder"—and he shifted focus to the King—"in service to the Lord of Eskalind."

Dalock King leaned back slightly. His chair creaked. "Good. Your next posting will be as far from Havadra as one can get and still be in a border kingdom."

Every ounce of his Ambassador's training was summoned to keep his breath steady—he would be unable to see Melande anytime soon. His Lady inclined slightly toward him.

"Favik, when Dalock drew the tiles, Amkland was drawn as your next Ambassadorship. A much more pleasant posting. Are you pleased?"

"His pleasure has nothing to do with it; it is the Will of The Powers." The King stood, and Favik rose quickly in deference. "I have other business to attend to. Now tell my Queen as much as her schedule allows, and I want a quilled report delivered to me by this time tomorrow. Tell us everything you could not say in your correspondences from Mavold or Havadra. Leave nothing out. In either report." He nodded to his wife and departed.

The Queen's shoulders rose as though she might sigh, but instead she spoke. "Do sit again, and remind me why Dalock sent you directly to Mavold after Havadra?"

He lowered himself onto the window seat by her side. "Our Ambassador Savsa was with child."

"Ah, I recall. The babe came very late. Unusual for a second child. But you fulfilled her role prior to the birth."

"Yes, and as soon as Ambassador Savsa was full recovered, I returned home. Per my Lord's instructions."

His Lady had placed both her hands by her side. "Mavold. One of the few borderlands that accept women as ambassadors. Well, you must be hungry, dear Favik. I will call for bread and sauces, if you like."

"Thank you, my Lady, that would be most pleasurable."

At this she smiled, raising an arm to yank the bellpull. The polished red beads forming the cord glittered in stark contrast to the dull linen of her smock. "Then we will talk of Havadra, and you will tell me what I should not mention to my husband." She shook her head. "Ah, Dalock."

Someone rapped at the door. "My, that was quick." Marna Queen raised her voice. "Come in."

A fat-cheeked Page that Favik did not recognize entered. "Lady Dara here to see you, my Lady. She waits at the bottom of the stairs."

"Dara? Oh, she wants to discuss my clothing for my Naming Day next month. By The Powers, so much fuss and foolishness for one feast. Avnil, tell her there is no need to come up. I wish to wear the same skirt from last year, if she can provide it with more of her lovely embroidery and embellishments. Perhaps more book designs." She winked at Favik. "That will soften the blow." Turning back to her Page, she continued, "Then fetch bread and sauces, and tea, for myself and Ambassador Favik."

"Yes, my Lady." The lad dipped his head and departed.

Favik grinned. "My Lady, Lady Dara will be crushed to not design an entire new gown."

"No doubt. Dara means well, and a Queen is expected to dress the part on formal occasions." She smoothed her brown smock. "When I was a young girl in our home county, I thought royals could wear and do as they wished. Ha!" His Lady laughed lightly. "Well, we are making progress in that area." Her voice lowered. "Slow but steady. Someday, I will speak with Dalock about it."

The young Ambassador nodded, silent and patient as his diplomatic training had taught: *Allow others to speak and reveal.* But the Lady of Eskalind did not continue her thought, instead asking, "Have you seen my son since you arrived?"

"Indeed, while I waited in the Library. He has grown!" It surprised him to hear the warmth in his own voice. The Ambassador paused a quick moment, then dropped his tone to a confidential one, like a gossip imparting a delicious tidbit of information. "My Lady, I must tell you, I saw King's Son open the Cabinet of Trelich King."

"Truly?" Her face lit with pleasure. "That is good news. Tell me all of it." Favik told the tale, listing the names of the Kings whose scrolls the boy had retrieved. Marna Queen said nothing until he finished.

"I thank you for telling me. Now, about your time in Havadra. Do you really think poor Ambassador Hornil's death was not suspicious? I begged Dalock to recall you when we received your letter. I felt certain you were in danger." She glanced away, eyes moist.

"Only The Powers know for certain, my Lady, but Hornil complained of fatigue for several days prior to his death, and slept a great deal until the day he no longer woke." Favik exhaled, the memory hard upon him of finding his superior's unresponsive form in the veil-draped bed. The same bed that he would later sleep upon as newly promoted Ambassador to Havadra. Though after a few nights, he had reverted to his Apprentice quarters, unable to shake the memory. "I spent his last wakeful hours with him. He complained of no pain or ailment, save exhaustion."

"Hornil was a good man. Perhaps his heart failed him," she mused. "I guess we will never know." Her mien hardened, and he felt a young lad again under her gray-gazed scrutiny. "Still, crisis proves the man, and thus the young Apprentice Ambassador stepped into his role. Tell me what it was like."

"An ever-changing cast of nobles vying for the throne—one would think they were traveling players with a hard case of attrition. The general, Yirlofts, is still the true strength behind their king. Kings. Three rulers in my two years there, and always a clatter of men springing forth to fill the throne."

A knock announced the return of Page Avnil, who entered carrying a bronze tray laden with sliced breads and a rainbow of sauces. Leaving it on a low table nearby, the lad exited quietly.

The Queen offered bread to her man, who pinched a thick, nutty slice. "They do not make bread this hearty in Havadra." Favik dunked it into a green sauce laden with flecks of spices. The herbs coating the bread exuded a familiar scent of rosemary and mint as he brought it to his mouth.

"Perhaps that is why the Havadrans all scheme to be king, so that they might obtain satisfying, nourishing food."

"My Lady, should we send Eskalinder cooks there, and end Havadrans' grand ambitions once and for all?" The pair laughed.

The Queen wiped a bit of sauce from her chin. "What are your immediate plans, Favik?"

"Quill my report for the King." He shut his eyes and leaned back against the cushions hard enough for them to lose air in an exasperated puff.

"What is it?"

"I cannot believe myself! There was a letter I was to give the King."

He opened his eyes and sat up. She raised an eyebrow as he reached into his letter sack. "The day before I received my Lord's missive recalling me, this letter came. As you can see, it is impersonally addressed to the Ambassador of Eskalind to Havadra." He brought forth the blue parchment envelope, handing it to his Lady.

"Parchment, even." She studied the waxy red fragments of the two broken seals. "I cannot discern the symbols."

"Inside, there are more seals, unbroken, with identical insignia."

Lifting open the parchment folds, she found the smaller inner envelope and examined the intact seals. "*A* and *S* for Acta Sua, the head of a noble house. So this was sent by a Strange Kingdomer. And *N* for—I do not know. Red seals and blue parchment, that could be houses founded under the Kings Saanlich, Maaylich, or—" Her lips tightened over her teeth. "Ah. The House of Adril, Narlock King's Friend. The Acta Sua is Lady Nalya." Her voice tightened at the end of the lady's name. "By The Powers, why is Nalya sending you a letter in Havadra?"

"A letter for the Havadran ambassador to deliver to the King."

"Why quill Dalock in such a roundabout manner? Why even quill him at all?" She flipped the envelope around. "Deliver unopened to the King of Eskalind," she read. Marna Queen dropped her hand to her lap. "This is most odd. No one but Nalya's Steward has heard anything from her since she went abroad, right after you and I arrived in Eskalind. That was over fifteen years ago. Do you know her tale?"

He recalled a bit, but wanted to hear the tale in her own words. He shook his head.

"Lady Nalya attended me just prior to my joining with Dalock, remember? Then she went journeying in the borderlands."

"Oh yes, I recall her. The blond Lady. Very nice figure and very poor demeanor. She wore a large hat."

"Yes, that one. After she departed, her estate paid no tributes for a year. Dalock sent a Records Keeper to investigate." His Lady leaned deeper into her crimson cushions. "Her Steward claimed she had demanded all her funds sent to finance her journeying. Her estate was a wreck—the people and livestock running out of food, their harvest poorly managed—and she had ordered all the laid-away stores sold for coin." Her eyebrows rose slightly. "Dalock was furious. He threatened to rescind her title and estate if she did not set aside a portion of the land's income for the care of its people and property. Nalya was using all the funds to live grandly in the borderlands."

"What of Lady Nalya's family? Surely they must have tried to stop her draining all their assets, even if she is head of the house."

"She is her house, the last of it. Nalya was the only child of her generation, and she joined young, without a babe in her belly. Her husband died before they had issue. As one schooled in Eskalind, you know it is against the ways of this land for one to re-join." The Queen shook her head. "I think it a foolish custom, but Dalock will never hear me breathe that thought. Nalya was a young woman at the time; perhaps a new husband and the children that may have followed might have soothed her loss, and saved us much trouble." His Lady laid the letter by her side and grasped a slice of bread. "In the end, Nalya signed the documents allowing the portioning, and that was the last word from her, until this."

"I wonder why she seeks contact now."

The Queen sponged her bread deeply into a shallow sauce bowl and held it dripping over the bronze rim. Her Ambassador could tell her mind had moved forward to other thoughts, and to bide the time, he reached for more bread.

"Favik, tell me more about Havadra. Was it odd to be there, in a land where they hide their women?"

In the midst of lowering bread into an aromatic brown sauce, his hand froze for the briefest of moments. Then the Ambassador immersed the bread deeper into the bowl to soak up more of the unfamiliar sauce, to make it appear his pausing was purposeful. "Odd indeed. It seemed as if the whole of Havadran society was at the ready to form a sword-earning circle, never a woman to be seen. Even the markets were devoid of feminine forms, buyers or sellers." He hoped he sounded normal. He looked at the Queen, trying to replace the rising image of Melande in his mind, her wavy blond hair cascading to her bare shoulders. Clearing his throat, he continued, his demeanor serious. "Havadrans deny female merchants the right to sell. If foreign women merchants enter the country, they sequester them while their male associates staff the stalls."

"And what if the women merchants have no male associates?"

"Then they cannot ply their wares in Havadra."

Her eyebrows rose toward her hairline. "I did not know their restrictions spread that far. By The Powers, I cannot imagine such an existence, kept caged all of one's days." It surprised him to see her suddenly smile. "Then you, young man, must want to make up for two years without female companionship. I am certain you will find several unjoined women in the King's Halls who will show their feet to the handsome young Ambassador." She gave his arm an affectionate squeeze. "There is a new cook, very pretty and talented with spices. That brown sauce you seem fond of is one of her inventions."

Favik realized he still had a nugget of bread submerged in the sauce. Rescuing it, he squeezed it slightly so the sauce would not drip and brought the soggy, earth-scented lump to his mouth. It dissolved quickly, leaving a tantalizing woodsy flavor of mushrooms mixed with a tangy hint of a spice whose name he could not recall. "Ah, my Lady, would that I could, but I believe my Lord has plans for me. Unless The Powers will it, I do not think I should form any attachments before journeying to my posting in Amkland."

"Ah yes. Well, despite living in Eskalind these many years, this former Hudikslander's mind still strays to matchmaking on occasion." Marna Queen paused, her voice pensive, "I thank The Powers every day for bringing Dalock to me. I would see you happy and settled, if that be Their Will."

Her concern touched his heart. How he wished he might tell her of his love for the general's daughter, but his Ambassador's caution forestalled him. "Thank you, my Lady. You have shown me much kindness these many years."

She patted his sleeve with one hand and with the other reached for Lady Nalya's letter. "I will deliver this to Dalock immediately, on your behalf." She rose, a shower of bread crumbs bursting from her smock and trailing to the carpet. "I hope your report quilling is not as tedious as it sounds."

"Thank you again, my Lady." Favik stood, bowed, and made his exit.

———

Marna Queen tapped the envelope in her hand against her palm, facing the diamond-paned windows of her semicircle-shaped chamber. Placing one knee upon the window seat, she held the folded parchment against the sunlight. She saw an indistinct tangle of quilled letters, massed like hair pulled from a brush. Peering closely, hoping The Powers might guide her eye, she discerned an *i* followed by an *l*, but could decipher no more.

"So, '-il' is a common ending for an Eskalind man's name. What is Nalya plotting?" The Queen lowered the parchment. "By rights, I could open this before passing it to Dalock. I have opened many Ambassador's letters in the past. But only when Dalock was away, or inaccessible." Her eyes narrowed. "And he might think I was trying to shield Favik in some manner." Marna raised the envelope again to the light, and this time clearly perceived one word, which tumbled from her mouth as she read. "Jinil." She shook her head. "Nalya quilling about King's Second, how odd. Yet it seems somehow familiar that their names go together." She wavered over the attached seals, then turned and marched to the door adjoining the royals' quarters. Opening her door, she found his unlocked and pushed it open, leaning her head into the room.

Dalock sat at the head of his dining table, a male Records Keeper she did not recognize standing by his side and pointing with a rod to a map of Eskalind that crested a tall stack of parchments before them. Both men glanced in her direction, and the Records Keeper, lowered his red cloth wrapped head to bow. She dipped her chin slightly, gazing seriously to her husband, a silent gesture they had long ago established to communicate that they needed the other's confidentiality.

Dalock tapped his long fingers on the map. "I thank you for your report. Leave these records with me. They will be returned after I confer with my Queen."

"Certainly, my Lord." The Records Keeper bowed, his brown robe billowing from the slight motion. "My Lady." He left the room as the Queen came toward her husband and sat by his side, placing Lady Nalya's letter in her lap.

"Come, Marna, this map shows I have but one estate to grant if I ennoble Jinil and his family. But it is too small to my liking." He pointed to two side-by-side *X*'s, one purple, the other green, marking a parcel in the northeast of Eskalind. "The former estate of the House of Aalpip, Narmlich King's Friend, defunct these many years since my uncle died."

"Your mother's house." She spoke tenderly, as though tending their son as a wee child after a nightmare. "Surely Jinil would be honored to be granted the estate where Treya Queen was born and raised, near where your parents were brought together by The Powers. Did he not serve her early in his career?"

"Yes, and he was fond of her." He groaned. "But may The Powers forgive me for thinking it too small a granting for my loyal Second." He flattened his palm over a lower section of the map, pointing to the northwest corner of their land. "But there is nothing else available unless Lord Radil, the sole member of the House of Valip, Palich King's Friend, dies without issue, and he has not yet earned his sword. Radil may yet father children, or live a long while. Or perhaps Nalya, the last of the House of Adril, Narlock King's Friend, will succumb while on her luxurious travels." He growled, "I had word from Ambassador Moril in Thislin that she finally quit their capital for the outerlands." He lowered his voice. "There was even word that she had taken lovers, but Moril could not establish firm proof. If I could confirm it, I would have full cause to seize her lands and end her house."

"Perhaps The Powers are at work on this subject, my husband. Favik carried this from Havadra for you." She brought forth the letter, placing it before him. He examined the seals, frowning.

"Favik had this?"

"Nalya sent this letter to him in a larger sealed envelope that was addressed to the Eskalind Ambassador to Havadra. He received it the day before he received your summons."

"Then it may have been delayed as well." He split the seals, and the wax flaked into burgundy crumbs dotting the table. "We need to use wax as brittle as this in our correspondences."

"I agree. But Dalock, I wonder why Nalya sent it to an Ambassador, rather than to you directly."

Her husband drew forth a folded parchment from the envelope. "So someone other than she would know it was sent. An old Ambassador's ploy. I believe her father served as such."

"Ah, I wish I had known that."

He unfolded the letter. "Please do not tell me you now wish to study the Ambassadors' training regime."

"I might find it useful." She smiled. "*We* might find it useful." Marna leaned by his side to scan the document. He angled the blue parchment so they both could read the studied script, bright and wine colored, tracking across the sheet in orderly rows that the Queen could never hope to achieve with her own clumsy hand.

Quilled this Tenth Day of the Sixth Month of the 2,900th Year
since the Founding of Eskalind
My Lord Dalock Strange King,
I quill you about a matter that has long been upon my conscience.

"Ha!" Dalock barked. "She has a conscience! That is indeed news worthy of Ambassadors' tricks."

It concerns Jinil, King's Second.

Marna brought her hands to her face.

"What is it?" He turned to her.

"Oh, Dalock, I just remembered—" Her eyes raced over the quilling.

"What?"

She pointed, "There. It says she was Jinil's lover. Twenty years ago."

He gazed back at the letter. "So it does. But what of it?" He read further, his eyes darting swiftly over the lines. "Ah, *after* her husband died." The King lowered the missive. "How could he commit such an heinous act? Jinil, my steadfast Second, my loyal Counselor all these years! No, there must be some treachery on her part." He rubbed his forehead. "I wonder who else knows of this."

Marna found it difficult to look at him. "I did."

"What? How?"

"Jinil told me. I had forgotten, till I read the words here before me. Dalock, it was so long ago, just before you and I joined. I was unfamiliar with Eskalind customs, that widows and widowers cannot re-join or take lovers."

He closed his eyes. "My wife and my Second keeping secrets from me. For years."

"I truly forgot about it! You must realize, at the time I did not think it much of a secret; it was an unfamiliar custom to me. Now, of course, I know differently."

Her husband opened his eyes, staring straight at his hearth as if she were not there, and rose from his seat. Wordlessly, Dalock strode to his main door that led to the stairs, opening it and calling to the Guard, "Send for my Second. Immediately." He shut the door firmly, pacing back to the table. "How could Jinil lie with her, knowing Nalya was a widow? And why, by The Powers, would he tell anyone, even you? Such a secret, were it to out, would ruin his position, his career."

"At the time I believed he told me to gain my trust. I still believe that."

The King said nothing, but sat and picked up the map, studying it as though he might glean new information on the situation from it.

"Jinil told me he did not know Nalya was a widow until after the affair had begun."

Her husband snorted, which struck her as behavior more fitting their thirteen-year-old son than the Strange King. She nearly said so. After several calming breaths, she could keep silent no more. "You are not thinking of dismissing him for this long-past indiscretion?"

The Lord of Eskalind replied in a tone sharp enough to halve a week-old loaf of bread. "I am thinking."

A knock at the door interrupted what seemed an eternity of tense silence. "Come in," called the King, still directing his eyes to the map. Jinil stepped into the room.

"You sent for me, my Lord?"

Dalock grasped the edges of the map and did not lift his eyes from it. "Yes, come, read this letter, here." He nudged Nalya's parchment with the edge of the map.

King's Second stepped toward the royals, bowed to them both, his eyes lingering on the Queen, who did her best to not betray the turmoil raging in her heart. Jinil removed the letter from the table and read. After a moment, he lowered the sheet to the table, exhaling slowly.

Dalock raised his eyes from the map to his Second. "Is it true?"

Jinil sounded remarkably calm, but the scar across his graying beard puckered, a sign, Marna knew, that he was anxious—according to her husband, who had been close to the man for nearly a quarter of a century. "By The Powers, I wish it were not. Lady Nalya took me for a lover, over twenty years ago. That part of her missive is correct. Yet she does not relate the full truth." He glanced between the royal pair. "I did not know she had been joined, and once I did, the moment I discovered she was a widow, I concluded the relationship."

"How did you find out." It was a question, but delivered in a flat tone like a statement.

"It was so long ago. She was unusually secretive about our couplings, careful to arrange any meeting only after her servants departed from her quarters. At first I thought it was perhaps shyness on her part, or some game, or even a defect in myself that she didn't want anyone to know." His green eyes seemed to sharpen. "I was as silent as she, telling no one, yet after a visit to her estate where she insisted we keep separate sleeping arrangements, I returned to King's Halls to investigate the Records Keepers' logs to see if there had been some past trauma, some reason for this secrecy. I was horrified to discover her a widow."

"Had you hoped to join with her?"

"My Lord, I always hoped to join in the way unique to Eskalind's traditions, with the woman who carried my child. Which is why I would not join with Saralya until she got with child."

The corner of Marna's mouth nudged slightly downward at the recollection of the distress that choice had caused his future wife, who was her closest companion and Reader.

"Why did you tell my wife of your affair, and not me?"

"Your pardon, my Lord. At the time, The Powers forgive me, I was afraid of losing my position over an innocent trespass on my part. As Lady Nalya had her entire estate to lose, I knew she would not breathe a word, and would not wish me to do so either. Yet when Marna Queen was newly brought to Eskalind, you asked me to familiarize her with our customs." He glanced and nodded to his Lady. "I felt—it is odd, but The Powers know I speak truth—I literally felt compelled to tell the Queen."

The King seemed astonished. "I have never heard you say The Powers compelled you to act."

"It is true. I felt strongly that King's Betrothed needed to trust me."

The Lord of Eskalind looked to his wife. "Why would you not trust my Second?"

"Dalock! Of course I trust him now, but when I first came here, I was the ignorant daughter of a Hudiksland bladesmith, betrothed to a King, and fully uninformed of the ways of Eskalind. I still remember when Lady Nalya first attended me. Her cutting comments and lack of respect made me worry that her family might be scheming to overthrow you for joining with a commoner." At this, the hint of a grin appeared on her husband's face.

"In all seriousness, Dalock, I am embarrassed of my initial ignorance of your customs. I did not fully realize then how protected Eskalind is by The Powers." Marna sank back into her chair, her cheeks hot and flushed, convinced her face was the color of a beet.

"Ah, I am embarrassing my wife." He folded his fingers together. "I am not pleased that you both kept this information from me."

"My Lord, I cannot ask forgiveness for my transgression, despite the circumstances. I hope you will understand that I felt directed by The Powers to tell the Queen in confidence. I will resign my position immediately."

Marna glanced at Jinil in shock.

"Stop, Jinil. There will be no resignation by my Second. I will not judge against you in this case, though I am disappointed." He raised his head to eye his man with a triumphant air. "The only evidence of this indiscretion is Nalya's word against yours. While your record shows over two decades of loyal service to my family, hers is a well-documented history of misconduct in managing her estate. Gah, the Records Keepers will bear that out if it should come to a challenge." He shook his head. "I only wonder why she quills now. By revealing this, she exposes herself to the loss of her estate, her title, her wealth. Do you have any idea why she would risk such a thing?"

"No, my Lord. I can speculate that Lady Nalya is bitter over her position as the last of her house, but I also wonder if her circumstances have changed so that she believes she no longer has anything to lose."

Marna added, "Perhaps she is ill, with no hope of recovery."

Dalock grimaced. "So she wants to bring Jinil down with her. Is there Havadran blood in her line?" The King shook his head. "Well, that is all speculation, but I think the three of us can keep this a secret"—the King circled a hand in the air—"amongst us." He waved at his Second. "You may go, Jinil."

"Thank you, my Lord." Jinil bowed and left, the closing door leaving an odd, reverberant thud in the silent room.

Dalock grinned at his wife. "You did not anticipate that outcome, my Queen."

"No, I did not. But I am pleased by it." Her nerves were jangled, and she placed a hand on his arm, seeking the comfort of his warmth.

"So am I. More than you know."

"Why, Dalock?" His grin deepened. She frowned. "Are you thinking you will seize Nalya's estate and grant it to Jinil?"

"I might. By The Powers, I just might. She took Jinil as a lover; there may be others she has lain with since her husband's death." He folded his hands together. "If proof of other lovers could be found, that would be grounds to rescind her title and lands."

"How will you find out?"

"Add it to all my Ambassadors' agendas to actively investigate and report anything they discover about her. Once we find out where she is, I can send a Records Keeper or trusted person, incognito, to investigate." He stood, and his Queen released his arm. "Meanwhile, I will begin quiet legal proceedings to put everything in order, so when Nalya is removed from the scene—by her death or her indiscretion—the transition will go smoothly. Though I may delay the bestowal."

Marna rose to her feet as well. "I see you have this all planned. Yet what if Nalya has some proof that she and Jinil were lovers? That would pull him down with her."

"She makes no mention of proof in this letter. If she had evidence, I expect she would have mentioned it, yet she gives only her word—as if that were good enough." The Lord of Eskalind sneered. "I am surprised she has not traveled to Havadra. She would flourish in their society. "

The Queen raised an eyebrow. "I think it risky, husband, to challenge her. A scandal for Jinil would affect not just him; his wife and young sons would suffer the blow as well."

Dalock nodded. "True. We shall see what comes. Nalya cannot offend The Powers and the King forever and get away with it."

A week passed, and then another, so that it came to be the Fourth Day of the Sixth Month, also known as Marna Queen's Naming Day. Celebrations were held. King's Son presented her with a carefully quilled rendering of the number forty-three, in honor of her age, and a short poem of his own hesitant verse, quilled in a tight scrawl that opened into a fluid flourish at the end of each line as he gained confidence in his hand, as though he had at first clambered cautiously down a steep hill but found his feet running near its end.

"This is wonderful! I thank you, my sweet son." His mother's joy manifested in hugging him tightly with such a pure, open love, he wanted to hide in embarrassment.

His father merely nodded, coolly patting him on the shoulder. Perhaps his Lord expected more. Since the King returned from Eastlant, anytime the two shared company, his eyes never left his sole son. Under this intensive scrutiny, Dalich silently wished an Ambassador's letter would arrive to call his Lord away to duty in one of the border nations.

That night, King's Son retreated early to his quiet chamber, startling the Candlelighter as the matronly woman brought flame to the wicks of the stout wax pillars lining his headboard. She departed, the closing door sealing out the revelrous sound of music and laughter echoing along the corridor leading from the Great Hall. The merrymakers seemed altogether more joyful, and more plentiful, than at his own recent Naming Day celebration.

His bed now was bathed in an island of candlelight, floating amidst the intense darkness that crowded from the chamber's stone walls, as though the rock emitted concealing black wherein other things lived.

Dalich flopped upon the coverlets, pushing aside teetering piles of scrolls so numerous that he could no longer lie full down to sleep without scroll knobs poking his sides or tangling his dark hair. The youth unfurled a faded blue manuscript, the thick, textured parchment rough under his fingertips. The volume bore the not very intriguing title *Customs of the Strange Kingdom,* but its scratchy sheets were unusual compared with the smooth, sanded parchment of the other scrolls. The texture drew him.

King's Son scrolled past the lengthy title section that dutifully listed the Librarians and Scriptors who had contributed to the text. Coughing on invisible, but pungent, dust, he read that the scroll was initially quilled during the reign of Daavlock the 16th King, recopied and recopied again until this copy, quilled during the reign of Mavlich, the 109th King. "That means this scroll must be at least . . ." Dalich strained to recall the dates drilled into his mind by his tutors. "Over four hundred years old!" He belched loudly, pleased with the pulsing reverb of its echo in the huge, hollow chamber, and wondered if the Guard outside his door heard.

King's Son read aloud: "'Noble households bear the name of the King who founds their house and the person whom the King ennobles, henceforth known as King's Friend.' Oh, everyone knows that." The youth hastily twisted the polished lapis scroll knobs to an inner section of the scroll, which had not faded and bore the original deep blue hue. There he found a section that caught his interest, for it mentioned his title.

"'It is expected that King's Son will spend much time alone.'" Dalich's long fingers traced the lustrous gold letters that seemed to float above the cobalt-colored sheet. "'The Powers forbid his lodging with others in King's Halls from the time King's Son leaves the nursery until he earns his sword. Then he can live as a man.'" The boy pondered. "Why must I wait three more years to earn my man's sword? Maybe there could be an important battle so I receive it sooner?" His eyes darted to the shadows, half expecting an answer. Groaning, his gray eyes reverted back to the text.

"'A room of his own must be found for King's Son so that he may find his Gifts, whatever they may be.'" He glanced up at the long row of lit candles lining the shelf crowning his bed's headboard. "That is why I sleep by myself here, and Father forbids me sleeping in the same room as Saril and Marnil, like I did before—before I was … I guess, five?" Dalich's departure from the nursery seemed ages ago. He raised his gaze higher, toward his chamber's ceiling, invisible in the unlit, lofty reaches high, high above his head. A vague memory of seeing the rafters once, just once, floated through his mind, though on rare occasions he heard creaking footsteps from the room above.

That chamber was his former nursery, and once King's Son left it, a few visitors had lodged their young children there whilst convening above with the Queen. For far above the nursery chamber were his parents' quarters, at the top of the royal tower, encircled by over a hundred stone steps and an outer wall to shelter from the nightly rains.

In his quarters at the wide base of the ancient structure, Dalich thought aloud. "Hmm … I wonder, if I told my tutors I knew my Gifts, would they let me stay with my companions? Marnil and Saril are more fun than these stone walls, and all these scrolls and books." He lobbed the open scroll past his bare toes and grabbed another from the stack under his elbow, the dark around him silent as a glowering beast.

———

Months flew by. The girl came into Dalich's mind now and again, but always when he sat without companionship, and most often in his chamber. *"King's Son,"* she would say. He would speak aloud his replies as though she sat by his side. Her voice was a comfort, a kind companion in his lonely room, a glad distraction from reading or watching the candles shrink in their holders.

Her name remained a mystery. He often thought to ask her, next time they spoke, but oddly never remembered to ask whilst they conversed. She was simply "you" during their exchanges.

Perhaps he was not meant to know.

He was not certain if the stones had whispered to him or if the idea came from his own thoughts. But from the moment the notion bloomed in his mind, Dalich began studiously avoiding finding out anything specific about her—not the names of her sisters or brother, nor the name of her town. Instead, the pair traded stories about their daily lives, or unusual things they saw. The girl told of the people who lodged at her father's inn, of the purple Lamorda flower stalks and the green waving grass pulsing in the fields behind her stone and timbered home. She could be anywhere in Eskalind.

The night before Dalich's fourteenth Naming Day, he received the best present of all, for as he lay in his bed reading yet another dreary tale of one of his ancestors, he wished for her, and her voice came to him. *"King's Son,"* she said in his thoughts. *"What is that before you?"*

"Hullo! I was hoping you might visit me. It is a book, the chronicle of a King who was a great healer."

"What does it say?"

"You cannot read?"

"I can quill sums and the date well. Today is the Sixteenth Day of the Fifth Month, 2902. I wrote and read that today. But I can't read more than that yet."

"I can teach you. Close your eyes." He pointed to a word. "These letters spell *queen*." Thus he began teaching her to read, an enterprise kept from his mother, though it would have gladdened her beyond anything to know of it.

The Powers saw fit to grant King's Son's other wish as well, though They dawdled a few months longer than the youth had hoped. In the Ninth Month, an Ambassador's letter arrived from the borderland of Thislin, calling for aid from the Strange King and his armies against invaders from an outerland. But while Dalich had initially desired his father to leave, as the day of departure approached, his parents' hushed conferences and closed doors reversed his wishes, so that in the end he wanted instead to go with his Lord and be privy to all plans. During this time of crisis and haste, he followed the proper etiquette at King's Halls, same as anyone else, submitting a respectful request for a private audience with his male parent.

The request granted the night before the King's departure, King's Son rushed headlong into his Lord's candlelit quarters. "Please, Father, allow me to journey with you!"

"Sorry, Son. Not until you are a man." His father lifted a book on his desk, placing it over an unfolded papyrus sheet.

"But I am King's Son without an heir! Let me fight in your stead, and earn my sword, and spare our Soldiers' lives!" The youth gripped the thick carving that crowned a high-backed chair and realized he must have grown; it was a more level reach than the last time he touched it.

"Those words are *never* to be shouted, Dalich." The Lord of Eskalind's angry glare clove the lad's confidence, leaving his next utterance a pathetic whimper.

"But … Father … what good is my Gift if I cannot use it?" He paced forward, and slumped into a chair, squeezing his eyes shut hard so he would not cry. He would not cry.

"You are only fourteen. And it may not come to battle, I hope to The Powers."

As his father spoke, the youth realized the voice was before him. He opened his eyes. His father had brought another chair and plunked it in front of his son. Dalock King sat, hand on his knees as he regarded his son through weary eyes. "I realize this is not what you want to hear, but you must apply yourself to your weapons studies. A new Swordmaster, from Mavold, will arrive in a fortnight. I want you to learn all you can from him. Edvain is the best and will train you well." The King's tone was gentle and persuasive, but Dalich wanted to run away. A Mavoldian Swordmaster would be a taskmaster. Battle seemed a more pleasant prospect.

His mother's voice surprised him. "I did not expect to find both my menfolk here at this time of night." She stood in the doorway that connected the royal couple's chambers. The Queen wore a sleeping robe and clutched a caramel-hued letter, backed with two round, red wax seals. An Ambassador's *A* marked the leftmost seal, while the rightmost seal would reveal which Ambassador—*F* for Favik in Amkland, *M* for Moril, newly transferred to Kaymif, and so forth—but he could not quite discern the character.

The Queen followed his eyes, flipping the letter over as she walked toward the pair. "How fares my son?"

"Fine." He leapt to his feet and fled the room, thankful to be rid of their irksome company.

During the absence of her husband, Marna Queen sought companionship in the King's Library, amiably chatting with the many visitors from the borderlands. "Onath of Thislin, wonderful to see you again. How goes your research; have you found any references to your red-barked tree in our records?"

The lanky man nodded, his thick lips strained over his toothy grin. "Why yes, two, my Lady, thank you. One in Humiksland, in the Forest of Fambay, and the other in Kursak, in the garden of their Healers School at their king's seat. I hope to journey to both soon to collect samples."

"I do hope you will send me one if your search is successful."

"I will deliver the bark and a seedling personally to you, my Lady, if you will allow me back."

"You are always welcome here, Onath."

He bowed, his eyes closed as though he might weep. "Thank you, my Lady. Your hospitality to people such as myself is legendary." Straightening, he continued, "I hope my research is fruitful, that the tales of the red bark's healing qualities are not exaggerated. And there is one thing I hoped to give you now, if you allow me." He fumbled through a scroll sack, and retrieved a single pine-knobbed scroll of plain papyrus.

"There is much of interest in this copy of this scroll, particularly near the end of the coil."

The Queen nodded, having heard this coded reference before. "Then I will give it my full attention. Onath, if you have any research you hope to share with me while you are abroad, do not hesitate to borrow some of my books and make notes for me. You may return them through my Ambassadors."

"Thank you for allowing me the privilege, my Lady."

"I will have one of the Scriptors, Palika, deliver the books to you tonight." With a nod she placed the scroll in an empty basket, picked it up, and departed for her office, pausing to gather a few more scrolls from a nearby shelf. One of her favorite privileges as Queen of Eskalind was enjoying the liberty of the Library, to choose and borrow any scroll or book of her own choosing, unhindered, at any time. Along the way, she acknowledged Benasa, a scroll merchant from Ghemif, then the healer Melkain from Mavold, and lastly a tutor from Kaymif as he sat with two young charges, helping them copy their alphabets.

Once in the privacy of her quarters, she unfurled the scroll Onath had given her to find, near the end of its length, a tissue-thin parchment. Thislin script flowed over the sheet. The decorative dots the Thislins placed atop all lowercase letters rendered it a bit difficult to decipher, but nonetheless, Marna read these words:

Lord Edlaych of Eastlant secretly supplies and fortifies an Askvit army to invade Thislin, in hopes of expanding his estate across the Eastlant-Thislin border.

The Queen exhaled, realizing this meant an attack might come from two sides as Dalock and the Thislin queen led their armies to fight the invaders. She flew to her desk to draft a warning note to her husband. Finding her inkwell devoid of its cork stopper and rattling dry, she searched for another, annoyed at herself for forgetting to insert the stopper. To avoid delaying her letter further, she decided against calling her Page for a fresh bottle of ink; she would find a closer replacement. Marna marched to the door linking the royals' quarters and entered Dalock's side of the tower.

A fresh breeze traced the curtains of an open window in his chamber. It surprised her that someone had left the window open in the uninhabited room. And the bedsheets were missing. Surmising that the maids had turned out the room for fresh air, she went to Dalock's desk and grabbed his bronze inkwell to find a generous slosh of ink inside.

A startling crash sounded behind her. The Queen jumped. Turning, she noted that one of the two baskets of Ambassadors' tiles had spilled onto the small portion of the stone floor not covered by carpet.

"Oh, by The Powers! How many broke?" Groaning, she approached, and was dumbfounded to see not a single one of the oblong ceramic tiles in pieces. Odder still, each tile had fallen name side down, except for one. "'Favik,'" she read. "This is extremely odd." The Lady of Eskalind gathered the tiles, replaced them in their basket, and brought the basket back to its table. Yet as she made her way to her quarters, another noise sounded behind her, and Marna turned just in time to see the other basket of Ambassadors' tiles splat onto the floor. "That Powers-cursed window!" The Queen marched directly to the window, shutting and locking it firmly with a screeching crank of the latch.

At her feet, the tiles again lay unbroken, and again all names were down except for one. "Eskalind? But that means the Ambassador is to return home." She studied the tile. The prospect of sending for Favik appealed to her immensely, but that meant another Ambassador must be sent to Amkland in his stead, which could mean a huge reshuffling of Ambassadors. "Still, if this is the Will of The Powers . . ." Righting the basket, she returned the Eskalind tile and the other ceramic lozenges into the woven container, placing it atop the table by its twin.

Closing her eyes, she reached with one hand into the basket of Ambassadors' names, and the other into the basket of nations. Retrieving a tile from each, she opened her eyes. "Favik and Eskalind again! Well, this is clearly the Will of The Powers. But who will replace him?" The Lady of Eskalind set the two tiles aside and reached simultaneously, again drawing forth one tile from each basket. "Havnil and Amkland. And Havnil is here at King's Halls, without a current posting. My, The Powers planned that well." She grinned, pleased as a child granted another helping of cakes. "I thank you!"

Speed in her steps, she went to the outer door to alert the Guard to send for a Swift Rider, then sat at Dalock's desk to quill a short note relaying Onath's information, without revealing her source. *News has reached me,* she began, wasting no time on information other than from Onath's report. Just as the ink sank steadfastly into the parchment, the messenger arrived to whisk it away. After sealing the missive, the Queen reached for another blank sheet. "Now to send Havnil to Amkland to replace Favik."

Chapter Five—An Exchange of Letters

20th Day, 10th Month
My Beloved Queen,
I thank The Powers for the timely arrival of your note. With your
news, we were able to block the second assault before it began,
much to the surprise of Lord Edlaych and his supporters. The
borders of Thislin are secured, but at the price of over fifty of
our men, though the cost would have been higher had your note
reached me later. I grieve for the lost men and their families, and
continually thank The Powers for my wonderful wife and our
strong son.
Send more of your salve when you can. There were many injured.
Tell Saralya that Jinil weathered the battle without injury.
Give my love to Dalich, and quill me with any further news, be it
of great or little import. It is good to hear from home.
Your loving husband,
Dalock King

Twenty-Fifth Day, Tenth Month, 2902

Dearest Husband,

I am grateful and relieved to hear of the victory in Thislin. I too mourn the loss of the many good Eskalinders. May The Powers keep us close! Yet you make no mention of how you fare, or when you will return home. Please send word as soon as you are able.

The Mavoldian Swordmaster you sent for arrived and tries Dalich continually. He believes in preparing King's Son for any attack situation, and one never knows where one may encounter the pair at practice. The kitchen staff has complained, and I preemptively forbade Master Edvain and his charge from sparring in the Library or our chambers. Dalich seems pleased with this immersion in weaponry. I believe he feels himself reliving the legends of his ancestors.

Our son has made no mention of the girl appearing in his thoughts again, and I have seen no evidence of it, though trying to keep an eye on the constant combatants tries a mother's nerves. I recalled Favik from his Ambassadorship in Amkland, and sent Havnil in his place. No other news save that I await your swift return home.

A dozen jars of my mint salve should accompany this letter, and I will send more once they are prepared and properly aged, but do not wish to delay further.

With love,

Your Marna

———

3rd Day, 11th Month

Marna,

Why did you recall Favik from Amkland? I do not understand why

you would do this.
The salve has healed many. I thank you for sending it.
You asked if I was injured. I am fine.
There may be more trouble here, thus I am uncertain as to
our return.
Your husband,
Dalock King

Ninth Day, Eleventh Month, 2902
My Dear Husband,
I thank The Powers for your note reporting your fine health,
though your Second quills his wife with different information.
Three dozen jars of salve accompany this letter, and as a Healer,
I suggest using a full jar yourself for the cut on your arm, even if
you consider it minor. May The Powers grant you swift healing.
You asked why I recalled Favik from Amkland. The Powers made
it clear to me that it was Their Will, first by knocking over the
baskets of Ambassadors' tiles when no one but myself was in your
chamber. Not a single tile broke, and only Favik's and the Eskalind
tiles faced upward. I then retested this strange phenomenon by
reaching blindly into each replenished basket; Favik's tile and the
Eskalind tile came up again. A second drawing yielded Havnil's
name, and the Amkland tile. I can only interpret this as the Will
of The Powers. I hope we are in agreement.
Upon his arrival at King's Halls, Favik reported that an odd
rumor had reached him regarding a certain widowed Eskalind
noblewoman and a re-joining. He departs soon to investigate
further and find proof, if it be true. I hope this news pleases you.
Your obedient Queen,
Marna

The new Swordmaster's lessons filled Dalich's days and occasionally his nights, as Master Edvain insisted the lad learn to fight in all manner of conditions and weather. Thus, King's Son honed his skills either by the glint of blue moonlight or, as The Powers deemed that rain must fall only at night in the Strange Kingdom, the soft sizzle of torches struggling to remain lit against the drizzle. One misting night early in 2903, Edvain asked the Queen if Guards would keep clear the terrace of King's Halls and the stone colonnade bordering the wide veranda so that the pair could practice without fear of injuring any passersby.

From the shadowed archway lining the terrace, the Queen, behind two Guardsmen, watched, knitting her hands and stalling herself from the inevitable solace-seeking trip to the kitchens for a quick bite. Concern and anxiety about her husband's letter coursed through her veins like an icy river, and the clacking of wooden practice blades seemed a staccato echo of her worries. But when Swordmaster Edvain and King's Son leapt into view, the youth was laughing.

Dalich defended well, and for a moment she enjoyed watching his graceful, sinuous parries and thrusts, the fluid ease with which he met the Swordmaster's attacks. But the fight turned more serious as Edvain bore down hard and unrelenting. The Queen departed, and forgetting her initial plan to visit the kitchens, traipsed the long curve of stairs that led to her chamber. With a nod to the Guard at the door, she entered the empty, candlelit room, closing the wooden door to pace about as though by some chance numerous circuits about the room would yield new counsel. Nothing came of it, and she lay abed, falling asleep dressed in her day clothes.

In the morning sunlight, a glance at the door to her husband's quarters purchased a thought she spoke aloud. "I hope the maids kept his windows shut." Rather than speculate, she marched forth and entered his chamber, vacant now for months. Pleased to see each window dutifully shut and latched, a new concern presented itself: a tall pile of green-leather-bound books of unknown origin teetering upon the King's neatly made bed.

"Whose are these?" Marna walked toward them, reaching a curious hand just as the first book fluttered open, its jade-colored pages rising into the air. The Queen hiccuped as the other books slid to the floor, gliding into a ring around her, translucent pages flying away from their spines and winging upward to shape a wide, domed parchment bubble from floor to just above the head of the Lady of Eskalind. Parchment fluttered and pulsed, crackling as if conversing in secret, then stilled to silence.

One last book skittered across the carpet toward her feet and sprang open soundlessly. Suddenly, a woman clad in green fabric alike to shimmering poplar leaves stood before the Queen, who backed away. No breath came.

The woman spoke—or seemed to speak, for though her mouth moved, her voice rang only in the Queen's thoughts.

Marna Queen

The apparition's irises were green pools of calm and command.

"*Who are you?*" Marna asked—or tried to ask, for she certainly thought the question, but no air moved in her lungs or throat.

> *One charged with the protection*
> *Of Eskalind*
> *Of the King*
> *And his family*

Marna nodded blankly, wondering if this golden-tressed woman could be one of The Powers herself. Her knees wobbling, she managed to stay upright, lungs sapped of breath, certain that all air had been pulled from the room.

> *Doubt will come by flame*
> *By candlelight*
> *You must prepare*
> *By the light of the sun*
> *Find the blank scroll of Treya Queen*
> *Read and act upon what is quilled there*

"*I … will.*"

The woman smiled, the sympathetic expression of a concerned companion who wishes to say more but has thought better of it. Then she vanished. The hovering pages of parchment collapsed to the floor, subsuming into the carpet, along with their bindings, so that not a trace remained.

Marna inhaled deeply, pressing a hand to her forehead to steady herself. Then she fled into her own chamber, bolting the door to the King's quarters behind her. At last gulping enough air to begin breathing comfortably, she opened the door to the stairway and raced down the stairs and through the corridors to the unpopulated King's Library, straight to the Cabinet of Trelich King. There she stood, panting again, attempting to gather her thoughts. Fear pulsed within her, yet just then an odd calm smoothed her forehead and trickled through her limbs, as if an outside force sought to soothe her.

"All right," she breathed. "I would see the blank scroll of my maither, Treya Queen." Marna reached for the lock, which separated for the Queen of Eskalind as effortlessly as a lazy sigh. When she pulled open the doors, the cabinet appeared empty, completely empty, a deep, dark void. She peered inside, for a moment wondering if Dalich had retrieved every single handscroll in the cabinet without bothering to replace them. Then a gold glint in the darkness sparked like a warning beacon. Marna tentatively stretched her hand into the black, pulling forth a knobless scroll the color of deepest shadow, edged with glistening yellow metallic ink. Black and gold, the colors of Treya Queen and Farlock King.

Drawing forth the scroll, Marna closed the cabinet doors and replaced the lock. Unrolling the coiled tube of parchment, she found gold quilling lining the top of the scroll:

A Chronicle by Treya Queen in 2877, by Her Own Hand, for Later Members of Her House

As the current Queen unfurled the document further, not a single letter nor drop of ink could be discovered. "It is blank!"

A shaft of sunlight pierced the high, arched windows and lovingly illuminated a polished, uncluttered table nearby. Marna strode to it, laying the parchment upon it and uncurling the empty sheets to bare them to the light. She scrolled through the crisp sable lengths of the blank scroll. The light faded a moment, and she paused, glancing about the unoccupied Library. Then the sun returned, like a flame unlooked-for that rekindles spontaneously, lit by a secret source. There before her, gold-writ, were these words:

The Powers are terrifying.
They must be obeyed.
Yet They do not obey one another, nor the rules They agreed upon, long ago.

War is brewing amongst Them.
You must prepare.

"Me?" Marna's hands trembled as she struggled to remain calm. She must do something, must devise a plan, to prevent damage or hardship. Marna Queen unfurled the parchment further, searching through the rest of the roll, hoping for more words that would direct a course of action. No other script revealed itself, as though the parchment's very surface shunned all quills. Raising her head from that velvety black, she closed her eyes. The colors of Treya Queen reversed, the gold letters appearing dark against a lighter background in her mind.

"My Lady?"

When she opened her eyes, there before her was Onath of Thislin, with his long, hooked nose that protruded far from his face. He stood before her bearing an open book in his upturned palms, as an eager reader who walks and reads simultaneously. For a moment the last words on Treya Queen's scroll flashed across her vision. *You must prepare.*

"My Lady, with your permission, I have returned from my search for the red-barked tree. My journey was cut short before I discovered it, but allow me to tell you, I met a woman along the way, a scholar, like us, in herbcraft, who gave me much new information."

"A Scholar…" The word felt imbued with new significance.

Onath waited. When she said no more, he continued. "Yes, my Lady. Allow me to present you with her book; I copied it myself." He grinned, his plump lips revealing large front teeth. She lowered her eyes to the book, its pages covered in tight, even Thislin script, and reached to accept it, her hands cupped. Onath gently laid the small volume in her open palms, as lightly as if draining water from his own.

They stood facing each other, the Queen with the open book in her hand, and the scholar from Thislin, his hands open before him as though he still held the small volume himself. The sunlight felt brighter. Marna pondered a moment. "Onath, are there any pages in this book I should pay especial attention to, as in the scroll you gave me when last we met?"

"No, my Lady. But with your permission, if any news of import reaches me, I will provide it to you. I am a swift copyist."

"I thank you, Scholar Onath." The Lady of Eskalind smiled, lowering her shoulders slightly, clearheaded and calm, as though a path had been set before her and she need only step forward. She wondered if the woman in green had anything to do with it. Marna closed the book, and a muffled thump reverberated through the Library like the proclamation of a weighted judgment.

I will use knowledge and Scholars to prepare for what will come. Together we shall protect Eskalind if The Powers fail us.

Onath folded his palms together as though his hands were book pages and bowed. "With your permission, allow me to depart on my search again, and with your permission, to thank The Powers for allowing me to serve you, and to serve Eskalind, in any way I am able." The Thislin man raised his head, expression bright, wide lips almost separating in a smile.

The Lady of Eskalind nodded her dismissal, and Onath departed, passing her Page Avnil near the entrance. "My Lady?" called the boy, his tone pinched and high.

"Yes? Is something wrong?"

"I went to your chamber with breakfast, but you were not there." He paced toward her.

The Queen nodded, placing her new book upon the table. She rolled the blank parchment of Treya Queen into a single coil quickly, as if she were late for an important appointment. "Avnil, has Favik departed yet?"

"No, my Lady, I just saw him in the kitchens."

"Good. Fetch him immediately, then procure my Lady Reader. Have them meet me in my chamber, now."

"But, my Lady, what about your breakfast?"

"Yes, have the morning meal sent for the three of us." Marna handed the lad her new book. "Bring this to my quarters as well."

Her Page dashed away to do her bidding. The Lady of Eskalind reopened Trelich's Cabinet, finding it still empty, and placed Treya Queen's scroll inside. A slight scrape in the orange paint on the edge of the middle shelf drew her gaze to where the color of the shelf faded gradually into the dark void of the empty cabinet. She shut the door and fastened the lock.

The Queen turned to see her son standing in the long aisle, clutching at least a dozen handscrolls arranged in a haphazard, teetering fashion across the brown-velvet tunic covering his chest. His face mimicked that of a lad caught stealing a morsel of Queen's Recipe Roast Chicken whilst turning it on the spit.

"Oh, hullo, Mother." A blue parchment scroll with red-jeweled handles slipped from his grasp and clattered onto the floor, momentously loud. Dalich stood immobile except for his gray eyes, which quickly glanced at the pair of cylinders rocking on the floor, then back to his mother.

"Dalich. While I am pleased to see your newfound interest in the chronicles of your ancestors, show some care," Marna groused. "Use a carrying basket next time!" The Queen unlocked the Cabinet again, pulling the doors apart to find the shelves full to nearly overflowing with handscrolls of every King's color. "It . . . seems The Powers have much reading planned for you, Son."

She stepped aside to allow him to replace his scrolls whilst she retrieved the scroll he had dropped. A close inspection for damage yielded none. Marna placed the scroll in a nearby basket, handing it to her sole child. He accepted it as automatically as if he had expected her to do this for him. She huffed, gathering the hem of her smock, and hurried back to her quarters, glad to continue her business without further delay.

The Queen found Favik waiting for her, standing by one of her window seats. His odd gray eyes, colorless but for a rim of blue about the irises' edges, lit with curiosity as he turned to face her. "My Lady, Page Avnil intercepted me en route to the stables. His timing was most fortuitous."

"Almost as if someone wanted you delayed so we might talk." She smiled as he tilted his blond-bearded chin in a quizzical manner. "Please, sit." Marna gestured to her dining table, as always littered with scrolls and books. The Ambassador did so as the sound of slow footfalls and a gentle rustling came up the stairs. Her Reader, Saralya, entered, slowly bowing in her red silks. Her deep brown eyes were unfocused, betraying an uncharacteristic weariness.

"Are you well, dear Reader?" asked the Queen, laying a pale hand on the cool, dark skin of her companion's arm.

"Yes, my Lady. Merely a late night helping my sons with their studies." The half-Guerish woman wiped a strand of long black hair away from her eyes. "Saril has his first Ambassador's assessment today."

"I am sorry to have interrupted your rest, but the matter is timely. Know that I am very pleased to hear your eldest is advancing to the examination level." The Queen led her Reader toward the council table. "Saril may be our youngest Ambassador yet." A glimmer of pride at her closest companion's son's progress warmed her chest as she settled into the cushioned seat at the head of the table. With a wave she gestured to the empty chair across from Favik.

"Thank you, my Lady."

Saralya sat as Avnil entered the room, bearing a tray of sliced fruits and bread still steaming from the oven. "Lay the plates between us here, Avnil. Yes, on top of these parchments is fine. Close the door as you leave." Her companions exchanged looks as the boy followed her commands. The door closed. All eyes were aimed at the Queen.

Marna pressed her palms together, then unhinged them as if opening a book. She nodded to her companions. Favik raised his eyebrows, leaned forward slightly, and mimicked her gesture with his short, thick fingers. The Queen nodded, gazing a long moment at Saralya, who slowly raised her graceful brown hands before her, following their lead.

The Lady of Eskalind spoke, subdued but commandful. "Saralya of Eskalind, Favik born of Hudiksland which is now Humiksland, this gesture shows we speak solely of our own private business, and that we speak truth. Guidance from afar, from . . . higher authority . . . has led me to this moment. It has long been in my mind that Scholars can provide information to Eskalind beyond that which Ambassadors and their staff glean. I want us to weave a network of trusted Scholars who can formally, but secretly, aid in the protection of the Strange Kingdom and its allies."

Saralya's voice was hesitant. "Scholars as spies?"

"Scholar Spies, yes."

"Ah." Saralya smiled as though she had just rediscovered a beloved scroll thought lost. Or perhaps she had had the same thought herself.

Favik lowered his hands slightly. "My Lady, in some ways, this network already exists. Ever since you opened the Library to all, King's Halls have seen multitudes of scholars from numerous lands. Their gratitude at the opportunity to pursue their research in a peaceful, unfettered environment is almost tangible. There is much they are willing to share."

"True, former Ambassador." She watched his face as she spoke the words, but he gave no hint of reaction to her form of address. Just as one would expect from his position. That was one of many reasons she needed him in this new role. "I want to formalize this, amongst the three of us, if you are full willing."

Saralya opened her mouth, but Marna interrupted her. "Before you reply, this must be concealed amongst us three and those whom we name as Scholars. While we work for the protection of Eskalind, no one else must know; neither our husbands nor our children." She glanced from her Reader to Favik. "Not lovers or companions, no one else."

He dipped his head, while Saralya said, "I thank The Powers to serve you loyally as a Scholar, my Lady."

"As do I, Marna Queen."

"I thank you both, my dear companions. Now, before our hands get tired in this position, we need a secret phrase by which we can identify one another as our associations grow, but I have not discovered it yet."

Saralya spoke. "Knowledge knows no borders."

Marna looked at her. "Perfect. What is it from?"

"I don't recall where I came across it, but it has been in my thoughts lately, like a tune that repeats over and over."

"Excellent. Then that will be our secret phrase." The Queen of Eskalind, Gifted by The Powers, gazed out the window, calm and clearheaded again, relishing the peace and promise of the moment. But more must be discussed. "Is there anyone you would nominate as a Scholar?"

Her Reader replied, "My blood cousin, Kermon of Guerland." Saralya raised her hands slightly, just as she would when she peered closely at a document she was reading. "As you may know, he is a Merchant Master with an abundance of associates in the trades throughout the southern outerlands. Just before my sixteenth Naming Day, I lived a year in his household; I personally know him to be a man faithful to The Powers and the ways of Eskalind. Kermon would have immigrated here long ago were his livelihood less tethered to his location."

"I had already considered him myself, Saralya. Kermon's connections will be most valuable. Favik?"

"I believe Onath of Thislin has served you well, my Lady."

"Yes, I will recruit him myself." Marna folded her hands closed and waited till her companions did the same. "Now for breakfast. Pass the bread."

Favik paced behind Saralya as the pair departed the Queen's Chamber after their morning meeting and meal. At the bottom of the stairs, he stayed her. "My Lady Reader, might we share a quiet word before I depart?"

"Certainly. Come to my family's quarters. My sons should have left for their lessons by now." The pair walked through the long corridor toward the rooms reserved for King's Second and his kin. The door Guard nodded to Saralya. "Saril and Marnil made their leave a short while ago, Queen's Reader."

"Thank you." She opened the door, ushering Favik into the main room, windowless and occupied by a table set with four chairs, though it could easily accommodate more. Books and scrolls were strewn about the stone-topped plank as if they contested for the least orderly position possible. A wooden practice blade lay atop the chaos.

Saralya sighed. "Ah, boys! I doubt daughters would have been as messy. Thank The Powers for the housekeepers; without them, I'd spend my days in quarters tidying after my sons." Shaking her head, she gestured Favik to a corridor that led to a small library, complete with a couch large enough for sleeping, two reading chairs, and a quilling desk topped with tooled leather, all upholstered in the King's colors.

Morning sunshine poured through the tall windows behind the deep reading chair Saralya sank into. Favik sat opposite her.

Neither one spoke for a moment, perhaps gathering their impressions of the morning's events. Finally, Favik ventured conversation using an old Ambassador's method: the compliment. "Your quarters are lovely and spacious, my Lady Reader."

"Ah yes, thank you. I know some of the Lords and Ladies have grumbled that Jinil and I, neither of us nobles, are allotted these sizable rooms." Her lips creased into a slight smile as if she expected he too was familiar with this problem.

"They should consider your position as Reader to the Queen, and your husband's as King's Second."

"Yes, that makes us an exception to the usual order of things. You are rather an exception too, Favik of Humiksland."

"One would say we both are, given our conversation with our Lady today."

The corners of her lips rose slightly as she gazed to the long window, festooned with scarlet draperies, then returned her dark eyes to his. Her irises were such a deep brown, even in the sunlight, he could barely distinguish the pupils. "I am quite pleased with the outcome. Long have I thought to aid Eskalind in some way through my family in Guerland, and to make use of the knowledge, and the potential knowledge, of the many scholars who visit and trade here in King's Halls."

"Had you spoken earlier with our Lady of this idea?"

"No, but I sense she had it in her mind too." The Queen's Reader leaned into her chair. "Saril may earn his sword soon, as will King's Son." Again she glanced out the window, and he felt her attention lay elsewhere.

"I wonder if our Lady is receiving direction."

Saralya faced him. "From The Powers?"

"The Queen did say 'guidance from afar' and from a 'higher authority.' I wonder why such a network would be needed now."

"It is not for us to judge."

"I meant no judgment, my Lady Reader, just curiosity."

"Perhaps it is just a mother's wish for protection of her son, and as Queen of Eskalind, a higher authority assists in the matter." Saralya knit her hands, leaning forward slightly and speaking quietly. "Our Lady has *asked* The Powers for things, and They have granted her askings."

He lifted his eyebrows. "I was unaware."

"I am intimately aware. Marna Queen knew I hoped to join with Jinil, and that he would never join unless we had a joining babe. She told me she would ask The Powers to send me a child, and They did."

Favik somehow doubted the Queen's wishes had anything to do with the conception of Saralya's first child, but as one well acquainted with the beliefs of Eskalinders, he nodded appreciation of the anecdote, adding, "Now that child trains as an Ambassador, in service to our Lord and Lady."

"Yes. But what of you? Are you no longer to serve as such?"

"It appears our Lady has other directives for me at this time."

"Ah."

He countered the look of expectation on her face by holding up his hands. "Well, who knows what The Powers plan for me to discover along the journey?"

"Knowledge knows no borders."

He smiled, in part because she did, and in part because of the obvious pride she found in the phrase. "Whatever knowledge I encounter, I will impart it to our Lady."

The threat of hostilities kept Dalock King away from his Halls longer than anyone expected—nearly eight months. As the chronicles of Dalich's ancestors related, it was not unprecedented, in a reign of over twenty years, for the King to be separate from home and family for such a duration. Yet the Powers saw fit to see Eskalind's Lord returned home for King Son's fifteenth Naming Day. At the celebratory feast, and again to his wife and son in private quarters afterward, the King stated how pleased he was to find the lanky thinness of his son's youth fading into the beginnings of the molded muscles of a trained, but untried, warrior. Dalich cringed at each utterance. To complete his mortification, his Lord requested, in an insistent tone, that he observe Dalich's next sword practice. King's Son would have preferred exile alone in his compassionless room, but he complied.

Thus the Lord of Eskalind watched as King's Son fought, wooden blade in hand, lips set in a determined line, his opponent, circling, arms tense and ready for the man's next move. Suddenly, the blade lunged at his chest. He scooted away to dodge the blow, then leapt forward with a stabbing downstroke, catching Swordmaster Edvain on the wrist.

"Good. My Lord." The Mavoldian's deferences always sounded like an afterthought. Edvain rubbed his wrist and adjusted the high cuffs on his long, padded glove, a bead of sweat dangling on his clean-shaven chin. He backed away along the stone terrace. "Again."

Dalich stood ready, watching the man's exposed neck, trying to read in his attitude which way he would move this time.

"King's Son?" came the girl's voice, clear as if she were standing next to him. Dalich turned to glance behind him just as the wooden blade thwacked hard upon his shoulder, sending him to his knees.

"Are you well?" The Swordmaster stooped to his charge.

"Fine." The man helped King's Son to his feet.

"Mine was an obvious move. My Lord."

He was accustomed to Edvain's scolding, though lately he heard less of it, but this time it perturbed him. Especially since his father watched. "Fine," King's Son whispered, "Where are you?"

"I think I am near you. On the road." Her voice was anxious.

"You are nearby? Which road?" He walked to the edge of the terrace, peering into the distance.

Behind him, the Swordmaster shouted, "Where are you going?"

"There is someone I must talk to," Dalich retorted, his tone imperious. At long last, he might be able to see her!

"You cannot walk away in battle! My Lord!"

———

From the far colonnade bordering the terrace, the King watched his son fall. Distress sank his heart. Then Dalich leapt to his feet, abandoning the Swordmaster, and Dalock surmised that the youth had immediate need to speak with him. But King's Son made away, toward the stairs leading to the balcony above the walnut-wood archways.

"Dalich, what are you doing?" Dalock called, stepping forward. His son did not reply.

———

"Where are you?" King's Son asked, scanning the distant road.

"Outside King's Halls. Your halls!" Her voice rose with excitement. *"Do you see two pairs of horses pulling two small wagons?"*

He shaded his eyes against the lowering sun. "Yes! Wave to me." A light-colored cloth wiggled from behind the last wagon. "I see you!" His heart leapt. If only he could swing off the ledge to the ground far below and run to her.

"I cannot see you." She sounded sad.

"Here I am!" He proudly thrust his wooden sword skyward. The pale wood reflected the amber light in a blaze of gold.

"I see a yellow … something … is it you?"

"Me and my practice blade." He grinned. "Are you coming here?"

"No, we are journeying to bring my brother to his army posting. Oh, I must go before my sisters catch me. I'm so happy I saw you! Goodbye!"

"Wait! I want to meet you." But the girl did not reply, and he knew she had not heard him. He sighed, wishing he could go to her. Perhaps he could slip out, run to the stables—

"Son, what are you doing?" He turned to see his father approaching, the King's eyes narrowed and focused like a hawk spotting a rabbit.

He did not want to argue, or lie. "She is out there, Father." Dalich pointed with his practice sword. His voice was wistful; there would be no chance to leave now.

"Who? In that traveling party?" The King gazed into the distance, which seemed hazier than a moment ago. Perhaps The Powers veiled her.

"My wife. Or rather, she who will be my wife. I have not met her yet." Maybe that would convince his father to allow him to go see her. Dalich lowered the blunted blade.

"You have a strange Gift, my boy, but you must be careful. I observed how you reacted with the Swordmaster. Distraction in combat would be fatal."

"I am King's Son without an heir," Dalich stated in a whisper, turning to stare at his father's jaw, crooked from when he fell from the royals' tower as a boy. "The Powers protect me, as they protected you."

But the King said steadily, "Someday you will have a son, and that Gift will be gone."

Dalich stared at his feet. Through the maroon leather of his shoes he could make out each of his toes as he tensed his feet against the hard stones. "Then I will be more careful, Father."

"Good." His Lord's voice tempered. He tapped a hand on the balcony rail. "If she is to be my future daighter, would you tell me a bit about this girl, hmm?"

"Certainly, Father." But uncertain where to begin, no words came.

The King cleared his throat. "Perhaps you could begin by telling me her name."

"I do not know." The youth turned to his father, chin held high. Someday Dalich might be tall enough to stare his father in the eyes without craning his neck. "What does it matter what her name is? It does not matter at all!"

His father studied his face, keen brown gaze darting over the lad's features, settling at last on a glowering observation of the eyes. Dalich aimed to appear firm, yet his heart beat loud in his chest. Dalock King laid a hand on the thick padding covering the youth's shoulder. "Then speak with this … girl. Tell her she cannot come into your mind unbidden." He gazed to the north. "I fear we may be called to battle soon." The King paused, then spoke, stern as though issuing orders to an errant Guardsman. "Do *not* share that news with her."

King's Son bent in a reluctant bow, his mouth set in a tight line. "As you command, my Lord." He turned, watching the road and wishing to The Powers his father were far, far away.

The King lingered a moment, then left the youth on the high balcony. The haze dissolved for a brief instant, and Dalich caught a last glimpse of the traveling party as it diminished into the west.

Dalock King called his Guardsman, speaking low, eyes intent upon his son on the balcony. "Trevil, a traveling party of two wagons and four horses are on the northwest road. A girl journeys with them. Find her and bring me back her name."

"Yes, my Lord."

"And send a man or two or three to see that King's Son does *not* leave my Halls."

Trevil nodded, glancing to see his Lord's child standing in the expectant posture of one readying to dash away. He gave the commands, soon leaving with two men to do his Lord's bidding.

The King's Guard found the group described in the crowded tavern of the nearby Old Quarry Inn. Leaving his men outside, Trevil entered through the broad doorway.

Several people flocked about, laughing, eating, and swilling drink as if it were King's Naming Day and the ale casks were open to all, regardless of coin. Perhaps this would be a good place to visit on his next leave. The Guardsman stayed the Innkeeper: "I would speak with the leader of the travelers with the two wagons and the four horses."

The Innkeeper gestured to a barrel-shaped man sitting at a table stocked with heaped plates of food and brimming crocks of ale. Trevil paced to him. "A word with you, sir."

The man regarded the red-garbed King's man with a furrowed brow and hazy gaze. "As you wish, Lord, sir . . . uh, Sergeant?" His speech possessed the lazy lilt of an Eastlanter. He heaved his bulk off the bench to follow the King's man.

Two thin girls, of equal height and old enough for a hint of bosom in their bodices, flitted into the room, the blond-braided one laughing uproariously, as if she had just played a trick on someone and relished her cleverness. The darker-haired youngster chased after, batting her companion's shoulders and scolding. Someone began pounding on a drum.

"Do those girls travel with you?" The King's Guard raised his voice over the din.

The large man glanced at the girls as the laughing one shielded herself by hugging a skinny youth standing by the hearth. She guffawed, "Oh, Haril, save me from Yamina's blows!" Strips of red cloth decorated her hair.

"Have my daughters done something wrong?" The man's dark eyebrows rose high on his wrinkling forehead.

"No, but I was sent to ask their names."

"It is not them you want, but me," said a small, barely audible voice from behind the King's man.

Trevil turned to see a slight girl, much shorter than the other two, a bit of baby fat still about her jaw and a black braid, threaded with brown cloth, ringing her head. A second long braid dangled at an odd angle by her ear, as though recently freed from its pins.

"How do you know this?"

"It is my Gift to know." The child regarded him with a lofty gaze that reminded him of his Lady the Queen in a peevish mood—as if the girl had made a personal study of such an expression—though her eyes shone a soft violet color rather then a piercing gray.

"I'm Trevil, King's Guard, sent to know your name," he stated.

The child considered this, small hands folded daintily one over the other. "It's Damina."

Trevil lifted his brow to the girl's father, who nodded and replied, "Yes, this is my youngest, Damina. Her sisters, over there, are my twins, Yamina and Pamina."

"Then, Damina and company, I make my leave."

The girl nodded in dismissal of the King's man. Trevil turned to leave, chuckling softly at the strange circumstances.

———

"Daughter, tell me what this is about. And what happened to your braids?"

"Pamina pulled them." The girl's violet eyes widened. "Just a moment, Father." Then Damina chased after the King's Guard. "Wait!" He was standing on the brick pavers outside the wide doorway. Men in similar uniforms awaited him on horseback. "Please wait!" Her dangling braid drooped further and she caught one of the ribbons entwined in it, trying to pull it into place as she pleaded, "Tell me, please, what does he look like? The son of the King?"

The mounted Guardsmen grinned at one another. "He's a handsome lad, King's Son is," the Guard who questioned her replied. "His hair is brown like his father's, and he has his mother's colorless eyes. His beard is just coming in."

"Oh!" she gasped, looking away. "He's older than I thought." She bowed her neck, the loose braid falling against her ear.

"Aye, he must be nearly twice your age," reported the King's man, accepting his horse from one of his men.

Damina nearly cried. "But will he wait for me to be of age?" she whispered.

"Till we meet again, my Lady," offered the head Guard with a merry grin. Damina raised her face to his as he sat his steed, her mouth open, but no words came. The Guard winked at her, then spurred his horse, leading his men away, the hooves a-clatter upon the pavers.

———

"King's Son," came the girl's voice, *"your father's men were here."*

Dalich sat straight suddenly on his bed; one end of the long scroll on his belly cascaded down the sheets, unfurling to clatter hollowly onto the floor. "What did they want?"

"Only my name."

"Did you tell—"

"Yes."

He breathed. "Then he will tell me when he knows."

"Did I do something wrong?" Her voice sounded as if strained through tears.

"No."

"But why did he ask me my name?"

"I think to break our speaking."

"Why would your father want to—"

"He fears it will distract me in battle. I was to talk to you about it."

"I'd never do anything to harm you!"

"I know, but he fears you might, unwittingly."

"Oh, but I wouldn't, ever! What will we do?"

———

The sound of Trevil King's Guard marching the many stairs to his Lord's chamber was a relief to the Queen's ears, though her eyes lay steady upon the book before her. The King's former Page made his report, mentioning the girl's name, and said he believed her father hailed from Eastlant.

"Send Dalich here," Dalock ordered when his Guard had finished. Trevil lowered his head and left the royals alone.

Marna closed her book, then leaned into the crimson-cushioned couch. "I do not understand what all this fuss is about."

"If you saw our son heedless of an attacking blade, you would." The King rose to pace before his hearth.

"He is King's Son without an heir. The Powers will protect him, as they did you, yes?" She glanced at the fire.

"That Eastlant girl has a sway over him. I saw it," retorted Dalock, tone tense. "I will not have my son in thrall to an infant."

"Surely she is old enough to speak."

Her husband turned to her. "Did you not hear? Trevil thinks she is no older than seven or eight. She will not be of age for years. The boy is fifteen. She is too young for him."

"Would you prefer his wife be older, following the example of his mother and father?" She invited him toward her by reaching out her arms.

"Aye, I would," he said, softening as he settled into the couch next to her again. "Though who knows what The Powers have planned for him."

"Our son would know his future, if he could." She stroked his long fingers. "You told me he believes this girl will be his wife."

"Aye, but if it is to be, then not for a long time to come." Dalock sat straight and turned to her, eyes earnest. "Marna, he told me he did not know her name. How did he converse with her for two years, two entire years, without knowing her name? Tell me, how is that possible?" A candle on the candelabra closest to the couch fizzled loudly.

The Queen replied, "That is odd. Strange even." Marna pondered what plan The Powers had at work and tried to sound calm as worry iced her veins.

Her husband interrupted her thoughts. "By The Powers, if you saw his outburst on the terrace after I asked her name—Marna, it was the reaction of a scared pup." He withdrew his hand from hers. "I looked into his eyes and I saw fear, fear that knowing her name will break their connection." He stood. "Let us settle this tonight. I will not allow our son to be distracted by a child."

On the ground floor of the King and Queen's tower, King's Son heard iron-shod footsteps outside his door. "Wait," he whispered to the girl. "Do not tell me your name now."

"You're afraid of what will happen if I tell you," she said in his mind. *"I can feel your fear. Why are you afraid?"*

"My Lord," came a voice from outside his head as the room filled with light from the torchlit passageway. Dalich turned, raising a hand over his eyes, to see one of his father's men in the doorway. "Trevil?"

"It is, my Lord."

"That is the voice of the man who came to me!"

Dalich jumped to his feet and shouted, "Trevil, do not tell me her name!"

The Guard sounded troubled. "No, my Lord." He bowed. "Your father sends for you."

"Did you tell him? Did you tell him her name?"

The King's man nodded. "As he commanded. Now follow me, my Lord."

"I need a moment alone," ordered King's Son, and he turned to the bare, windowless stone walls of his room, the candles atop his headboard worthless against the bright broadcast of light pouring in from the doorway.

"Just a moment, then." Dalich listened as Trevil shut the door. "Will you wait for me, please?" he whispered to her.

"Wait for . . ." She caught his thought. *"Do you think we will be joined?"*

"Aye, but I also think we will be broken from each other. When I know your name, we will lose the other's thoughts. It is my Gift to know that." His eyes darted about the room, a strange sense of supremacy growing within him. "And somehow, my father knows it too. But I will come to you," he breathed.

"My Lord," sounded an outer voice. It was his father's man again. This time it was he giving the commands. "The King is waiting." Trevil stood in the doorway, one foot forward, as though he might enter the room and grab his Lord's son by the scruff of the neck.

"Coming," moaned Dalich, standing. He followed the Guard out, and up the stairs. Behind Trevil's red-cloaked back, he murmured to the girl, "Wait! He's bringing me to my father now, and I must tell you something." The pair strode up the King's stairs. "When you first came into my mind, I was startled, then wary." King's Son stomped loudly on the stairs so the Guard would not hear his speech. "I even thought it a curse, to have someone else know my thoughts." Trevil began mounting the stairs faster. "But I have grown to consider you a part of me; I can share myself with you and lose nothing." Dalich breathed hard, trying to keep pace with the Guard's rapid ascension. "Before I knew this strange Gift of ours, I would have rejected it, but now I need it. I need *you*." On the top landing, Trevil stepped aside, leaving King's Son to face the door to his father's chamber.

With a resolute sweep of his arm, Trevil King's Guard pushed the door open, revealing Dalich's parents standing side by side before the King's fireplace.

Always he was alone against them.

"King's Son?" the girl called.

"Wait," he whispered.

He knew his mother read the trouble in his eyes. "Come my son," the Queen called, holding her hands out.

"King's Son, I'll miss you, I'll wait, I don't want you to go either!"

Dalich approached his mother, eyes intent upon her as though only she stood in the room. Accepting her kind hands, he drew to her side, away from his father. She gazed at him with sympathetic eyes.

"I feel she sees me," said the girl slowly.

"You will meet again," whispered the Queen, her gray eyes for once kind and understanding. He wanted to trust her, to believe she was on his side. "Now say goodbye, for now."

Dalich bowed his dark head. "Goodbye," he whimpered. "But tell me your name."

"Damina."

It was as though something evaporated inside his chest. He clutched his heart, mindful of its pounding.

"Damina?" he said, raising his face to his father.

"Yes, that is her name," said his Lord. "I do this to protect you, my son."

Dalich stared at the caramel-colored carpet under his feet, the pattern of *M*'s and *D*'s interwoven along its curved border blurring then sharpening as water dropped from his eyes. Many months passed before he could look his father in the eye again.

The Queen stood in the doorway, anxiously watching the stairs as the last of her son's heavy footfalls reverberated along the stone corridor.

"Marna, my dear wife, do not worry after Dalich like a mother hen!"

She gathered her smock hem. "He needs comforting. I am going to the kitchens to make him a plate of bread and sauces. If he will not accept them, then I will bring them to my quarters for us to enjoy." Not waiting for a reply, she cascaded down the stairs, pausing only when she reached the corridor. Eyeing Trevil, guarding her son's door, she asked, "Is he within?"

"Aye, my Lady."

The Queen nodded and continued toward the kitchens, glad to see Page Bafnil approaching. "Send for Favik to meet me in the kitchens," she ordered the boy, slowing to a stately pace.

Reaching the kitchens, she set about mixing sauces and fussing over the bread selection. Given the late hour, the cooks were gone, and only a wide-eyed serving girl was there to assist her. Twice she sent the youngster to the kitchen garden to select fresh herbs, and just as she had exhausted every stalling tactic she could conceive, and the last sauce bowl was crowded onto a tray, Favik arrived. "Oh Favik, would you help me carry this?" asked the Queen, a bit peeved at waiting so long. He did, and the pair glided from the kitchens.

Once in an empty passageway, she touched his sleeve and leaned to his ear, "There is a party of two wagons and four horses at the Old Quarry Inn, just north of here on the King's Road. A girl named Damina travels with them. Go there immediately and speak with her parents. Make them this offer: I will send tutors to their daughter Damina, and if they have other children who wish to participate, to them as well. I want Damina to learn to read, quill, and reason." The Queen released Favik's arm. "I will carry the tray from here."

Favik nodded, intrigued, but said only, "As you command, my Lady." Handing her the tray, he made his departure, wondering what called this girl to his Lady's attention. Perhaps she possessed some Gift that would make her a valuable Scholar someday, with the proper education. Whatever it was, he hoped it was worth the interruption from his current lover's bed.

Grateful to arrive at the Old Quarry Inn before the nightly rain started, he slipped into the tavern to find a muted fiddler quietly entertaining a few patrons, each solitary at his table, mug of ale in hand. Inquiring with the Innkeeper, Favik learned that the family he sought had retired for the night.

"You are not the first King's man to visit tonight," the proprietor reported.

"I come on the Queen's business, and I need you to wake the parents of the girl called Damina. I must speak with them at once." He leaned slightly forward.

The Innkeeper pursed his lips—a comical expression, as his upper lip was much larger than the bottom. Nodding, he departed, pausing along the way to push a chair out of his path with his elbow. Not long thereafter, a stout man—a woman that size could be thought to be carrying twins in her belly—entered the room at a dragging pace behind the proprietor. The owner of the Old Quarry Inn pointed to Favik, and the man waddled toward him. As he approached, the scent of ale grew stronger, and the former Ambassador assessed the man's gait to be the product more of inebriation than of his size.

The man's eyes swung over the interlocking *M*'s and *D*'s ringing the neckline of Favik's uniform. He seemed confused. "Sir?"

"Are you the father of the girl called Damina?"

"Yes, yes, what is this all about? We have done nothing wrong. I served my full military service, I pay my allotted tributes to the Records Keepers—"

He inhaled as if to go on, but Favik interrupted. "Good man, I'm most sorry to wake you and to cause you undue concern. I am brought here by the explicit request of none other than Marna Queen." He introduced himself formally, offered the man a chair. The pair sat alongside a copper-clad table. The former Ambassador signaled the proprietor for two ales, then relayed his Lady's message.

"Why would the Queen send tutors for my little girl?"

"She did not tell me."

"Oh." The man accepted this information as if it were the expected natural order of things.

Favik inquired with gentle earnestness as to the man's name and family situation, discovering him to be called Gamin, a widower, born in Eastlant but emigrated to Eskalind as a young man. Serving five years with the army, Gamin gained his citizenship, purchased the Lamorda Meadows Inn, just three hours ride east of King's Halls, joined, and fathered four children. Damina, at eight, was the youngest. "Eight long years since The Powers claimed my wife. May They keep me strong and healthy to raise three girls on my own!" The large man burped, just as the Innkeeper deposited two mugs of ale on the table. Gamin pawed at one, then seemed to think better of imbibing more. He shoved the mug toward Favik as though the Queen's man were an undeserving customer who did not deserve such a fine brew.

"Gamin, you have a son in addition to your daughters?"

"Aye, my eldest, Haril. He reports for his first military service training in two days. The girls and I came to see him safely to his barracks. Haril wanted them to dress in the costumes of my home county, said it's important Eskalinders show that our families originate from many nations. I think his Sergeant said that first." Gamin moaned. "If only my wife had lived. I never thought I could raise them on my own." The former Eastlanter seemed about to weep.

Favik lowered his chin and eyes as the man's open grief played on his sympathy. For once he allowed himself a moment of self-pity as his thoughts drifted, not to the lover he had left tonight, but to Melande, left behind long ago in Havadra. "I'm sorry for your loss, Gamin. I too have lost a great love."

"Any children?" Damina's father seemed to brighten at the prospect, despite the fact that just a moment ago he had been decrying the burdens caused by offspring.

"No, we were only together a short time." The former Ambassador folded his hands in his lap.

"My Kaya got with child the second time we lay together. Or was it the third?" Gamin raised a hand to his broad cheek, the fingers dimpling the round flesh. It reminded Favik of a gesture he had seen in Havadra when one silently wanted another's attention: a finger placed against the cheek and a long glance until the gaze was met.

Raising his eyes to survey the room, he noted a blond man with brown eyes under prominent brows and a small nose—classic Havadran features—making that exact Havadran gesture, and staring directly at him. Fighting the instinct to twist around to see who might be behind him, Favik turned his head toward Gamin's reflection on the coppery table. As his tablemate blubbered through a monologue of calculations concerning his son's conception, Favik nodded attentively, and studiously avoided showing any interest in the light-haired man across the room. Why would a Havadran want to make contact with him? He hoped to The Powers that Melande had somehow found a way to reach him, across the miles and the border that separated them. But no one knew he was at this inn except the Queen, unless he had been followed.

Suddenly the surface before him shuddered as Gamin stood, his belly bumping the table edge. "Forgive my fatigue; I must return to bed. We had a late start today and must rise early to make up the time." He cleared his throat. "By The Powers, I never thought I'd thank a man for waking me from a dead sleep!" Gamin patted his belt with one hand, and with the other raised his mug of ale, having found the temptation of a beverage within reach undeniable. "Favik, tell her Highness I am delighted to accept her offer of tutors. All of my daughters will be delighted."

"I will, Gamin. I anticipate meeting your family someday soon."

"Yes, yes, you must come to my inn. Just as nice as this one, if I may say. Better brew than I can find readily, though." Gamin chuckled. Lowering his mug to the table with a hollow clank, Damina's father saluted in the Eskalind military manner, palm and forearm parallel to the floor, then a lift of the wrist so that the palm faced Favik. Then Gamin departed.

Marna's man sat a moment in silence, giving the Havadran no regard. A young couple entered the room, the woman dressed in a water-soaked yellow cloak trimmed with evergreen embroidery patterned into a series of the letter *F*. She complained loudly about the rain. Many turned to look at her, and Favik profited from the distraction to glance toward the blond man again. The fellow was still looking directly at Favik, but this time his hands were before him, in the position of an open book. Once Favik made eye contact, the man closed his hands together.

A bit shocked that this stranger might be a Scholar as well as a Havadran, Favik gazed back at the man and nodded toward an upholstered booth in a corner of the room. Rising, he grabbed his ale and made toward the booth, settling into the cushions. The rain-soaked young woman, who appeared to be not long past her sixteenth Naming Day, called for wine, while her male companion tried to soothe her with promises of a warm bed if they laid aside their journey and spent the night at the inn. A man nearby snickered. Favik's Havadran rose, tankard in hand, to approach while the woman berated the snickerer.

The snickerer made a lackluster apology as the Scholar slipped into the booth across from Favik. "You were once Eskalind's Ambassador to my country?"

"I was. What do you do in Havadra?"

"I leave, as often as I can." The man smirked sardonically, as though he had made peace with a poor situation.

Favik began with a traditional Havadran inquiry. "What is your profession; what is your status?"

"You are familiar with our common greetings. I prefer the Eskalind custom of introducing oneself first before crowing about one's connections and standing. But I will assume you asked to be polite, in the manner of your employer. The rulers of Eskalind are famous for their *knowledge* of the customs of the other lands, and for honoring them." He ran a thin finger around the rim of his tankard. "Ah, knowledge. Knowledge knows no borders."

The loudly complaining young woman shrieked with laughter. "Not again, Aknil! Thank The Powers I am not with child now, as I will never lie with you again." The Innkeeper hesitantly presented the warring pair with a thick mug of ale and a stout glass of ruby-shaded wine; he tiptoed away. Then the couple tittered in a manner indicating that the woman's last utterance might not turn out to be entirely true. The inn's other patrons watched the antics appreciatively—even the fiddler, to the detriment of the tune.

Favik opened his hands before him in the sign of the Scholars. The Havadran repeated the gesture and spoke very quietly, the first words out of his mouth solving part of his mystery. "I am Deenofts of Havadra, sent by Kermon of Guerland with word for the Bladesmith's Daughter."

Surprised by this obscure and coded reference to the Queen, and at Kermon's swiftness in recruiting a Scholar, Favik regarded the Havadran expressionlessly. "Go on."

The fiddler squeaked another wrong note, then began playing a bit louder, as though the volume would smother his earlier error. Deenofts leaned closer. "The Lady of the House of Blue and Red intends to re-join in Nordak near the start of the new year. When she does, by the law of Nordak, a registration will be made in their record of nobles."

"This, this Lady . . . will join with a Nordak lord?"

"It is truth."

"What is her name?"

The Havadran mouthed the name *Nalya*, then said aloud, "That is all my report."

Each closed their palms together. Favik sipped his mug, finding the brew smooth and crisp as he pondered how pleased his Lady Queen would be with this news. Attending again to his tablemate, he asked, "What news of your homeland? I have been away for over two years."

"Fortunate you. You must expect to hear we have had at least three changes of rulership." They both grinned, though a tinge of unease needled Favik, to be joking about the unstable regimes of Havadra with one of its citizens. "No, I jest, only two coups, and the general still keeps rule under the king."

"You know of the general?"

Deenofts replied, "I will tell you, my father and brother are in the army. My father always said, he who controls the warriors controls the throne. Our king is dependent on the soldiery, which means the general." He swallowed a bit of ale. "Divide the army's allegiance, and Havadra will face disaster."

"Has anyone tried recently?"

"Colonel Sirish."

"Ah, I met him when I was Ambassador. Blond with brown eyes . . ."

"That describes nearly all of Havadra."

"A largish man, with a broken nose."

"Makes a hideous sound when he exhales, that's the one. My father served under him. The Powers be thanked it was only for a brief time." Deenofts's small nose wrinkled as if encountering an unsavory scent. "Yes, the general halted Sirish's scheming in a most efficient way."

Favik grinned, certain a tale of serpentine intrigue and conspiracy followed. Most Havadran plots ended with a corpse; the only blank piece of the tale was filling in the method of death. "Do tell how the general eliminated him?"

"He joined houses with him."

Favik's chest tightened as though he might cough, but he managed to say calmly, "Ah, the general joined with a woman of Sirish's house."

"No, the general joined a daughter of his to Sirish."

Melande! She had told him she was the general's only child, a state secret. He felt something fly away from him, felt as though he were a rose stem whose last fading petal had suddenly released, gliding slowly to the cold earth, to its inevitable decay.

"Do I know you?" It was the young woman at the root of the earlier commotion. She planted both her hands on the table to steady herself and stared at Deenofts with eyes as green as her emerald-hued dress.

"Good woman, I do not believe we have met."

"She's a Lady! Address her as such, Havadran," called her companion in a surly tone as he rose from his chair across the room. Favik inhaled as slowly as he could to calm himself.

She sounded like an inquisitive child. "You are from Havadra?"

"Yes, fair Lady. Regardless of popular folklore, I have only one head, and I do not eat children." Deenofts smiled, then leaned forward, whispering, "Except on my Naming Day."

The young woman raised a hand to her wine-stained lips, losing her balance in the act. She fell toward Favik, who reflexively rose to catch her, and slumped against him, soft with the scent of citrus-noted perfume and fresh rain mixed with pungent wine. She cackled, "I was flirting with a Havadran!" How odd to hold a woman against his body when all he could think of was how Melande now shared a bed with a man she called husband. He had no chance of ever holding his great love ever again. She was as gone from him as a grain of sand blown by the wind.

The Lady's companion approached. "Lady Ala, I must insist you retire. Come, let me bring you to bed."

He reached for her, but Favik tightened his awkward hold. In this moment, she was his world. "Is that what the Lady wants?"

"Who's asking?"

"Ambassador Favik of Lord Dalock Strange King's Court." His voice glazed with the chill of restrained pain and a hardened will burned in his eyes, as though he could manifest his intent by mere thought.

All the man could manage was, "Oh."

Lady Ala leaned softly against his shoulder. She murmured, "No, I do not wish to go with him now."

"Innkeep!" the Ambassador called, spotting the proprietor gathering empty beer mugs. "A *secure* room for this Lady." Ala was limp in his arms, her lips brushing his neck. He leaned away, making ready to hoist her feet from the ground and bear her away.

"Certainly, sir." The Innkeeper motioned Favik to follow him.

With a stern nod to Deenofts, Favik scooped Lady Ala into his arms and carried her toward a safe chamber.

"We will talk more soon," said the Havadran from his seat. His voice trailed away as though it were he who was in the act of departing.

The dawn of the year 2904 found Favik bundled in nested coats at the entrance to the House of the Records of nobles in Nordak. Snow swirled around him, the flakes seemingly playing tag with one another.

The document he sought did not appear that day or the next, not until the start of Fourth Month. When the Nordak copyist haggled on the stated price, former Ambassador Favik reminded the woman that the document was for Lord Dalock Strange King. Further discussion ceased, and an elegant record was hastily quilled. Favik's long journey home culminated in his Lady welcoming him into her quarters on a bright Summer day in the Seventh Month.

"Favik! I thought you might be clad entirely in furs. Is Nordak as chilly as they say?"

"Nordak is cold, but not unyielding." From his travel pouch, he pulled forth a snow-colored document cylinder and presented it to Marna Queen with a flourish.

"You found it!" Her ink-stained fingers flashed along the tube, unlocking the clasps. She yanked the coiled certificate from its housing and unrolled it. "Well, Favik, this is most pleasing news, in a way." Marna Queen scanned the creamy Nordak parchment, tilting it slightly against the sunlight. It reflected soft light onto the slight droop of the Queen's chin and unadorned neck, as if lit from within. The seal at the bottom of the certificate glistened: a small, globular, pearlescent wax button enhanced by a shock of thin ribbons emerging from its base, which mimicked the rainbow of hues found in an ice stone. "My, the Nordak records keepers use unusual wax."

The Lady of Eskalind lowered the document atop a stack of others, in the King's colors, that crowded her quilling desk, saying quietly, "At last, proof that Lady Nalya joined with a Nordak lord. The owner of an ice stone mine, no less. Ha! Well, Dalock will be most pleased to rescind her estate and title. I wonder how she will explain to her new husband that by re-joining, her Eskalind property is forfeit." Marna smiled at her man. "I am most glad your visit to Nordak was fruitful. Would that all news were this good." Her hand strayed to a brick-colored papyrus, which she retrieved and passed to him. "Damina's progress report, from her tutor."

From his Ambassador's training he knew to read beyond the page, to delve for hidden or implied meanings. That skill was unnecessary for this document, as Damina's tutor was plainer-speaking than most, and her report was not favorable. Favik encountered one nugget of good news though. "The girl's arithmetic skills are good."

"As one would expect from an Innkeeper's daughter." His Lady groaned. "Damina is but nine years old. I suppose she will need time to adjust to her new circumstances of structured lessons. Though you were quite a quick study at her age."

"I can never thank you enough for your kindnesses to me, my Lady."

She flicked her wrist at him. "I cannot expect such performance from all children of a mere nine years, much as I would wish it. I do wonder, though, if her progress would have been better if you had been here to introduce Damina to her tutor. But I needed you to go to Nordak."

"My Lady, I only met her father that one night. I never met the girl herself."

"True, but I cannot help but think it would have been a smoother transition for everyone if you had overseen it."

Favik savored her confidence in him, though, not for the first time, he was left wondering if she thought he possessed abilities beyond his actual capabilities.

"Ah, Favik, the ill news continues; Scholar Benasa reports that her sovereign plots to conquer our Ever Ally Kaymif."

"My Lady?" He raised his eyebrows. "Scholar Benasa?"

"Benasa of Ghemif. She came to me whilst you served in Havadra, and has provided much useful information. I made her a Scholar while you were in Nordak. She is unusual: Ghemiflanders frown on educating their women, but her family was more enlightened, recognizing her talents. Benasa has spent much time in the Library." It was her turn to raise an eyebrow, and he could see an idea igniting in her expression. "I think you would truly like her."

Without controlling the urge, he lowered his gaze slightly.

"I am sorry, Favik, did I upset you?"

It should not have surprised him that she caught his mood. "No, my Lady. But my heart is … not engaged in finding a sweetheart at the moment." It had not broken his heart that his last lover quit him whilst he travelled to Nordak; rather, Deenofts' tale of Melande joining another had done the deed.

"Ah." She glanced at the Nordak document again as though it held new interest. A knock sounded on the door. "Come in."

Her Page Avnil entered. The lad appeared to have consumed more than his share of Queen's Recipe Roast Chicken since Favik last saw him; Avnil's round cheeks were wider and redder than before. "My Lady, Reader Saralya is at the bottom of the stairs and hopes to come up."

"I will meet her downstairs later."

"She said you would say that, my Lady." The boy grinned. "She also said," Avnil made a thoughtful pause, "she would a-ppre-ci-ate the exercise."

The Queen shook her head. "If she insists, send her." The lad left, while the Queen turned to Favik. "Have you seen Saralya since you returned?"

Her gray eyes twinkled. "No, my Lady, I have not."

"You may be surprised." But she would not elaborate, instead rolling Lady Nalya's Nordak Joining certificate back into its cylinder, which she tucked inside her desk. Reaching for a quill, the Queen added a few more lines to a piece of brown papyrus upon her desk, then sat with her hands in her lap and waited.

A few minutes later, Saralya entered alone, puffing for air, one hand on her back and the other on the expansive swell of her belly. Favik had been away from King's Halls longer than he realized. The former Ambassador rose, smiling, and walked to her. "My Lady Reader, I see congratulations are in order."

The half-Guerish woman's deep brown eyes lit, but her manner bordered on tired, the usual dark glow of her complexion exuding a pallid hint. "Thank you, Favik. The Powers gave me quite a surprise on my fortieth Naming Day. I never thought I would be with child again."

"When will the little one's Naming Day be?"

"The babe will come the end of next month, but as for her Naming Day, it depends on when my husband returns with the King."

"Her?" asked Favik, but the Queen interrupted, her tone edging toward aggrieved.

"Dalock and Jinil's return may also depend on our Scholars' news. If Ghemif invades Kaymif, our army will aid the Kaymiflanders. As our Ever Ally, Kaymif must be defended."

The former Ambassador said, "May The Powers not let it come to that, my Lady."

"Aye." There was no zest in her agreement. "Please, Saralya, I tell you again: I have no sway with The Powers whether the babe be a girl or a boy. I ask only for a healthy mother and child." The Queen shook her head. "And I cannot believe you insisted on all those stairs." The Lady of Eskalind rose from her stout desk and traversed the room to her pillowed couch. She sat, patting the seat next to her. "Come, dear Reader, sit."

Saralya laughed tightly. "I cannot believe I insisted on the stairs either. I thought stretching my legs would do me good." She laid a hand on Favik's offered arm. He guided her toward the Queen. "I have been abed for two months, but our Lady gave me some sweet herbs, and I'm much better."

Favik glanced quickly at the Queen. A slight frown pulled her lips, as though she didn't entirely believe Saralya, or perhaps was simply concerned for her companion's health. The Reader sat next to the Queen, and Favik settled into the chair opposite. "Tell me, my Lady Queen," he said, "how many Scholars are there now?"

Suggesting that she found favor in this line of questioning, the Bladesmith's Daughter replied in a lighter tone. "I am courting more, but currently eight. The three of us, Onath of Thislin, Benasa of Ghemif, Melkain of Mavold, Saralya's blood cousin Kermon of Guerland, and Deenofts of Havadra." Looking to Saralya, she added, "Favik encountered Deenofts by chance at an inn some months ago. That meeting led Favik on the journey he has just returned from."

Her Reader nodded. "Ah, so you met our Havadran compatriot."

"I did. It was a surprise, as I did not know Havadrans would be included in our circle." Saralya bristled slightly. Favik added in an Ambassador's fluid tone, "His information proved most trustworthy and accurate."

"Of course Deenofts's information was genuine," Saralya said. "He was judged by Kermon's father to be worthy of trust long ago, when the Havadran was just a boy. And Kermon himself judged Deenofts the same." Saralya folded her arms over her chest. "My mother's family comes from a long line of Merchant Masters, and their livelihood depends on accurately sensing whom to trust. That is one of many reasons I suggested Kermon as a Scholar."

"I meant no discourtesy to your family or their customs, my Lady Queen's Reader."

"It is a Gift from The Powers that some Guerlanders are able to see one's true character. Those individuals are acknowledged as Merchant Masters, held in the highest esteem," Saralya said. Her gaze hardened on him, and Favik wondered if she thought herself in possession of such skills that she could divine flaws within him. It conjured up the Tension Trials he had undergone during his Ambassador's training, in which Apprentices are subjected to intense scrutiny while confronted with stressful or surprising situations. Like most successful Eskalind Apprentice Ambassadors, Favik had found the Trials a challenge he relished confronting.

The Queen's gaze darted between the pair during this exchange, but she said nothing. Favik countered Saralya's opposition with a deferential nod. "Then I am most glad Kermon uses his Gift in service to our Lady." He spoke gently, with a hint of mirth in his next utterance: "If I must ever return to Havadra, might your blood cousin have a Gifted son he could lend me to see me safely through the journey?"

"Kermon's wife died in childbed. He has no living children." Saralya gazed out the windows. "My poor cousin. Such a good man."

The Queen intervened, laying a hand on her companion's back. "Saralya, dear, I know this is a difficult time for you. For us both." She raised her gray eyes to Favik. "We are both anxious about our husbands and our sons. Dalich and Saril are with their fathers, overseeing army maneuvers in preparation for possible battle in Kaymif."

Favik puckered his lips slightly, eyes sympathetic. "What can I do to make your burdens lighter, my Lady?"

The Lady of Eskalind leaned into her cushions, running both hands along her hair and smoothing back the intermingled gray and reddish-blond tresses. "End all wars." Anxiety tightened the cords of her neck. "No, that was a weak jest. We must prepare. It is the best solution. The Scholars' network alerted us to this Ghemif situation, and we must keep their news flowing to Dalock and Jinil so they can prepare on the front lines."

Saralya whispered, "May The Powers help us all."

"Favik, I am naming you Queensman."

He had never heard of such a position before and was uncertain what it entailed, but before he could inquire, she continued. "I want it clear to all that you work solely for me, that you are free to move about under my sole direction."

"Thank you for your trust, my Lady."

Directing her gaze to her Reader, the Queen said, "My husband will see the value in it when Favik brings him the reports we have from the Scholars."

Saralya cautioned, "Are you certain this appointment will not vex the King, my Lady?"

"It may, but I need Favik free to move about. I cannot leave these Halls with war brewing; I must remain to receive and direct fresh reports from the Scholars, or sit judgment on any Ambassador's letters that might arrive."

The dark-haired woman stared at her belly. "And I am clearly not going anywhere."

"Saralya, I need you here with me for your counsel." Marna Queen's eyes stared across the room, to nothing in particular that Favik could discern. "And your companionship."

"I thank The Powers I am in your service and in your care, my Lady."

The two women gazed at one another. Tears welled in the Queen's Reader's eyes, then flooded her cheeks. Their Lady leaned to embrace her companion. "Dear Saralya, it will be all right."

Favik looked at his hands.

The tent flap fluttered closed behind the heavy Guard escorting the Ghemif messenger from the Strange King's pavilion. One could never be too cautious in the borderlands before a battle.

Dalock drummed his long fingers on his elbows. "So much for a word from their king," he grumbled. "An ultimatum from their king was more like it." He sniffed, finding the air still potent with the courier's cologne. "If King Grufmit is as perfumed as that overgroomed whelp, then his judgment is surely clouded by the stench. Gah, I can taste it in the air." Were it not for the fine rugs carpeting his pavilion, he would have spat. He gestured to Jinil, his Second now for twenty-six years, to come to his side.

Jinil's face held a neutral expression, but Dalock read a multitude of worries in his man's eyes: a treacherous enemy, the eve of his eldest son's first battle, and his wife, over four hundred miles away in Eskalind, ill, at last word, and heavy with child. "My King, I do not trust their terms."

"We are in agreement." Dalock peered toward their sons, standing at attention at the far end of the tent, opposite the door. "At ease, boys." Dalich and Saril bowed in unison, their crimson cloaks and shoulder-length black hair rendering them more twin-like than the King could ever recall. After a long summer spent out of doors, Dalich's skin was tanned to nearly as dark as his companion's natural tone, while Saril's Ambassador's training had kept him deep in the caverns of the Library much of the time, save for the last few weeks. Their new beards were similar too, full on the chin but thin on the cheeks.

For an instant they looked the part of straight-backed, disciplined young Standers, youths not yet come to their swords and thus not yet eligible to be called Soldier. Then they dropped their poses to sink onto the carpet with youthful enthusiasm, scrambling to replace their chess pieces and resume their interrupted match. The King felt a glimmer of pride that the lads had not once complained about not earning their swords yet, despite having both passed their sixteenth Naming Day months ago. Dalich and Saril seemed content to forgo earning their manhood in a prearranged tournament, instead opting to wait for combat. Now the battle was just hours away.

The two men seated themselves at a small table. Jinil retrieved the rolled maps of the area, set aside before the Ghemif messenger entered the tent. He stroked the scar that cut through his gray beard. The King gestured for him to speak.

"We will meet on the field at noon if the negotiations fail," Jinil said.

"And they will fail," Dalock predicted. "The Ghemiflanders will not give an inch, having stolen half of Kaymif and killed King Koulai. And his heir but a six-year-old boy." He nearly thanked The Powers his own son was nearly a man, but Dalock was in no hurry to have the youth inherit.

King's Second murmured, "My Lord, I fear an ambush."

"Where?"

"We should prepare for anything, but," Jinil glanced at the youths, "I saw the messenger's eyes roaming this pavilion." He leaned slightly toward the King, speaking softly. "It was not just the glance of an anxious man. I suspect he gathered information for an attack on you, or King's Son."

Dalock nodded. He too had had an uneasy sense about the Ghemif messenger. "Then Dalich and I will remove from my pavilion for the night, and post extra Guards to watch for anything suspicious. Though in a camp of two commingled armies before battle, anything may seem so." The Lord of Eskalind folded his fingers before him, studying the maps of their current environs. "Order the cooks to serve drink with the small ladle. A lesser ration of ale tonight will keep our men alert."

"The cooks are roasting Queen's Recipe chicken; the men may not notice the decrease in drink."

Dalock could not help but smile. When this was over, and thanks to Marna's diligence and information, he would finally reward his Second for his many years of staunch service with a title and the grand estate that once was Lady Nalya's. Aloud he called, "How goes the game, Dalich?"

"I am thinking four moves ahead, Father," the youth responded, voice terse.

"One should always think ahead," cautioned the King, his eyes tracing the map.

"And of doing two things at once," Jinil replied. Dalock nodded, bending closer to the parchment.

Saril said, "Check."

"What? How did you do that?" King's Son exclaimed.

"Doing two things at once, my Lord."

Dalock grinned at his Second. "Think backward, Dalich," he advised, leaning away from the table. "Jinil, this strikes me as a fine place for an ambush." He pointed to a choke point on the map, just as his Page Bafnil entered the tent.

"My Lord, Favik Queensman is freshly arrived with urgent messages from home," the boy reported.

"Show him in," the King answered, peripherally noting sudden tension on the faces of Jinil and his son. Saril stood, mirrored by Dalich. Jinil placed a cautious hand on his long knife's hilt.

The blond man they expected entered, bowing to the assembled males, who relaxed slightly.

"What news?" Dalock grunted. While he was still not entirely pleased with his wife's naming the Humikslander Queensman—an ambiguous designation, to his mind—some work of The Powers must be behind it. Marna was his Queen after all, Gifted beyond the measure of most of the Queens of legend. Still, that would not spare the man any love from his Lord.

"Glad news, my Lords." Favik smiled at Jinil. "On the Twenty-Ninth Day of the Eighth Month, your wife, Saralya, was safely delivered of a healthy girl child."

"Thank The Powers!" Jinil's green eyes lit with the release of a great worry. He raised his hands to the tent ceiling, then glanced at his son, who smiled broadly. The King gave his man a congratulatory slap on the back as the two embraced.

Favik reported, "My Lady the Queen attended the birth, as did your son Marnil."

"Marnil?" exclaimed Saril. "My brother did something?"

Dalich gave a high-pitched laugh.

"Ah, then she had the best of care," Dalock said, turning from his Second to shoot a stern glance at his son.

The blond man continued. "I have other messages for the King from my Lady, regarding," he lowered his voice, "the situation here, and," his eyes shot to Dalich, "a message for King's Son, which I am bid to give him in private."

Dalock turned to his son, raising his eyebrows, but the youth tilted his head down, deep brown hair sliding before his eyes to hide them.

"So my wife and my son have secrets." The King glanced at his Second. "Perhaps they conspire on my Naming Day present." The jest served to lighten his mood, and he turned to his man. "Well, Jinil, we will have the Naming of your daughter to celebrate when we return. For now, I am hungry. Let us leave the conspirators, for a brief moment." The King reached to accept the red-wax-sealed envelopes Favik offered. "Dalich, meet us at the kitchens the moment you are finished." To the Queensman he commanded, "Make it quick."

"Certainly, my Lord."

To Jinil he beckoned, "Come, my Second, new father of a daughter! Let us see what information my Queen contributes to our plans." He left the tent, followed by his Second and Saril.

———

King's Son held his head high, hoping he mimicked his father's demeanor. His mother's messenger handed him a tea-colored note impressed with the Queen's seal. Dalich ripped it open, the sticky wax caking under his fingernails. It was quilled just over a week ago.

First Day, Ninth Month, 2904
My Dear Son,
Soon you will earn your sword and become a man. It is a mother's
fondest wish to be proud of her child, and to see him glad in
his days. While the former is accomplished with ease, I must
remedy the latter. Forgive your father for trying to protect you.
He does this only out of love for you. Your father says The Powers
protect you, and that you must use this Gift in service to others.
Remember your training, my son! May these many years of
preparation serve you well and see you safe.
Lastly, accept the small token Favik carries and find that which
you know, and yet do not know.
Your loving mother,
Marna Queen

He glanced at Favik. "Where is this token of which my mother writes?"

His mother's man reached into a pocket to retrieve a small bundle, no bigger than his thumb. He handed it to King's Son, who untangled the braided string with purposeful fingers.

Inside was a fine chain. Dangling from its end was a stonesmooth locket. Along its glossy bronze curves unrolled a delicate scrolling pattern akin to the flourishes at the end of a line of poetry. The carving was of such delicate quality he could not feel it. The youth flipped the minute latch, which sprang open to reveal a miniature portrait of a lovely girl. Dark braids encircled her head; her eyes shone a deep, enchanting violet. She looked about to speak.

Damina. Gazing into her eyes, he felt certain the image would bring her voice, her thoughts, back into his mind. But nothing happened. He touched her image. Still nothing. After a sobering breath, he queried, "Where did you get this?"

"Your Lady mother bid me give it to you, with no more words than I have spoken." Favik bowed his blond head.

Dalich nodded, a slow smile growing. His mother knew where Damina could be found, perhaps had even met with her. Against his father's command, Mother wanted him to reconnect with the girl! Rejoicing inside, he said, "Tell our Lady she gives me hope." King's Son fastened the chain around his neck, tucking the locket inside his tunic.

"As you wish," replied the man, a cool, impassive expression on his face once more. "To the kitchens, my Lord?"

Dalich suddenly remembered his father's orders. At least this was a command he wanted to follow. "Oh yes." He wondered when he would get a chance to study Damina again undetected. Perhaps later tonight. For now, he followed his mother's man toward the kitchens, paying no mind to the mud along the way, feeling he floated above the soppy ground.

Ahead, Saril stood just inside a large tent, holding one side open, his red cloak a keen match to the fabric wall. He waved as they approached. "Favik," he called, "My Lord King bids you meet him at the ale tent. The one near the smithy."

"Then I wish you both well," the native Humikslander replied, nodding at Dalich. For a moment, the man's visage reminded the youth of his mother in an unnerving way, as though she herself gazed at him in this moment. Then he recalled how often folk of her birth country of Humiksland gave him that sense, and he shook it off.

The Queensman made his leave, and Saril motioned Dalich inside, then dropped the tent's fabric wall, closing it. Inside were washtubs and a table covered with dirty pots, stained platters with lids askew, and sadly empty tankards. A bundle rested on the sole chair. Jinil's son reached for it. "My father said we must wear these cloaks." He unfurled one of the cloths, handing Dalich a brown-colored, coarsely woven cloak akin to the attire of Standers.

"He truly is worried someone will try to attack us." Dalich unfastened his rich crimson cloak, exchanging it for the plainer one. He patted his belt to make certain his short sword and dagger were in place.

"Hmm. Now see what else . . ." Saril reached for a large covered pot atop the table. "Queen's Recipe chicken!"

"Four?" Dalich gushed when his companion lifted the lid to reveal two pairs of freshly roasted birds side by side.

"Two for each of us!" Saril exulted, the youth's voice triumphant. The encompassing aroma of mint and rosemary rose into the air as though pridefully announcing its source.

Dalich hoisted the bird pot to the floor and sat. He reached for an herb-encrusted leg. "I *may* forgive you for beating me at chess," he mumbled, biting into the savory meat.

Saril brushed his own red cloak from his arms, reaching into the pot. "Ah, but we did not finish the game. You may beat me yet." Standing, he crunched into the crispy skin. "My Lord, what did your mother quill you about?"

Dalich thought for a moment about whether to share his secret. "Mmm, she was wishing me well." It was true, but not the whole truth. Still, he felt clever for not lying outright. "Saril, do you remember when my mother's wishbone was thrown away?" He reached for his second chicken.

"Hmm?"

"Some special wishbone from when she and Father met. She had it on her desk, and one of the servants thought it was left over from a meal and threw it away."

"Right, right!" Saril laughed. "I remember everyone going through the compost trying to find it. That was gross!"

Dalich chuckled too. "And when they found it, Father had it bronzed for her so it would not happen again."

Chicken leg in hand, Saril walked to the tent wall, pulling aside the fabric to gaze out. "Do you think it was the right wishbone they found?"

"Aye. My mother would know. She knows everything." Dalich reached to his chest, touching the small lump of Damina's locket under his rough cloak and tunic. "Hmm."

"I cannot wait till we earn our swords." Saril gazed intently as two young women carrying jugs approached.

"Me either," King's Son replied. Then he would go to Damina. They sucked the bare bones, watching as the women swayed past them.

Nudging King's Son, Saril ventured, "I heard one of the Guards say the Kaymif princess is very pretty."

Trying to think of something funny to say, Dalich gave a noncommittal nod. "I wonder how they could tell, since Kaymif ladies always have those beads hanging over their eyes." The pair snickered a moment, shifting their gaze about, hoping no one overheard. It would be unseemly for the sons of the most important men in Eskalind to be caught mocking the customs of others.

Chicken leg between his teeth, Saril tied the tent side open. King's Son suggested, "Saril, what do you think; would this be a good spot to continue our chess match?"

"Aye," Saril agreed, removing the bone from his mouth. "But I left the set at your pavilion. Wait here, my Lord, I'll get it." Pretending to aim his bare chicken leg bone at King's Son, he then flung it to the opposite side of the table.

"Watch it!" Dalich hefted a whole chicken in his hands as if it were a throwing stone. His companion ducked, whilst Dalich bit into the chicken. The pair laughed. Saril rose, turning toward the outdoors just as the same two women made their way by the tent again. "Enjoy the view," he whispered, his dark eyes glinting.

Dalich grinned, watching Saril trot back in the direction of the King's tent, his red cloak still bright against the graying light of nightfall. Dalich glanced back at the women, thinking Damina far prettier than the two of them together. All of a sudden, a strange feeling seized him; his skin prickled from his shoulders to his lower back.

"Saril forgot to change his cloak!" King's Son leapt to his feet, dashing to pursue his companion, nearly knocking over the passing women. "Saril!" he yelled, careening past Soldiers and Guardsmen. The familiar red cloak rounded a corner as Dalich pursued, calling, "Wait!" He thought Saril began to twist toward him, but a giant of a man appeared, blocking King's Son's path.

"The Soldier asked you a question!" the huge man bellowed, sweeping aside his plain brown cloak to reveal an Eskalinder Soldier's uniform of matching tunic and breeches. A red numeral 7 for the Seventh Company was stitched over his heart. His belt was studded with an impressive array of varyingly sized scabbards.

The youth stopped short. "What?" He craned to look around the man, spying Saril continuing toward the King's pavilion.

Someone approached Dalich from behind. The Strange King's heir turned to face a second man, who also wore the brown cloak and metal helm of an Eskalind Soldier. The youth did not recognize either of them. By The Powers, he must recall a man of such outstanding size in his father's army. Unless they were disguised Ghemif assassins.

The Soldier sneered, "I said, what Company are you with, laddie?"

"I…am of the King's Company." A vague, yet honest answer. Dalich balanced himself on the pads of his feet, readying to dash away.

The second man squinted at him. "King's Company?" he snarled. "Who's your Captain?"

Dalich met the man's gaze, but tensed at the unmistakable ring of steel as the enormous, weapons-laden man drew blade behind him.

He must convince them to release him, somehow, or run for his life.

"My Captain is Jinil, King's Second," he said as firmly as he could.

Two more uniformed Eskalind army members approached: a woman bearing a torch, and a man with a brown, crested First Sergeant's helm. The First Sergeant called, "Stop, you fools!" He hastily marched toward Dalich and his questioners. Removing his helmet, he said, "I know the face of my aunt's son when I see it. My Lord." A swift bow of his blond head followed.

"Narnik!" Dalich cried as he recognized his cousin. "Thank The Powers!"

The man who had been questioning Dalich asked, "First Sergeant, you know this youngster?"

"Aye, he is King's Son," Narnik replied, blue eyes steady, his free hand upon Dalich's shoulder. "Do you not recognize him?"

"I did," said the female Soldier with a nod, mindful not to lower her torch.

"He's King's Son?" began the huge man, as he too bowed. "My Lord, forgive us, we thought—"

Dalich raised a hand to stay the apologies. "Please, you must help me. Saril may be in danger."

Narnik stepped aside, "Saril, Jinil's son? Where is he?" He replaced his helmet.

"Follow me." Dalich guided the four at a fast pace toward his father's tent, hoping he followed the same route as Saril. There were more paths than he realized.

One of the Guards posted outside the King's unoccupied pavilion told the small company that Saril had just left.

"Back to the kitchens. We must find him!" Dalich led his group in the direction the Guard pointed. They splashed through the mud, coming to a split in the path. He tried to read the tangle of footprints on the ground.

Narnik said behind him, "Both those paths lead to the kitchen tents."

"I do not remember which way we came before." He felt foolish.

"My Lord Cousin, Saril may have gone a different way."

"We should separate, then," Dalich said, twitching with frustration. Why was it so hard to find his companion when he was but a moment ahead of them?

"I will go this way," Narnik headed to the left, gesturing for the torch-bearer to follow him. "We meet at the kitchens," the First Sergeant told his young cousin.

Dalich nodded, dashing down the path on the right, followed by the two men who had questioned him earlier. It was getting darker, but some of the way was lit by staked torches. Ahead, he caught sight of a man shoving what appeared to be a red bundle between two tents.

"That was Saril!" King's Son dashed ahead of his father's men. He unsheathed his short battle sword as he approached the man from behind, just as the man raised a cudgel over Saril's head. Jinil's son was now crouched, his back to the cudgel lifter, facing two more opponents. One held an axe and the other a long knife. Saril too held a blade, assessing his adversaries as he recovered from his fall.

Dalich swung his weapon into the club-holder's neck. The man and his stout stick fell with a thud, just missing Jinil's son.

"Saril!" Dalich yelled to his companion, and the other youth glanced back. "Watch out!" Dalich barked as the man with the axe threw a net toward them. King's Son scooted to the side, but Saril, attempting to leap away, was entrapped in the black web. He lost his balance, toppling to the waterlogged ground.

The two attackers rushed Dalich. He flung mud at them, hitting the axe-bearer in the eyes, then parrying the other's blow with his short sword. "Help!" he called to his father's men, drawing his dagger with his muddy free hand.

The axeman cursed whilst wiping his eyes, then lunged at Dalich. Suddenly the man groaned, grasping his chest. A lance pierced through his tunic, and he collapsed into the dirt as the two Eskalind Soldiers came to their master's aid.

The last attacker, seeing himself surrounded by a trio of armed fighters, dropped his weapon to plead, "No, don't kill me! I have information! Please!"

"Stop!" Dalich ordered, stepping away from the man. The Soldiers pointed their weapons at the man's neck. He dropped to the ground, quivering hands held high in the air.

"Please, please spare me!" the man cried, as King's Son helped Saril untangle himself from the net.

"What can you tell us?" Dalich ordered, flicking mud from his hand. His lifelong companion broke free from the mesh and threw it aside.

"For my life?"

"If you answer truthfully, you will keep your life," the youth bargained. Saril stepped to his side.

"Yes, yes!" The man nodded with vigor.

"What were you doing here?"

"We … we were sent to kill the Strange King," the man admitted, eyes mindful of the sharp steel hovering near his throat. "But he was too well guarded. So we thought to capture the prince," his eyes jerked to Jinil's son. "For ransom."

Saril spoke. "Who sent you?"

"King Grufmit."

"The Ghemif king," Dalich said. "Father was right. What else? How many of you?"

"Just the three of us." The man's voice faded as King's Son added his blade to the others, close to the man's neck. "Only three!"

"You tried to harm my companion and plotted to kill my father." The Heir of Eskalind pressed his steel against the man's throat.

"*You* are the prince?" the man sputtered. "Please, kind, kind sir … I … I know other things. There is to be an ambush tomorrow . . ."

Dalich regarded him, recalling that his father did suspect an ambush. "Am I to trust an assassin?" He pictured this man sneaking into the King's tent, drawing blade against his father as he slept. Dalich need only flick his wrist to end the man's life.

"My Lord—" Saril began.

"No," Dalich stated. He studied the thickening blood on his short sword, evidence of the assassin he slew to save his companion. For a moment he thought the wet pattern spelled letters he could not quite interpret. His rage lessened as though a calming hand pressed his shoulder. "I am King's Son of Eskalind. We are the Strange Kingdom, and I will not kill in cold blood." The man gaped at him. "I will be true to my word and spare your life. Though you may not deserve it."

"Oh, thank you, kind, kind prince!"

"My title is King's Son. You will reveal all you know to my father." He wiped his blade on the inside of his rough cloak. To the two Soldiers he ordered, "Bind him and bring him to our Lord." Sheathing his blades, he turned to Saril, who smiled.

"I think tonight King's Son earned his sword." They clasped arms. "Thank you, thank you, my Lord."

Dalock's son grinned. "At last I outpace you at something!"

"Well, we still have a chess match to finish," Saril said, echoing his father's dry humor.

———

Dalock dropped his wife's note onto the large barrel of ale serving as an impromptu table for himself and his Second. "The audacity of the Kaymif queen! And she begged our Ambassador to send for Eskalind to avenge her husband's death." He ground his elbows into the wood.

"I hardly believe it myself," Jinil agreed from his seat on a smaller cask. "Her treachery would outdo a Havadran." He eyed his King's agitation with caution.

"Are we certain Marna's news is accurate?" Dalock queried Favik, who stood at attention before the older men.

"To the best of her abilities, my Lord," he replied smoothly, his expression neutral. Jinil watched him with a close eye. He often wondered how the Queen and this man came by so much information.

"So if Marna's knowledge is correct," Dalock King began, "then the Kaymif queen plotted with her brother, King Grufmit of Ghemif, to kill her husband, so she could place her six-year-old son on the throne and rule through him. But along the way, her brother decided to conquer half her kingdom and keep it for himself. Thus, she cries to us for aid." He shook his head. "Add to it that she has designs to join her daughter with my son. Ha! She should have been a traveling player. She acts the part of bereaved widow quite well."

"Perhaps when this is over, she will find a new occupation," Jinil jested, pleased to see his Lord's composure returning.

But the King did not smile. "Again our people risk their lives for unworthy men. And women. Tell me, Jinil, remind me, again, why ours is the better way. Why cannot we stay at home and let these fools kill each other as it pleases them?"

Nearly thirty years of service to Dalock King had taught Jinil to expect this request. Often it came on the field of battle after the slaughter. Sometimes before, like tonight.

"My Lord, The Powers guard our land," he began, aware he was slipping into his routine. "Never in all my years, or those of my fathers before me, has an attacking army crossed our borders." He looked at Favik, watching him with keen gray eyes. He read doubt there. That challenge inflamed his convictions. "But they exact a price for their protection."

The King nodded, his gaze turned away, perhaps thinking about his father's death in just such a battle over a quarter century ago.

"My Lord, if we did not pay here, in foreign lands, with our Soldiers, and maybe our sons, we would pay at home, with all our family at risk." He thought of his wife, safe within the Strange Kingdom's borders, at home in King's Halls with their newborn babe. "I may not live to see my daughter," Jinil whispered. "But I know," and he reached for his usual tone, "that if she grows to womanhood in our lands, The Powers will see to it that no war will touch her there, ever."

Dalock King nodded noncommittally, but his countenance softened.

"Then we fight tomorrow for Jinil's daughter." His voice was quiet, but hardened with resolve. "Soon you will see her, and together, you and your wife will name her." He stood, laying a hand on his man's arm "Now I want to question King Koulai's widow. Let us see what she will tell us, without revealing Marna's news."

As though beckoned by The Powers, King's Page Bafnil rushed into the ale tent. "My Lord, King's Son and Saril Jinil's son have returned with a prisoner," the boy announced breathlessly.

"Prisoner? Show them in, then send for the Kaymif queen. Tell her I have urgent news that awaits her judgment."

Bafnil swept his head in a bow and departed.

Jinil watched as his crimson-cloaked child and King's Son, in brown, filed into the tent, followed by two Eskalind Soldiers, one so tall his helm brushed the fabric ceiling. The Soldiers held a bound man between them. Closer inspection revealed mud staining Saril's clothes. The coppery scent of blood tinged the air, but both youths appeared unharmed. He scolded under his breath, "Saril, I told you to wear the brown cloak I gave you!"

"Yes, Father, I'm sorry," his son replied, dark brown eyes shamed.

Then King's Son told the full tale, to Saril's enthusiastic nods. Jinil experienced both great relief that his boy survived and deep annoyance that the youth had made such a foolish, easily preventable mistake. By The Powers, he had thought his son's judgment keener. Saril would not be ready for an Ambassadorship anytime soon.

Dalock King glowered at the Ghemif prisoner. "Tell us about this ambush."

"My Lord," quavered the man, "the prince said my life would be spared—"

"On the condition that you tell us the truth," interrupted the King. "Unlike your master, we do not traffic in treachery. Continue. Now."

"There is to be a...force, hiding in the trees. The trees on the—" The prisoner's eyes bulged. For a moment, Jinil wondered if the man had been poisoned. But the Ghemiflander continued. "The east side of here, along the road that leads to the field where the battle is to be."

The King rapped his fingers on the ale barrel. "How many?"

"A hundred. With nets. And men concealed on the ground as well," the prisoner stammered. "And the farmhouse on the—" Again his eyes widened as he searched for the proper term, or perhaps for his imagination to catch up to his mouth. "On the west, the farmhouse has men hiding in it. Fifty men. In a door in the ground. In the cellar."

Jinil drew closer to the King. "Too elaborate," he whispered.

"What else?" Dalock asked the bound man, who shook his head.

"That is all I know, my Lord," the would-be assassin said with a gulp. The Ghemiflander directed his eyes longingly at the bread and sauces and the plate of chicken bones residing on the large keg in the center of the tent.

"Soldiers, see that this man is chained, fed, and looked to," Dalock ordered. His men led the captive away. The King shifted his gaze to his son. "What do you think, Dalich?"

"Father, fifty men hiding in a farmhouse cellar seems unlikely."

The King grinned at his Second, who added, "Most unlikely. We are in full agreement, my Lord." Favik was nodding.

"Good," Dalock began, shifting his brown gaze to the youths. "Given Dalich has proven himself in combat tonight, now would be a good time for King's Son to receive his sword."

King's Second asked, "Just present company, my Lord?"

"Aye. Given the circumstances, the ceremony will be brief. Come forward, Son."

With a quick glance at Saril, the young man stepped forward to kneel before his father, gray eyes solemn and serious as only an earnest youth's can be.

The proud father surveyed their surroundings, chuckling. "Well, my boy, who would have thought you would be granted your sword in an ale tent?"

Dalich tilted his forehead downward, a hint of reddening in his cheeks before his dark hair fell forward and shielded his face.

The King turned to his Second with a look that Jinil read as saying, "Well, what can I do?" but he said aloud, in a serious voice, "Bring his sword."

Jinil retrieved the designated blade from a plain brown cloth, tucked between two barrels earlier by the Guard whose duty was to see that these swords stayed near the King. As he unwrapped the sheathed blade meant for Dalich, he caught sight of the scabbard meant for his own son. Again disappointment brushed his heart. He gripped the carved bronze sheath of King's Son's blade with both hands, holding it lengthwise to present to the King.

The Lord of Eskalind spoke. "As is our custom, let this sword pass through the hands of all men present."

The King passed the sheathed blade back to Jinil, who handed it to Favik. All the while, Saril kept a fond gaze on King's Son. It pleased King's Second to see his eldest appear happy for his companion. The youth might make a courtier yet, though he might not always be so lucky as to serve one he truly liked. The first lesson as a royal's servant was to wear the face expected, regardless of one's true feelings, though The Powers knew this to be less true in Eskalind than elsewhere.

Favik passed the metal scabbard back to the King, who grasped it. "This night, Dalich King's Son proved himself before The Powers to be fully a man by defending his companion Saril. My son, wear this sword in defense of yourself, our family, our Kingdom, and the borderlands."

The youth raised his head slowly and reached for the sword. Father and son gripped the bronze sheath, and for a moment it did not matter that this formal ceremony occurred amongst barrels of ale in a land beyond their home. The King spoke, his voice both warm and choked. "This sword was made by your grandfather of Humiksland." His brown eyes gleamed in the torchlight. "It is carved with the devices of your father and your mother." Dalock King stroked the bronze decoration on the locket, at the top of the scabbard. It was an open book, its pages a smooth gleam of unscratched metal. "Marna said, 'If my books bear the symbol of a sword, then your sword will bear the emblem of a book.' I wish she were here," murmured the King.

"As do I, Father," replied the new man with resolute sincerity. A slight smile curved Favik's lips. Jinil did not doubt the Queen would receive a thorough report.

Dalock King released the sheath into his son's hands. Dalich stood and extracted his new blade, slow and steady, careful not to endanger anyone in the tight space of the ale tent. The Heir of Eskalind admired the sheath's crafted length whilst his father watched with a joyful smile, similar to the one he had worn on King's Son's Naming Day, over sixteen years ago.

A rustle sounded from the tent flap, and the King's Page made his way inside.

"My Lord, the Kaymif queen is here," Bafnil announced. His eyes grew wide when he noticed King's Son holding his fine blade.

"Delay her." The Page left. "Come, Dalich, belt your sword for now. Though soon," and the King's eyes narrowed as they tracked to the tent's entrance, "you may have opportunity to use it."

Dalich bowed to his Lord, still aware of every quick beat of his heart, for he was a man now and could go to Damina. He sheathed his new blade. Saril's exuberant smile and embrace only clouded his thoughts. He wished to The Powers that his companion too had earned his sword this day. King's Son fastened his scabbard to his waist, stepping to his Lord's side just as a pair of his father's men entered the tent, followed by two Kaymif guards.

Bafnil reentered, his hands behind his back. He pronounced, with all the solemnity a boy of twelve years can summon, "Her Grandness, Queen of Kaymif, Mostaza, born of Ghemif."

A blond woman clad in a high-waisted, low-cut, wispy purple gown floated into the tent. She curtsied low to the King. The amethyst beads draped across her forehead made it difficult to read her true expression, though she parted her lips in a manner that most would account a smile.

The Page announced, "The Queen's daughter, Princess Kostaza." A slender young woman, dressed similarly to the Queen but in a blue gown trimmed with purple, followed. Despite the sapphire and violet beads draping her eyes, Dalich sensed the princess glance curiously between himself and Saril. Hoping to attract more of her notice, he casually brushed aside his rough brown cloak so that his new sword might be admired, whilst he studied the soft curves of her cleavage.

The Kaymif princess curtsied low to his father, which gave King's Son a most enjoyable view. Then she assumed a position next to her mother, but with an anxious flit of her head toward the doorway. Wanting to appear taller, Dalich straightened his back and leaned forward slightly on his toes.

The King cleared his throat. "I sent only for—" But Bafnil, urgent to finish his task, interrupted: "And the Queen's son, Prince Moulai."

A sad-faced boy stepped into the tent, bowed stiffly, then scooted to his sister's side, wearily placing his head against her elbow. He stared at the floor. The princess reached her arm around him, pulling him to her hip as if to shelter him from a grave threat.

The Strange King addressed the Kaymif Queen directly. "Prince?" Exactly what Dalich thought, for surely by the laws of his land, the little lad was now king, since his father had been killed.

The Ghemif-born woman smiled weakly, bringing a finger to her mouth as though silently shushing a child. Dalock King's eyes glinted. For a moment Dalich thought his father might snarl at the queen, but her daughter interrupted. "Your pardon, Lord of Eskalind. It is a great honor to meet you, but my brother is not well. May I return with him to our quarters?"

The tension in the King's neck relaxed slightly. "That would be best for all involved."

"Thank you." The princess bowed and turned to leave.

King's Son flushed with a sudden desire to not see her go. He inclined toward his father, speaking quietly and urgently. "My Lord, allow me to see to their safety by accompanying them to their quarters."

Dalock King squinted. "An excellent notion." To the gathering he announced, "Dalich King's Son will lend his sword and escort the queen's children."

This time, the Kaymif queen's smile bore the sparkle of genuine pleasure. "Kostaza would be most pleased to accept the honor." She nodded to her guards.

Dalich bowed impassively to her and to his father, but could not help wondering why the queen had not included her son in her statement. He also withheld a grin at her phrasing—his father had offered the woman no choice in the matter.

The young man stepped toward the princess, gazing at the azure and purple beads draping her brow, hoping she looked upon him with favor. He gestured for her and her brother to precede him. Following the Kaymif royal children, King's Son exited the tent, following a tantalizing hint of hips under the princess's gown.

Outside, torches flickered along a brightly illuminated path of straw that stretched to two canopied carts, one draped in violet hues and the other in soft blue trimmed with purples. Several liveried men stood in small groups chatting in hushed tones. Upon spying their young lord and the princess, they swooped into position, four of the broader men at the front of each cart, making ready to pull their burden. In pairs, lankier men with the alert bearing of Soldiers assumed positions at the sides and back of the carts. To Dalich, it seemed an excessive amount of guards, but this was a Kaymif war camp, not the road to King's Market in the Strange Kingdom. A tinge of pity at the need for such caution in the borderlands brushed his heart. A keen desire to protect his companions inflamed his thoughts.

Kostaza gestured a graceful hand toward the blue and purple cart. "That bounche is ours. The other is Mother's."

"And Father's too, when he comes back," interjected her brother, showing a bit of spirit.

Dalich saw a hint of a quiver on her smooth lips. Without another word, the trio walked upon the straw toward the designated bounche. One of the men stepped forward. "My lady, is the queen coming?"

"No, Voukai. You may do as you like."

"Very good." It was a phrase one might hear a thousand times from a servant, but this utterance carried an air of relief and mischief within it.

Voukai lifted the young lad up to a thin step, then parted the curtains to reveal a pillow-flocked interior. Prince Moulai spread his arms and whooped as he fell face forward into the soft cushions, which fluttered up slightly from his weight. It looked like fun, but Dalich, still reveling in his status as a new man, doubted the princess would receive similar treatment. Though he would not mind having her land on top of him, if they had a bounche with opaque curtains to themselves.

"You try it!" encouraged the youngster to Dalich.

"Shh, Brother. That is only for you, as a special treat, when Mother is not watching!" chided his sister. "Right, Voukai?" Kostaza spoke warmly, as if fighting laughter, as she tilted her head toward the servant.

"Yes, my princess." Voukai grinned as he helped her into the cart in a much more civilized manner. To King's Son's disappointment, she settled into the farthest position on the cart, which left for him only the vacant pillows on the other side of her brother.

With a firm, calloused hand, the servant assisted the Heir of the Strange Kingdom into the bounche. Dalich lowered himself beside Moulai, who sprawled and yawned exaggeratedly as if he were in his own bed. "I'm tired," the child announced.

His sister turned her head. "I know, but do you not want to speak with Prince Dalich? Maybe he knows a good story," she encouraged, reaching to pat the boy's leg. Behind those tiny, bright beads draping her eyes, there was no way to know for certain where Kostaza's gaze fell. Telling tales to a sleepy lad did not seem the best use of their time together. Still, Dalich hoped to make a favorable impression, even as the strong scent of lavender in the cart threatened to engender an embarrassingly large sneeze.

Outside, Voukai bellowed forth an order to march, and the cart lunged forward, then settled into a slight rocking motion, which caused a teasing swelling and then disappointing contraction of the gauzy fabric draping the sides of the princess's chest. It was difficult not to stare. To distract himself, Dalich swiveled his head away, noting the pair of guards marching alongside the bounche, their scabbards clattering in their belts. A second pair followed behind, their eyes scanning the torch-lined path, the supply tents, and the shadowy forms of Soldiers and camp workers making their rounds as the royal cart rolled past. He reached to pat his sword, mindful that it was still by his side.

"Is everything all right?" the princess asked. A moment passed before he realized she spoke to him.

"Um, yes, I—" He gently cleared his throat to buy time and hopefully recover from reacting like a man with too much ale clouding his head. The last thing he wanted was for her to think him dull-witted. "I was considering the best story to tell your brother."

Kostaza shook her head. "That is kind of you, but there is no need to trouble yourself. Moulai is already asleep."

"Oh." His mind went blank for a moment at this new information. A glance at the prone lad confirmed it, for Moulai's jaw dangled open. His eyes were partially visible through lowered lids in the same eerie manner as Saril's brother Marnil when sleeping. Were it not for the jiggling and creaking of the cart and the stomping of marching feet nearby, he likely would hear the boy snore. All King's Son could think to say was, "I am glad to see he is getting some rest."

The young woman must have felt equally at a loss for words, for her only reply was, "Yes."

In the face of the defeat of conversation, Dalich rallied to ask, "How much farther to your quarters?"

"Not much farther." She folded her slim hands over her lap, her profile fading into shadows and blooming into sharp relief in the ever-changing light. "Thank you for accompanying us."

He spoke his heart. "I would see you safe."

The Kaymiflander turned her face toward him, and he sensed she scrutinized him carefully. Perhaps it was the subtle tightening of her forehead. He truly wished she would remove those Powers-blasted beads so he might see her eyes! To his surprise, Kostaza leaned toward him, over her sleeping sibling, cupping a warm hand to his ear. She whispered urgently, her breath searing into him with an intensity that made him shiver. "My brother does not know our father is dead. Mother will not tell him." She withdrew to her side of the bounche, turning away, but not before he caught a trickling tear glinting on her high cheekbone.

"To rest!" thundered Voukai, and the cart rocked to a halt next to a sprawling pavilion with a canopied entrance. The Soldiers guarding the sides of the bounche pivoted in one synchronous motion to face outward, and Voukai turned to assist the royals from the cart. "Our lord sleeps?" he asked.

The princess replied. "Yes, let us not wake him."

"Allow me," Dalich volunteered, easing the king-who-did-not-know-he-was-king from the pillows and gently passing him to his servant's uplifted arms. Descending from the bounche, King's Son accepted the slumbering lad again, carrying him into the brazier-lit pavilion. Unlike in his father's quarters, not a single tapestry decorated the tent's sides. Instead, draped fabrics of shimmering textures undulated across the walls.

"This way, if you will." The Kaymif princess breezed past him toward a passageway he had not noticed on his initial inspection. The lustrous fabrics lining the corridor glowed from lamps lit on the opposite side. He followed her to a small room occupied by a curtained bed and a short table with a silver candelabrum. The candleholder was made of zigzag posts holding aloft several lit tapers. Kostaza pulled the curtain and then the blankets back, gesturing to Dalich to tuck the sleeping child there, which he did as gently as he could.

The young prince roused as Dalich released him to the covers. "Papa?" he asked in a sleepy but hopeful voice. The plaintive question burned Dalich's heart. He needed to find out why no one had told little Moulai of his father's death.

Kostaza brushed past the Eskalinder and bent to kiss the youngster's head. "Shh, Brother, rest." Kostaza smoothed his light-hued hair till his little eyelids fluttered closed. This time Dalich could hear his snores.

Another person approached. Dalich rotated swiftly, placing himself between the Kaymif royals and the impending footsteps, hand ready to draw his short knife.

A man called. "My princess?"

"It is Voukai," she whispered. "He guards my brother at night." Slightly louder, she replied, "Here, Voukai."

King's Son nodded as the expected man came into view, bearing a platter of fruits and small pieces of bread. "For you, my princess, and your guest. Do you wish it here?"

"No, Voukai, allow me." She grasped the large plate. "King's Son Dalich, will you accompany me?"

How lovely and soft she was, and he would follow her anywhere at this moment and forgive her confusion at his title's proper order, or anything else for that matter. Somehow he replied in formal tones, "As you wish, Princess Kostaza."

"Voukai, I will see you in the morning." The servant nodded whilst parting an opening in the cloth wall of the room, which the young woman passed through. Dalich followed his hostess, but not without receiving a withering glare from the guard. Wondering what to make of it, he shadowed the princess through a corridor of blue fabric walls, similar to the first, merging into another unpopulated area. Braziers burned near the center of this room; a warm, spicy smell, perhaps cinnamon, permeated the air. Kostaza lightly stepped toward a low table off to one side, placing the platter upon it next to a silvery ewer chased with the winding pattern denoting Kaymif royalty. Beside the ewer, a pair of tall metal goblets rested. Their stems bore the same zigzag pattern.

Gesturing to several long, low pillows, the princess offered, "Please, honor me with a seat."

He should return to his father, but he needed to find out more, and The Powers had clearly provided them with this opportunity to be alone together. Dalich sat upon the pillows. She knelt beside him, poured a bronze-colored liquid from the pitcher into each goblet, and proffered one to him.

"Thank you." Accepting, he drank the cool, aromatic liquid, which was flavorless at first, then warmed his tongue with hints of pepper. It emboldened his spirit. "Princess, might you say more about why your brother does not know about your father?"

Kostaza sat on her knees and placed the ewer upon the table, her filled drinking vessel in one hand. Not being able to see her eyes, he found his senses sharpened on how she held her head, tilted slightly downward, and on the placement of her hands—one tightening on the cup, the other languid on her thigh. The rhythm of her breathing was steady and controlled. "My mother—" She turned her neck slightly as if hearing a far-off call.

Returning her attention to her guest, Kostaza pointed to her ear, then swept a finger about the room. Dalich stared at her. She repeated the gesture, and he realized she was trying to tell him someone might be listening on the other side of the fabric walls. He dipped his forehead to show he understood. She continued. "My mother wills it. Thus I obey."

Her voice sounded tired and frustrated; it touched him. "I understand. My father discouraged me from a girl I fancy. Fancied." Dalich brushed the lump of Damina's locket in his tunic. A bit of guilt niggled for pretending he no longer cared for her, but he was alone with the pretty princess, he was a man now, there was a battle tomorrow, and who knew what The Powers planned for him.

The blond Kaymiflander drank a long swallow of her glass, holding the cup in both hands. "You understand how difficult it can be, being a young royal, don't you? We are trained to rule, to lead, to be decisive, and yet we must obey our parents." Kostaza made a deep breath. "I worry for my brother; what if he overhears the servants talking about Father? How terrible for him to find out in that manner!" She turned toward the opposite wall, perhaps hearing someone move.

Dalich whispered, "Do you trust Voukai?"

"I do. Why do you ask?" Her slender fingers claimed a morsel from the platter.

He leaned into the pillows, sipping from his cup. "He favored me with a look that would evaporate a lake." She nearly choked on her food at his jest.

Composing herself, she replied, "Oh, he is very protective of me and my brother. It is a long story, but my father saved his wife's and daughter's lives. Voukai guards us like family." A hint of a sob had crept into her voice.

"Princess . . ." He raised himself slightly, reaching to touch her arm. Kostaza gazed toward him.

"I am sorry. I am not much of a hostess." She bent her blond head in the posture of one sinking into despair. The beads curtaining her eyes leaned away from her face; tears stained her eyes.

Scooting closer to her, Dalich replied, "You are a fine and beautiful hostess. It is clear you love your brother." He smiled weakly, hoping she heard the honest truth in his words.

"Thank you." She sniffed. "I would do anything to protect Moulai. One of my first memories is Mother telling me to ask The Powers for a babe brother." Straightening, she added, "I must be boring you, going on about my family."

"No, please, it is interesting to me. I have no sisters or brothers. I sometimes wonder what my life would be like if I did." At this Kostaza smiled, her lips spreading broadly over her closed mouth, cheeks dimpled in a charming manner.

"Moulai is a good boy, except when he plays tricks on me, such as hiding my veil." She laughed, then crooked her neck to show the back of her head and pointed to the thin rope of glistening stones encircling her hair. "Will you unclasp it? I want to see you better."

Speechless with delight, he gladly performed the task, captivated by the smoothness of her tresses and the warmth clinging to the sparkling beads as he slipped them into her outstretched hand. Kostaza turned to face him, her eyes a lovely, inviting azure under fair brows. For a moment, the royal pair studied one another intently. The intensity of their gaze rendered Dalich breathless.

Kostaza withdrew. "Here, let me refill your cup." The Kaymif princess tilted toward him, gesturing for him to bring his goblet closer. He did so to find her leaning closer still, close enough to kiss, but her lips glided past his cheek to whisper quietly in his ear, "I think Mother had Father slain. You must tell your father." Kostaza pulled away and put down the pitcher, azure eyes quiet and serious as if repeating her message to him silently.

Several thoughts ran through his mind, but he murmured, "Should I go?"

"Oh no, please stay." Her voice sounded stilted and strange. Dalich wondered what she was truly trying to communicate. It felt suddenly wrong to be so physically close to the young woman. Odder still after wishing for such an opportunity.

She tapped a finger over her top lip, as if to say, "No more," then raised it to gently trace over his lips. Her touch was hypnotic, but her eyes pled with him in a way that confused him. "No, you are right. You should go," Kostaza said, quietly, but not quite in a whisper. Her languid tone suggested she was not entirely pleased at the prospect of him leaving, but the blue depths of her gaze bespoke urgency, as though The Powers themselves nudged him to make his leave.

He stood, placing his goblet atop the table, and bowed slightly. Kostaza gazed up at him as he raised her hand.

"Have I seen you home safely, Princess?" King's Son kissed her cool knuckles, watching her.

"This time, yes." The young man wondered what that meant. As he absented himself, a burning sensation of unsettledness and incompletion throbbed in his veins.

Despite departing through the same passageway he had entered, Dalich did not come upon the boy king's sleeping chamber. Instead, he found himself outside the pavilion sooner than expected. As it dawned on him that the fabric walls had been rearranged, he spied a light-haired man in his father's colors dismounting a horse. The man called to him. "King's Son."

Recognizing Favik, Dalich responded, "Aye."

"Come, my Lord, your father would see you." Favik gestured to a riderless horse kitted in brown leather with red medallions. King's Son claimed the mount, and the two men trotted the path back to Dalock King's war camp. Along the way, they passed a lumbering bounche heading in the opposite direction, dripping with the zigzag pennants of the Kaymif royals. Its curtains were drawn; he could not see if Kostaza's mother was inside.

Favik led him to yet another ale tent, where the pair found Bafnil waiting at the entrance. The lad dashed inside just as a woman in the plain brown garb of a Scout departed. King's Son and Favik entered as Bafnil finished uttering "Queensman."

The King and his Second sat before an upright barrel, not a goblet or food platter in sight, nor any sign of Saril in this impromptu council chamber. One glance at his father's posture—raised shoulders, drumming his long fingers upon the flat, stained wood—and Dalich knew he had done something wrong. Or the King had just received bad news. He hoped it was the latter.

His Lord spoke coolly. "You have been gone a long while, Dalich."

"Aye, Father." Dalich stood at attention like a Soldier under inspection. The ill mood in the room must be his doing. But perhaps he could deflect his Lord's ire by sharing Kostaza's news. "I have learned a few things."

"Such as?"

"The princess thinks her mother killed her father." Dalock King stared unwaveringly at his son, but next to him, Jinil's green eyes darted briefly toward Favik. Dalock continued, "She told you this? In the presence of others?"

"No, my Lord Father, we were alone. Though she believed someone may have been listening. She whispered *very* quietly."

The royal gaze narrowed. "You were alone with her in her quarters?"

"Um, yes." It suddenly occurred to him how improper that might be in Kaymif. At home, no one would think it inappropriate for a man who just earned his sword to visit alone with an unjoined woman who was of age. Dalich assumed she was aware of the custom in his land. Or maybe she was not of age. He squeaked out, "Is Kostaza not sixteen yet?"

"You call her by name and you did not ask her age?"

Dalich felt immensely stupid, and worried that he had committed a terrible breach of etiquette that would lead to The-Powers-knew-what trouble. Might he be expected to join with her? The thought caused panic. He liked her very much, but he barely knew her.

Meanwhile, the King glanced at his Second. "Well, Jinil, I think my son being alone and whispering with a borderland woman in her private chamber is the least of my worries right now." Then, to the young man's surprise, his father laughed. A quick glance at Saril's father yielded the slightest smile. Dalich turned to study Favik, but his mother's man stood by the entrance as impassively as a tent post. The King wiped his eyes. "Ah, Son, forgive me. This day never seems to end."

"Not unlike the Kaymif queen's pleas," interjected Jinil, leaning back slightly.

Peeved at their odd behavior, Dalich blurted, "Did I do something wrong?"

"No, Son, you did everything right." Perhaps in answer to the confusion clearly written on his face, his father continued. "This plays right into our hands. We believe the Kaymif queen hoped to entrap you with her daughter. Which is why I sent Favik to fetch you." He nodded to the man by the doorway. "Meanwhile, you were learning from the princess what we had already gleaned from your mother: that Queen Mostaza had her husband assassinated."

"But the princess was not certain of it. She only said she thought that was what happened. She gave no details." Dalich swallowed.

"It all fits together. Anything else?"

"The boy does not know his father is dead."

"Ah yes. His mother claims he is ill, and she wants to protect him. His 'fragile state' was the term she used. Is he well guarded?"

"The princess said a man she trusts more than anyone watches the boy."

"I do not think the mother would harm the lad; as the sole male heir, he is her key to the throne. Perhaps she suspects her daughter knows something, which is why she would see the young woman joined and departed from Kaymif."

Jinil nodded. "Speaking as one of the two former Ambassadors to Havadra in this room, I think the Havadrans would envy her cunning. What say you, Favik?"

The blond man raised his head with the gravity of a traveling player about to deliver a legendary oration. "Queen Mostaza could convince a chicken to pluck itself, roll in Queen's Recipe herbs, and jump onto a skewer above open flames."

Everyone laughed, including Favik, who seemed an entirely different person when a smile lit his face. As he shared the chuckle, Dalich realized the odd behavior and jesting was a way for the men to relieve the strain. For once, King's Son was included in a way he never had been before, a true comrade in arms, an integral part of their private world. If only Saril was with them.

The King spoke. "Tomorrow is nearly upon us, and when the negotiations fail, the battle for Kaymif will begin. Let us rest while we are able. By The Powers' Will, we shall rid Kaymif of both its duplicitous queen and her marauding brother tomorrow."

The gleam in the King's eye could kindle a bonfire. For the first time Dalich witnessed the full depth of will dand authority The Powers had invested in his Lord. How he hoped he could fulfill the expectations of their people and someday be a great warrior and leader of men like Dalock King. Perhaps even tomorrow.

The next day dawned to news that indeed, the negotiations had failed, for the Ghemif king would not depart without battle. Ambassador Moril, Eskalind's representative to Kaymif, bore the grim news to his Lord. Battle-dressed, Dalock King turned to his son. "Prepare yourself, Dalich. We will meet King Grufmit on the battlefield for one last private conference. May it avert much bloodshed. And may all those years of training with the Swordmasters pay off, aye?"

Dalich nodded, hummingly anxious, excited, and fearful, also curious what his Lord would propose. But the scrutiny in his father's eye warned him off asking.

Without ceremony or brave words, they rode without incident, side by side upon a matched set of geldings, each walnut maned and chestnut coated, his father's mount half an ear taller than his own three-year-old Haanip. Arriving at the prescribed place of battle, they found the armies of Kaymif and Eskalind allied against the orange-tunicked men of Ghemif. All bore swords or lances, the Allies carrying blue or red round shields whilst the Ghemiflander shields were copper-covered and akin in shape to the number eight.

It was an odd sight, so many men arrayed facing one another in long lines across a broad, open field, as though the space between repelled human presence. Father and son paused their horses, the Lord of Eskalind asking quietly, "Dalich, did you ever read the Legend scroll from Trelich King's Cabinet that said long-ago armies battled one another with pointed twigs that could fly great distances through the air?"

"Yes, Father."

"Thank The Powers we do not live in those times, aye?"

"Yes, Father."

Dismounting, they filed through the ranks, the scarlet and chestnut banners of Eskalind fluttering alongside the blue of Kaymif. Above, the sky glowered gray. Dalock called greetings and encouragement to the men in a hearty voice, slapping backs and helms amiably. Dalich followed, silent and stoic, trying to conquer the swift beat of his heart.

At last the honey-brown field of Autumn-cut wheat opened clear before them as they broke free of the army of Ever Allies into the no-man's-land to face the array of Ghemif warriors strung across the far side of the field like a rope. Shieldmen stood at the fore, their staffs painted green, their banners flying pumpkin-colored pennants, whilst bannermen and spearmen stood arrayed behind them. Unbidden, the names of each of the Strange Kings who claimed orange and green as their colors came into Dalich's mind, an incantation from the deep annals of Eskalind. *Daavlock, Sixteenth King; Aadlich, Seventy-Sixth King; Palock, One Hundred Sixteenth King.* The smooth syllables of the earlier Kings' names formed a calming lilt, punctuated by the staccato punch of the last, like a call to action. *Daavlock, Aadlich, Palock.*

He who would be the 125th King raised his eyes, spying Page Bafnil running toward the Eskalind royals from the enemy side.

"So?" asked his father.

"My Lord, King Grufmit will parley with you." The lad raised a hand toward the no-man's-land between the armies. A lone figure emerged from the line of the enemy. He wore a hammered copper helmet anchored to his jaw with strap, a green tunic covered with a breastplate of like make to his helm, and an armored skirt.

"Come, Dalich, let us go," grumbled Dalock King in a worn tone.

The young man followed as the pair paced through the short, stiff stalks of cropped wheat.

"At least the farmers had time to gather their harvest," his father stated, rather loudly. "Whoever wins this land will not starve." His Lord brushed a dried stalk from his leg, speaking quietly, as if to the earth. "Dalich, may The Powers let you use your Gift to win the day."

Icy fear clutched King's Son as he realized his father intended to use his Gift as the invincible, sole heir of the Strange Kingdom to fight.

Ahead, King Grufmit stood perhaps a hundred feet away from them, far short of the blue-flagged stick marking the center point of the field, where they should have met. The man called, "Who are you?"

"Dalock King. This is my son. I have a proposal for you."

"Then we meet at the stick. Leave the lad behind."

His father exhaled roughly, which meant he was annoyed. For his part, King's Son bristled at being called a lad. But from his training, he recognized the use of taunts to incite anger in order to throw one off guard. If anything, the pitiable tactic strengthened his resolve to defeat the Ghemif army and protect the princess.

"Stay here, Son. Hold your palms open so the man can see you have nothing in your hands."

Dalich obeyed, feeling oddly exposed in such a posture. Silently he thanked The Powers for preventing the use of airborne sharpened twigs, for truly he would have been the easiest target. Glancing quickly at his belt, Dalich double-checked that both his newly granted long sword and his short sword were still belted there. The two rulers paced to the center meetspot and stopped short, each with a hand on the pommel of his blade as though facing a mirror, in profile against the shorn field.

"King Grufmit?"

"I am, Eskalinder. Your negotiators failed; now what do you want?" A slight breeze carried the Ghemif king's speech to Dalich's ears, clear and crisp, as though The Powers wanted him to hear every word.

His father's hands flopped to his side in the manner of one deeply frustrated. "I have a problem."

"Ten thousand of my men facing yours?"

King's Son thought that a highly inflated figure.

"That is a symptom of my troubles. The root is your sister, Queen Mostaza."

At this the man laughed, raising his bearded chin to the sky as he did so, his fat lower lip rolled forward. It seemed an expression of genuine amusement. King's Son wondered what to make of it.

His father did not laugh. "You are familiar with my situation."

"For all my days." The man shook his head, the thick leather flaps of his armored skirt clanking with the motion. Grufmit's manner seemed conversational, as if he were speaking with an old companion. "Ah, when Mostaza joined with Koulai, my father and I drank thanks to The Powers to have her out of our court and beyond our border. That was a good day." The Ghemif king chuckled lightly. "And yet, here we are, you and I, about to draw swords on one another over her lands."

"Her son's lands."

"Ah yes, my nephew, the boy king. My sister would control his inheritance till he is a man." Again he chuckled. "Which she will delay as long as possible. I wager she will find a way to keep a boy from becoming a man."

"Yet you plotted with her to kill her husband."

"Kill Koulai?" The man straightened, drawing back. "I had no quarrel with him. That was Mostaza's doing." His tone returned to nonchalance. "Once Koulai was gone, there was the matter of much unguarded land into which I expanded my domain—ha! Do you truly think I want my double-dealing sister as a neighbor?" He chewed his lower lip, shaking his head. "My braither, Koulai, he had a giving heart. Truly, any man joined to Mostaza for nearly twenty years must have had a kingdom's worth of patience. Or a dozen mistresses to soothe the loss of the many weary hours wasted with his wife." Grufmit laughed as though personally acquainted with the problem.

Dalock King continued in formal tones. "As Lord of Eskalind, I am charged by The Powers since ancient days to protect the borderlands of my realm. As Kaymif borders my domain, it falls under my protectorate."

"Even for a faithless queen?"

"I would prefer to end this dispute with the loss of as few lives as possible."

King Grufmit said nothing, spinning his fingers over the pommel of his sword as if it rotated. Dalich found this curious. His arms were starting to ache from his open-palm posture. His father continued. "Let us make a challenge, rather than a battle: my best man against yours."

The Ghemiflander rolled his lips. "Show me your best man."

Dalock gestured toward his army. "My son, here." Dalich swallowed, nearly choking, but held his head high as he could; his spine could be no straighter. Setting his mouth in a grim line, he attempted to appear battle-proven, but he felt ridiculous with his palms still held aloft.

"Oh, come now! That scarecrow?" Grufmit craned his head toward Dalich whilst narrowing his eyes.

"Aye." There was no relish or life in his Lord's voice.

"I will fight him myself. It will be over in a short minute." Grufmit pointed at Eskalind's ruler. "And if you think you can sacrifice him to weary me out, then step in yourself to gain the glory, then you are The Powers' greatest fool."

"That, I am not." But there was a hitch of timidity in his father's voice.

The Ghemif king lowered his hand, replying in an autocratic tone. "Then these will be the terms: I will fight your son, your son only, and when he dies, you hand over Kaymif." King's Son bristled at the confidence with which the man spoke of his death.

His father countered, "When my son carries the fight, and *you* die, your men will lay down their arms, accept Kaymif overlordship, and retreat to their homes as Kaymiflanders. Ghemif will be no more. If you win, my men will quit these lands. You may have this place."

"This place?" The Ghemiflander gestured to the stark field surrounding them. "This sad field or all of Kaymif?"

"All of Kaymif, to its existing borders. But you must assure me that no harm will come to your niece or nephew. You may exile them to my land if you wish; they will be well provided for."

"My niece is a very pretty girl. I may keep her for myself."

Had the man been closer, Dalich would have drawn blade, but Dalock King seemed nonplussed. "Your sister will be yours to dispose of as you wish. Do we have terms?"

"We have terms." Grufmit raised his left arm. "I am calling my page to relate these conditions to my undercommander." A slender boy sped from the ranks of the Ghemif army and was soon by his lord's side. King's Son squinted to get a better view, for he appeared familiar. Then he realized the lad had the same small nose and fat lower lip as his lord.

Dalich called sternly, his voice a challenge, "Is he your son?"

Grufmit finished imparting his news to the Page, who ran back to the line. "Probably."

Dalock King trudged to his only child, gesturing for him to lower his still-raised hands. He reached a glove to grasp the young man's shoulder. The sun broke from its cloud cloak for an instant to catch the bronze threads of the embroidered swords stitched across the fabric. They glimmered brightly, bringing a host of images to the new man's mind: fresh water glistening in a bowl, afternoon light shining full across the royals' corridor back home, the smooth polished metal of Damina's locket, the sparkling jeweled beads encircling Kostaza's fair forehead. The glimmer of his newly earned blade as he balanced and swung it in training this morning. He blinked. His father's brown eyes gazed at him; a mix of tenderness, resolve, and courage tinged his voice. "I will see you soon."

Dalich swallowed hard, suddenly wanting to retch. His father departed, leaving him alone.

Thus King's Son gazed at his opponent, finding the will to mentally drill through the routines of the Swordmasters, measuring and evaluating his adversary.

This king was about his own height, but broader in the shoulder.

He wore his scabbard on the left, thus a right-hander.

Bare hands with many rings that a blade could catch upon.

A sheathed dagger strapped across his armored chest, but more might lurk on his back or be hidden in his boots.

The Ghemiflander's chestplate was fastened a bit loosely under his right arm; that would allow a clearer range of motion. It also left a gap a blade could enter.

Grufmit drew his sword, shifting crabwise across the shorn wheat stalks, eyes not leaving King Son's. "Your father must have many sons to spend you so readily, Prince."

Dalich pulled his own blade, pacing similarly, facing his opponent, whilst trying to breathe steadily. The young man was searching his mind for a clever retort when an odd sound, like a muffled woman's voice, came from behind him. Fearing some trickery on Grufmit's part, he glanced quickly over his shoulder. He saw no person, only the hacked strands of wheat shaved close to the ground, like small sentinels standing stoutly as a fresh breeze fluttered a few stray pieces of stiff chaff tangled amongst them.

Then some of the strands crunched flat against the earth. A length away from those, another grouping flattened, as though some unseeable thing stepped toward him.

———

Above, on the hillside, amongst the army of Eskalind and beside his Second, Dalock King watched his only son show his back to his opponent. His breath ceased as King Grufmit swung blade toward Dalich. "No!" he sputtered, clutching his sword grip. "That girl came into his mind!" Dalock stepped forward just as his son crouched and spun toward his adversary. Grufmit stood in a wide stance, his sword slicing clean across the vacant air above King's Son's head, as Dalich raked his own blade across the ground, angling the shining point up and under Grufmit's armored skirt and thickly slicing the man's inner thigh. The Ghemif king fell to his side, his mouth a silent *O* of pain and surprise. Dalich hefted his sword out of the man's thighbone and raised the gore-mired blade to drag it across the prone king's throat. Dalock gaped in disbelief as Jinil cried, "By The Powers!"

"Yes, by The Powers," breathed the relieved father, when he could find words, half sick with horror at the gruesome spectacle of his once innocent child slaying a man.

On the Ghemif side of the field, hammered metal shields fluttered nervously as the front-line warriors fidgeted. Strong shouts surged across the lines, and a man stepped forth, his breastplate polished and bright. The Ghemiflander drew his sword, held it aloft a brief moment, then flung it to the ground. He turned and walked away.

"What is this?"

His Second leaned toward him. "The surrender of Ghemif."

Ghemif warriors followed their commander's lead, some overturning their shields as though laying them to rest, others stacking them as if to cover a body, whilst spearmen spiked the earth with their shafts. Rather than a battlefield littered with the strewn bodies of men and horses, the losing side's abandoned weapons sprouted at all angles; a strange crop of tall spears and figure-eight-shaped shields. Here and there an halberd or axe stood out like an errant weed amongst a well-seeded field.

A group of Ghemif pages and standers came forward to reclaim their lord's body as Dalich trudged uphill toward his father, dripping blade in hand. All around him, cheers rose to the clouded sky as the Strange Kingdomers and the Kaymif army celebrated their victory, but all Dalock could see was the wonder *and* befuddlement in his son's dear gray eyes. He stepped forward to embrace the young man, who backed away, shaking his head. Dalich raised his sword before him, the flat blade at the King's eye level.

"Father, look! Do you see it?"

There, across the widest part of the blade, written in blood with the flowing, exquisite quilling of a Lady of the Strange Kingdom:

Dalich King's Son

"I … do."

"You are richly Gifted, my Lord," whispered Jinil, green eyes intent upon the blade. "Show it to the men, my Lord!"

"Father," Dalich cried, a pleading expression upon his face like a youth whose sixteenth Naming Day approached with no plans made for his Sword Earning. "I do not know what happened, down there. Something came toward me, I cannot say what it was. It pushed me down, and then I was spinning, and my blade found him. I did not do it; I was guided …"

"The Powers protect you, my son." The pride within the King's chest threatened to break free of his breastplate. Dalock stepped forward, placing a hand on the young man's shoulder. "Dalich, let our men see your sword. They must share in this day of Legend. Come." He guided his heir toward their lines.

———

Under his father's guidance, Dalich moved automatically, blade held lengthwise before his eyes. Eskalinder Soldiers gaped admiringly, jostling each other for a better view of King's Son's sword. Most of the Strange Kingdomers could read the words, but for the occasional man who could not, a companion would point to the letters, sounding out their meaning.

In his mind, the champion of the day replayed the strange occurrences, but could make no sense of them. As if in a fog, he proceeded down the lines of Soldiers, not noticing when his father halted for a lengthy conference with a Captain. Dalich ambled along alone, oblivious to the shouts of well wishes and praise from his grateful countrymen.

Gradually, the brown and red uniforms of the Eskalinders intermingled with the blues of the Kaymif army as lean Kaymif soldiers surged toward King's Son. Suddenly, a man was shouting at him. Dalich blinked to see a strong-jawed Kaymiflander, face flushed, cerulean eyes narrowed, the short purple tassel on his blue cap bobbing as he spoke. "The Ghemiflanders killed our king! You're letting them go unpunished?"

Another Kaymiflander, garbed in a homespun tunic with an army-issued blue vest over it, stepped forward. "They burned my father's farm and crops. I want revenge for my family!" A long, tanned, well-muscled arm reached across the borderlanders, separating them from the young champion. It was the giant Eskalind Soldier who had helped Dalich rescue Saril from the would-be assassins. "King's Son just saved your lives!" A vein in his thick neck throbbed as he glowered. "Read his sword. The Powers are at work here."

The first Kaymiflander challenged him. "I was guard to King Koulai; I demand revenge for his death. So do my men."

Dalich interrupted, the tension recharging his spirit. He lowered his sword hand to his waist. "Grufmit paid with his life." He shook his sword, the blood-writ words glistening. "There will be further payment to come." He nearly told of Queen Mostaza's treachery, but the hunger in the men's gaze bespoke more bloodshed. "King Koulai's young son and heir may be in danger. You king's men must guard and protect him." This got their attention.

"What? How?"

"Yesterday, Ghemif assassins tried to kill my companion, thinking *he* was the heir to Dalock King." He gestured to the large Eskalinder beside him, tall enough to stare a horse in the eye. "This Soldier helped me rescue my companion before he was harmed."

All the Kaymiflanders' gazes roved to the mountain of a man, a silent agreement forming amongst them that yes, indeed, this was a good man to have on one's side. Dalich nodded for the Strange Kingdomer to lower his arm. Then King's Son leaned toward the former guard of King Koulai, speaking intently, pronouncing each word loudly and carefully so that even those who strained to listen from farther back in the line could hear. "There may be more hidden assassins, seeking vengeance for King Grufmit's death. You must see that King Moulai grows to manhood, a man who inspires your well-deserved loyalty, as his father did." The Kaymiflander guard slowly nodded, though there was a glimmer in his eyes that suggested he was not fully convinced.

The second Kaymif soldier, his voice no longer charged with anger, asked, "But how will my family rebuild our farm? The Ghemiflanders carried off our animals and burned our property into the earth. Our barn, our house, our crops, even our chicken coop!" His blue eyes clouded. "There's nothing left, save our lives."

Dalich's heart clove with pity. A plan sprang to mind. "Soldier of Eskalind," he called to the giant. "Tell me your name?"

"Varmil, my Lord."

"Varmil, I charge you with retrieving the Sword of Surrender and giving it to this man."

Varmil nodded his great head. After a lingering look of warning to the Kaymif soldiers, the Eskalinder turned to do his Lord's bidding. Dalich placed his free hand upon the rough fabric clothing the Kaymif soldier's upper arm. "That sword will fetch a high price in your land. That should go a long way toward paying for rebuilding." Tears began to slip from the man's eyes. "Thank you, Lord."

Turning to the others, Dalich called, "This Kaymiflander is not alone in his loss. Bring carts to gather the weapons left by the defeated Ghemiflanders. Surely the metal and armaments will bring a sum of coins to the families who suffered this invasion. May many of Kaymif's famous long knives be wrought from this booty."

Several soldiers gave their assent and dispersed, but the man to whom Dalich had promised the Ghemif sword stood nearby still, now openly weeping as he tried to speak. The former guard to the Kaymif king slapped his arm. "What are you blubbering about, man?"

Wiping his eyes, the Kaymiflander raised his head. "What does this prince's sword say?"

"What?"

"The large man said The Powers were at work here. He said to read the sword."

"Well then, read it!" The guard turned to walk away.

"Halt!" Dalich ordered. The man paused midstep, pivoting back to face his questioner—such a perfectly executed maneuver, King's Son ascertained it must be part of his guardsman training.

"Lord?"

"You, what is your name?"

The man swallowed hard. "Kamkai, my Lord."

"Kamkai, read it to him. Can you?" He raised his elbow to hold the long length of the blade before the noses of the pair.

The guard nodded, clearing his throat as his eyes scanned the bloody letters. They widened slightly as he read them for the first time. "Here," Kamkai pointed, his voice gaining reverence, "It says 'Dal-' followed by '-ich.' Dalich. That is you, my Lord?"

"Aye."

"And this says 'King's…'" He slowly traced the air next to the sharp edge. The soldier by his side nodded. "'Son.' The blade says 'Dalich King's Son.'" Kamkai raised his hand in a showy flourish akin to that of a traveling player, but a finger brushed the flat part of the blade, and at his touch, the blood drained to the ground in a slim stream, the letters vanishing.

"Oh no," exhaled the soldier, while the guardsman gaped in disbelief, then fell to his knees to hang his head.

"Lord King's Son, forgive me!"

Something within Dalich was glad to see the troublesome man chastised. "Perhaps, Kamkai, you will find new employ as the cleaner of my sword."

The Kaymif guard gaped at him, face pinched, whilst the soldier at his side chewed back the beginnings of a grin.

"Rise," Dalich ordered, grasping the man on the shoulder. "Go serve your young king."

Chapter Fourteen—An Unpleasant Matter

Pacing back along the lines, Dalich held his spine straight as he weighed the last few moments in his mind. He hoped he had dealt well with the Kaymiflanders, that his father would not disagree with his command to give the Ghemif surrender sword to the Kaymif soldier.

"My Lord Cousin."

The voice jolted him. He must have been deep in thought. He glanced to the blue eyes of his cousin Narnik. "Well met, First Sergeant."

"Never better well met!" The blond man slapped his arm. "Thank The Powers you're safe! It was a thing of wonder to watch you annihilate that Ghemif scoundrel."

Dalich tensed. "I could not have done it without The Powers' help."

Narnik walked alongside King's Son. "I was sent to tell you, your father and King's Second want you at their council, back at camp."

"Let us go then, Cousin."

"One thing first, my Lord" Narnik stopped to face him, placing both hands on his shoulders, gazing straight to his eyes. "When I was a young lad, I wanted to be a Soldier. I dreamed always of the glory. I never considered what it would be like to kill a man. It is a hard, hard thing."

Dalich bowed his head; nausea hinted. "I know."

"Something you may not know, Lord Cousin." Narnik paused, which brought King's Son's attention back to his eyes. "No man who has done this will think it wrong were you to throw up, or not eat for a few days, or drown in a cask of ale . . ." Here he grinned, his face creased with the faintest radiating lines about his eyes and lips. "Or if you find the nearest woman who will show you her feet." The First Sergeant patted the young man's shoulders, a bittersweet, tender expression about his face. Then Dalich was released.

"I find your advice sound, my dear Humikslander." Dalich dipped his head slightly.

Narnik chuckled, returning the nod. "Now let us find my ayncle, the King. I imagine our Lord will want some ranks to escort the Ghemif army back to its lands, seeing to it that they don't pillage Kaymif again along the way."

Availing horses to convey them, the two men made the fastest time they could through the meandering Soldiers and Standers of Eskalind, many hoisting flagons in victory and shouting praise at King's Son when they saw him. "The ale tents have been breached!" jested Narnik to his royal relative. Reaching the King's Pavilion and dismounting, the cousins nearly collided with a messenger swiftly departing. Entering the spacious quarters, they found only Dalich's father, King's Second, and Favik Queensman huddled around a small table.

Dalock King rose, gesturing for the others to stay seated as he strode forward to heartily embrace his heir. "Ah, Dalich, my Gifted son! My champion!" He thumped the young man on the back and withdrew, slapping Narnik on the arm in greeting. "Nayphew!"

"My Lord." Narnik grinned, bowing. "A proud day for King's Son and Eskalind."

"Aye, but there is another victory to be sought." Dalock wrinkled his brow, locking eyes with his Second. "Confronting Queen Mostaza."

"Father, what are you going to do with her?"

The Lord of Eskalind gazed to his son. "She has been sent for. She and her children." He raised a hand. "The little boy still has no idea that his father is dead, that he is lord of Kaymif. Now I ask, Dalich, what would you do with the Kaymif king's mother?" He gestured for his son to speak.

King's Son considered. "For conspiring to kill her husband, I would exile her to one of our Ever Allies, but far from here. Thislin, perhaps, or Humiksland." He spoke quickly, hoping he made no mistakes in his father's eyes.

"Good, good. And what of her children?"

"Her son Moulai named king, and her daughter . . . as regent?" He could not help but peep at Jinil for a moment, hoping to ascertain if he mirrored his father's strategy on the subject.

"Yes, with our Ambassador Moril as shared regent to keep an eye on the situation and report back to us." The King raised his chin. "How should this life-changing news be imparted to a lad of six who has lost his father and will never see his mother again?"

Wondering why his father pressed this point, Dalich said, "Let Princess Kostaza tell the boy. They share a close relationship, and she is a gentle, caring sister."

"I see." The King sat, folding his long fingers together on the table. "Your counsel is sound, my son, but—" Bafnil burst into the King's pavilion so enthusiastically, one would have thought he was harkening to a claim that Queen's Recipe Roasted Chicken awaited inside. "The Kaymif royals arrive, my Lord!"

Dalock King lifted himself swiftly to his feet. Favik and Jinil stood as well. Their Lord spoke. "They must have already been on their way. Well, enough governance lessons for now. Jinil, signal our Guards. Bafnil, delay the Kaymiflanders a moment and tell them I specifically request the presence of only the women royals at this time."

The lad bowed, spun on his heel, and dashed from the pavilion, whilst King's Second paced to the fabric walls on the opposite side of the entranceway. He batted the cloth twice, then two more times. Rustling metal was heard, and a section of the wall folded away as Eskalind Guardsmen entered the spacious tent to ring its perimeter.

The last Guardsman tied the secret entrance closed. The Strange King motioned his man to summon their guests, which he did.

Bafnil entered, announcing the two women. The Kaymif queen entered with head and shoulders held high like a vigilant Soldier undergoing scrutiny from a commander. Her neck swiveled slightly as her beaded eyes marked the Guardsmen ringing the pavilion. Her daughter stepped lightly into position behind her, folding her hands before her slim waist as two Kaymif guards followed to flank the women. The guardsman next to Kostaza was Kamkai, King Koulai's guard who had confronted Dalich after the battle. Dalich suddenly wished he had not mocked the man about cleaning his sword.

"Lord Dalock King." Queen Mostaza bent her knee, the princess mimicking her movements. The Lord of Eskalind nodded ever so slightly. "We come to thank you for the great triumph today that saved our land. I am told your handsome young son claimed us the victory." Her blond head pivoted toward Dalich, her painted lips parting in a smile, though he sensed that the beads draping her eyes concealed a wandering gaze. He bowed, careful to regard solely the queen, though his regard would rather fall upon her lovely daughter.

Dalock King began. "I thank you, Queen Mostaza, but this day must contain some hint of hardship for you, as your brother is dead. I know the two of you enjoyed a close relationship."

Her spine straightened. "By The Powers, my Lord, I do not know what you mean. My brother invaded my land; his men burned my crops, driving my people from their homes and into my arms clamoring for safety." The guards by the women's sides went steely eyed.

The princess interjected in a quiet, yet potent, voice, "And he killed our good king." Kamkai nodded slightly, the tendons of his hands tensing as though he made ready to draw blade.

"Yes, and Grufmit slew my husband, fond father of my children," the queen acknowledged, her voice mounting in command. "So you see, I bear him no love. I do not mourn his loss."

"Interesting choice of words," Dalich's father began. "For I possess a letter," and he nodded at Favik, who Dalich noticed now bore a stack of folded parchment, "quilled by you, Mostaza of Ghemif, in which you say of your husband . . ." Favik's flicked quickly through the letters. He gracefully flipped the requested document to his Lord's waiting hands. Dalock King read:

The death of my husband is of no consequence; I bore him no love and do not mourn his loss. Forgiveness will be yours if you leave my lands at once to my rule.

"What false document is this? I see your scheme; you would seize my lands for yourself." She grit her straight teeth, but the Strange King shook his head solemnly, even-tempered brown eyes on her guards as though by his gaze he could quiet their mounting anxiety.

"Princess Kostaza, do you recognize the hand that quilled this letter?"

The young woman stepped forward, reaching a pale hand to accept the document. Before she could scan the quilling, her mother snatched the cream-colored parchment.

"My daughter will not engage in your treachery." Mostaza balled the letter in her fist and dashed it to the floor. Kostaza bent to retrieve it, the beads that draped her eyes swinging away to reveal a mien of determination and firm will.

"I *will* read it, Mother," she breathed, scooping the missive from the carpet and stepping to the other side of the guard Kamkai, away from the queen. Kamkai's eyes roved the page, as did the princess's. Her hands trembled slightly. "This is my lady's quilling." The princess's hand darted over her own mouth as if to stifle any further utterance.

Her mother huffed. "The Powers have stolen your reason, Kostaza! How can you—"

Kamkai interjected, "No, my lady. I know your hand, and that is plainly it."

"How does a guardsman claim to know his lady's hand?"

"While my lord king lived, I read your letters aloud to him," Kamkai related, voice raw with authority and anger, gazing to Dalich and holding his head tall. "King's Son knows I can read. Both ink and blood." All eyes turned to the young man.

"Kamkai speaks true; he read The Powers-writ blood on my sword after the battle." He could not help but gaze at the lovely princess.

His father spoke. "Mostaza of Ghemif, I charge you with the murder of your husband, and with inciting your brother to invade Kaymif."

"By The Powers, you all accuse me false."

The Lord of Eskalind waved at the stack of parchments in Favik's grasp. "There are more letters here with similar egregious statements. Your own hand condemns you."

The queen seethed, glaring at Favik as though he were the root of her plight. "How did you get those letters?"

Dalock King spoke to the room, "What sentence for a queen who kills her king, who willfully allows marauders into her lands?"

The other Kaymif guard replied, "Death, Lord Strange King."

Kamkai growled, "By my hand, if it pleases you, Lord of Eskalind." He ground out the words, reaching for his sword's hilt. Kostaza shuddered. Dalich used every ounce of will to stand in place and not dash to comfort her in a protecting embrace.

"Hold!" his father ordered. The Guards ringing the inner perimeter of the pavilion stomped a foot in reply. The motion and sound startled the Kaymiflanders. "The sentence is exile. Mostaza will be sent far from here. To Thislin, or an island off the coast of Gergelt."

"You will not do this to me." Disbelief, or perhaps guilt, sank the queen's features.

"I grant you one small redemption; tell your son that his father is dead and that you are departing. You need not tell the lad the circumstance, and by my word, I will not either. Only my son, as my representative, and your daughter will bear witness to your farewell. Everyone else, out." Deaf to her stammering, he nodded to the Kaymif royal guards, who snapped their blue-capped heads to Dalock King, the purple tassel at the top of each cap flicking forward with the motion. They departed out the main entrance. "Guards, Favik, Narnik, with me. Jinil, leave and tell Bafnil to send in the Kaymif king." With that, he gestured to the nearest Eskalind Guardsman to untie the secondary entrance. Dalock King and his appointed men filed away from the pavilion. Favik lingered to retrieve the condemning letter from the princess. Once he exited, Dalich and the two Kaymif ladies stood in tense silence.

"You stupid, stupid girl!" spat the former queen.

Making no reply, Kostaza stepped farther away from the purple-clad woman. Dalich paced to her side, assuming a formal stance, as if this were a coronation ceremony rather than a mother's final farewell to her child. Bafnil entered, announced Moulai, then left.

"My dove!" His mother knelt, yanking aside the beaded veil draping her eyes and holding her arms out to the boy. Moulai entered with cautious steps. The amethyst beads sparkled on his mother's outstretched hand.

The lad walked into her arms, hugging her stiffly. "Mother, what is wrong?" He gazed about, spying Dalich and his sister. "Are they getting joined? I thought you would be happy if they did."

"I have terrible news, my dove." His mother inhaled and released him, then reached forward to brush one of her tears from his round cheek. "Father, he is not coming home, and I am leaving too. It breaks my heart, my dove, my little king."

His small voice rose. "I thought Papa was coming home soon?"

The former queen of Kaymif shook her head. "Moulai, you are king now. You must be a strong boy, a strong king to your people. I will miss you." She swept a hand over her young son's blond locks, petting them feverishly as the boy wailed, "No!"

"Shh. Whatever anyone tells you, ever, know I lived only for you, my dove." That seemed to calm him.

She squeezed her son, then kissed his forehead and rose to her silk-slippered feet, eyes flashing at her daughter. In a low voice she scoffed, "May you suffer the fate of the Amkish queens and bear only daughters." As though readying for an appointment as mundane as breakfast, Mostaza draped her purple jeweled veil over her head with apathetic nonchalance. Smoothing the glistening stones to drape evenly across her eyebrows, Mostaza of Ghemif regally glided from the pavilion.

"Kosta?" whimpered the lad.

The princess gathered him into her arms, murmuring, breath ragged.

Dalich wanted to provide comfort, but considered it best to allow them a private moment, and also make certain their mother did not escape. He whispered, "I will be back," squeezing Kostaza's shoulder gently. Swiftly exiting Father's pavilion, he found Eskalind Guards escorting the traitorous queen away. She marched amongst them as if they were an honor guard.

Nearby, Kamkai and the other Kaymif royal guard who had witnessed the sentencing spoke separately with the Kaymif men staffing the two royal bounches. Kamkai pointed at his eye, pronouncing loudly, "I saw her betrayal of Kaymif myself, in her own hand, just as I saw the Eskalinder's blood-writ blade after the battle!" The gathered men muttered, their arms crossed in defiant postures, some eyes glaring in the direction of Mostaza's departure, others impatiently at Kamkai.

"Hold! The Eskalinders will see to her, but there may be others in league with the Ghemiflander against our lord. We Kaymiflanders must be vigilant in our protection of King Moulai. Our lord needs us."

The Kaymif guards rallied in assent as someone lightly punched Dalich's arm. Turning, he saw Narnik grinning at him. "You advised sending that shrew to Humiksland, my Lord? You would wish her upon the same soil as your aunt and cousins?"

Catching the jest in his eyes, Dalich countered, "Your mother has six sons to protect her."

"Ah, but two are in your father's service."

"Well, four sturdy Humikslanders against Queen Mostaza would be questionable odds."

"Ha! I think our Lord should exile her to Barrel Island."

"Where is that?"

"Anywhere he wants it to be. Simply put her in a weighted barrel, drop it in water, and call it Barrel Island. Till it sinks." They both grinned, but Dalich's smile faded quickly as he envisioned the cruel death it foretold. As if reading his thoughts, his cousin placed a strong hand on his shoulder.

"War is a brutal business, my Lord King's Son. A man may pass well-weighted judgment on another, yet have compassion in his heart for those who deserve it." Narnik inclined his head toward the departed party. "That woman proved herself brutally false. Think of all the suffering her actions caused. She deserves no pity."

One of the Kaymiflanders called out, "Where is our lord king?"

"Time for the introduction, my Lord," murmured his cousin, demeanor hardening into the firm gaze expected of an Eskalinder First Sergeant.

Dalich gulped air, but stepped forward to raise his voice. "Men of Kaymif!" All heads swiveled toward him. "I shall present your lord to you." King's Son reentered the pavilion.

The princess and her brother sat upon the carpets, talking quietly. The princess's veiling beads lay by her side. It pleased him to see the azure of her eyes, though her expression was doleful. "King Moulai, your men would greet you as their lord."

The lad seemed uncertain, but his sister smiled kindly. "It is time to present you to our people, my lord brother."

"What do I do, Kosta?"

"Follow Dalich King's Son." She tucked her slippered feet under her, rolled onto her soles and stood, a slim hand outstretched to her sibling. "Come. I will go too."

"Kosta, your veil beads." The boy swept the glittering jewels from the floor and into her hands. She gazed at Dalich a lingering moment before lowering them over her eyes and clasping them over her hair. The heir of Eskalind inhaled, then led the new king of Kaymif and his sister to their people.

Days passed as the Eskalinders lingered in Kaymif, at first ascertaining if the transition of power to King Moulai would go smoothly, and then that no further Ghemif plots arose. A detachment shadowed the Ghemiflanders' army to their previous borderline, leaving Kaymif soldiers to maintain the peace as Ghemif dissolved into Kaymif.

After all seemed in order, the Strange Kingdomers celebrated their victory with a tournament of skills for the youths who had hoped to earn their swords at the battle. The camp rang with the glad shouts of young men, including Saril, celebrating their Sword Earning. The few young women in the army's employ watched, heads bobbing as they compared the merits of the new men. Feminine feet were bared to both the new men and those more distant from their Sword Earning Day as the relief and exultation of surviving the crisis swept the camp in a wave of joy and feasting. However, Princess Kostaza spent every moment, both wakeful and sleeping, attending to her brother's new role and duties. Or so her notes to Dalich would lead one to believe.

As a new man, Dalock's son slumbered in his own private pavilion. His thoughts upon first inhabiting the tent bloomed with anticipation of entertaining the princess there. He called for tapestries and a screen to provide a sequestered private area in the airy space, and even floor pillows in a nod to Kaymiflanders' taste for interior furnishings. Instead, the secluded spot became his solitary retreat to gaze upon Damina's likeness. "Soon I will come to you and we will be together," he told her locket. Kissing her likeness, he clasped it shut, tucking it inside his linen tunic. Rising from the bed, he kicked at the pile of Kostaza's notes politely refusing his overtures. "Who wants a princess when one can have a violet-eyed beauty of Eskalind?" Dalich flicked his fingers as if dismissing an annoying person.

Outside, the Guards called to someone. King's Son went for the entrance just as his father's Page entered.

"Pardon, my Lord, your father needs you."

Grateful to be freed from pining alone in his quarters, Dalich replied with the air of a great philosopher. "It is good to be needed, Bafnil."

The boy puzzled this pearl of wisdom. "Yes, my Lord." He led King's Son to their Lord's tent.

Inside, Eskalind's ruler sat alone, his eyes distant and glassy. A heaping basket of bread and full bowls of aromatic sauces sat ignored on the table before him. "Father? What is wrong?"

"Ah, Dalich." The King glanced at a stack of spent envelopes near his elbow, his bearing hardening as though he addressed a vexing ambassador. "Fresh messages arrived from home; they do not bear good news."

"Mother?" Dalich blurted, his voice rising with panic.

Father raised a hand. "Will you let me finish? Marna is as well as can be expected, given what has happened. A terrible windstorm ... buildings collapsed and fires across the land, including our Halls. The worst damage at home was to her Scriptorium." His voice was heavy. "Three people killed, the Chief Scriptor and two visitors from Mavold. Most of the new books destroyed."

"How terrible!" was all Dalich could manage.

His father must have anticipated his question, for he continued with, "Your cousin Palika is unharmed, thank The Powers. Your mother named her Chief Scriptor, but there is not much for her to supervise, save the rebuilding. The Library survived intact." He groaned, uttering under his breath, "Marna would never be the same if she lost that."

So, it would not be the happy homecoming King's Son had envisioned. He planted his feet in a stance he hoped read as resolute, but stammered, "The Chief Scriptor, I cannot recall his face." It was as though the man never existed, as though only the confirmation of others would acknowledge the Scriptor's time on earth. "Father, what was his name?"

"It was Maknil. He was one of your first tutors." Dalich said nothing. He felt small and stupid. His father continued. "Elsewhere, extensive crop damage in the north; the harvest there may be completely lost. King's Market destroyed, buildings collapsed, many lost their lives." Dalock King exhaled wearily. "This is where I will need your help, King's Son." The older man folded his hands together, his brown gaze tightening in an appraisal akin to that of a Records Keeper querying during a trial. "Jinil and I shall return home. His daughter must be named; it has been nearly a month since her birth. I would have sent him earlier but there was too much to be done. Therefore, I place you in charge of the recovery efforts at King's Market. Saril will go with you."

"Yes, yes, Father," Dalich stammered, finding it difficult to contain his excitement. His first command, and Saril would be there too! He grinned.

"Dalich, this is an opportunity for you, but keep fresh in mind," the King cautioned, "terrible tragedies have occurred; the people will rely on you for assistance, and comfort. As King's Son, as my representative, you must provide both, as equitably as possible."

"Of course, my Lord." The younger royal sobered his tone, yet a rising sense of a freedom that he had never known soared within him.

Eskalind's Lord smoothed a hand over the table. "After, we may visit you, and tour the north. That is the plan for now. I will send you messages with regards to my wishes."

"As you wish, my Lord." At last his father trusted him. He would prove to his parents and to The Powers that he was a just and able administrator, then return to a glorious homecoming, find Damina, and take her as his bride. The future of his own making dawned bright and glad, unstoppable as the sunrise.

"Has it really been two months since we came here?" Dalich asked Saril as the pair toured the rebuilt covered stalls at King's Market. The scent of sawn wood still lingered in the air. Traveling merchants eagerly stacked their wares upon the freshly installed tables, pleased to no longer sell from blankets spread on the ground.

"Two months and five days," his companion sighed.

"You only remember so well because you met Falya the fifth day we were here," King's Son teased.

"Aye, my Lord." Saril grinned.

Dalich envied his companion's proximity to his lover; it made Damina's absence from his arms even more tangible. He was certain there were times Saril would rather go to Falya than keep his company. Perhaps even at this very moment.

King's Son looked aside to see Planil, the Chief Records Keeper of King's Market, approaching them.

"My Lord," the man called, raising a hand. Planil stopped before the two young men and bowed, his crimson cape spilling round his shoulders.

"What news have you?" Dalich asked.

The Records Keeper raised his head, brown headwrap rising as he lifted himself up onto his toes, as his profession required when reporting or making a pronouncement. "The final negotiation with the housed merchants has concluded. As you instructed, they are to owe no taxes from the last year, as a recompense for the loss of their goods and records from the storm. However, now that their shops are rebuilt at my Lord the King's expense, and are operational, they owe first month's rent immediately, and monthly taxes will be collected henceforth." He handed King's Son a rolled contract.

Dalich accepted the brown parchment and flicked his thumbnail on the red ribbon encircling it. "My Counselor," he glanced briefly at Saril, "and I will review this. Come to us tomorrow."

"Very good, my Lord," Planil replied, smiling the smile of a man pleased to be rid of a troublesome task. "And my congratulations to Jinil's son on the forthcoming founding of his house." The Records Keeper lowered his heels to the ground, made his deference, and left.

Saril leaned close, speaking under his breath. "That went well."

"Aye, it was a good idea to see the tavern rebuilt first." King's Son turned to admire the long line of reconstructed permanent shops, the well-oiled new shop signs swinging smoothly in the breeze as patrons scuttled in and out of the doors. "It provided the merchants with a place to discuss their trading and plans, plus a festive atmosphere, a pint of ale . . ."

Jinil's eldest son nodded. "Rebuilding all the shops to open at once was a keen idea."

"Avoiding petty jealousy and competition between the shopkeepers to be first to reopen." A glow of pride at their accomplishments spread across Dalich's chest. He silently thanked The Powers for granting him this time to savor his rapport with Saril. He placed his free arm around his fond companion. "I hope our sires think we have done well."

"We will know when we return home." Saril's voice carried a hint of wistfulness.

The heir of Eskalind slapped his companion's back. "Ha! I know *you* are not looking forward to returning." Then he caught himself. "Well. Mostly not looking forward to it. You have yet to meet your wee babe sister."

Saril grinned, brown eyes gleaming. "True, and Falya says she will follow when we return, so I will not be too glum." He laughed, leaning close to Dalich's ear. "Perhaps she has a cousin who might be of interest to you, my Lord?"

"Only if her father is an Innkeeper," Dalich replied, enjoying his companion's puzzled face. "Come, Counselor Saril, soon to be Lord Saril of the House of Jinil, Dalock King's Friend, let us review this covenant." He waived the coiled parchment, smirking as he relished his secret.

Chapter Sixteen—A Long Overdue Ceremony

In his last few moments as a commoner, Jinil stood before his King and the entire assembly of the royal household; ambassadors from the borderlands in their native dress—Kursaks in plain beige tunics embellished solely with embroidered cuffs and collars, Mavoldians draped in their renowned linens, Kaymiflanders with their small, betassled caps; and the servants and Lords and Ladies of Dalock King's Halls, clothed in the King's colors—soon to be the colors of his own house. Ranks of Tutors, Swordmasters straight in their bearing, Records Keepers clustered as a group, their crimson cloth wrapped heads bent in conference, merchants in gaudy finery, the ale maker slapping his belly as he joked with a builder from Teffle, Apprentice Librarians arranged behind the Master Librarian like obedient ponies, Scriptors rubbing their ink-stained fingers, King's Son at his father's side, Guards ringing the perimeter of the gathering, Nursemaids coddling their charges, Healers, Cooks in clean crisp aprons, freshly bathed Gardeners; it seemed the whole of Eskalind was represented on the crowded terrace and below in the courtyard, all basking in the bright sunshine on this Powers-be-thanked temperate and beautiful Winter day.

Jinil stood first in the line of his family, for he ranked eldest amongst them. Strange Kingdomers believed the order of age should be exhibited in ceremonies, thus the eldest came first, followed by the next eldest, and down through the line to the youngest. Thus, by his side, his beloved wife nodded to her blood cousin Kermon in the crowd, who beamed back at her, his teeth a pale flash in his dark face. Next to Saralya was Saril, followed by fourteen-year-old Marnil, and lastly, just a babe in arms—the Queen's arms, no less—Jinilya, comfortably napping through the founding of her house.

King's Second glanced to the empty space on his other side, his thoughts upon long-ago memories of his mother and father, dead nearly fifty years, leaving their young son bereft of parents, of all family, to be raised in a King's House. Now that orphan stood to become a Lord, the founder of his own house. Jinil nodded in grateful acknowledgment to The Powers that saw fit for him to be born an Eskalinder and Gifted with the favor of his King.

Across the terrace, near one of the the covered archways that ringed three sides of the open space, Favik Queensman stood near a trellis of King's Vine, the white flowers gracefully spread open to accept the sun. Jinil had never had a great fondness for the man, but for the first time, he considered that the Humiksland-born Queensman also had lost his parents as a small lad. Through Eskalinders' belief in meritocracy, Favik's talents and abilities too had been recognized, and he had risen to prominence. King's Second nodded again, an uplifting sensation of benevolence and brotherhood spreading across his chest. Perhaps The Powers moved Favik to the same feeling, for the Queensman caught King's Second's gaze and inclined his head in deference, his neutral expression for once replaced with one of camaraderie.

The Queen smiled lovingly at wee Jinilya, tracing a finger along the round curve of the babe's smooth cheek. She glanced up as her husband raised his arm for silence.

The King spoke. "I thank you all for coming to bear witness to the founding of the House of Jinil, Dalock King's Friend." Cheers erupted, and the babe's eyes flew open, her mouth forming a tiny *O* as though she might cry. Marna rocked her gently, cooing to calm her.

The King raised a hand again, his brown gaze upon the timber framework of the new Scriptorium. Marna dropped her gaze to the yawning child, not wanting to think of the lost lives and books, the wind and fire that destroyed the original building. During the storm, she had thought The Powers would raze King's Halls in their entirety, that all her work preparing for whatever war The Powers waged with one another would not suffice to save her adopted people. Now she wondered why her book making and copying had been targeted for destruction. Seeing her family return home safe had comforted her somewhat, and especially hearing Dalich's strange tale of his combat with King Grufmit. Yet still she wondered.

Better to think upon the warm weight of sweet Jinilya nestled in her arms, or to gaze across the crowd at familiar and new faces, all watching her husband, the light of expectation and joy framing their expressions. There, Lady Dara, in a highly embellished gown with bronze threading encircling her long neck, stitched by her own talented hand. By her side, Lady Yadla, whom the Queen had not seen in years, accompanied by her husband and her daughter, Lady Ala, whose life span of eighteen years also represented the length of Marna's joining to Dalock. Scholar Benasa, tall and pretty, shoulder to shoulder with Scholar Onath, who possessed a good heart and a keen intelligence, but by The Powers, was perhaps the least attractive man in the Kingdom. In one hand Onath held a small, glossy, brown earthenware pot, home to a tiny seedling of the red-barked tree he was so fond of, a present for soon-to-be Lady Saralya.

It pleased the Queen to see Benasa and Onath together in public; their outlander shyness about their intimate relationship was unnecessary in Eskalind, where nobles and non-nobles intermingled without regard to status. As if to demonstrate the mores of Strange Kingdomers, at

Onath's side stood young Lord Radil, hand in hand with his lover Synya, an Apprentice Librarian whose father tended the kitchen animals and whose mother served as a housemaid to the borderland ambassadors.

Dalock spoke, clear and glad for this moment he had desired for many years. "At the end of this First Month of this two thousand nine hundred and fifth year since the founding of Eskalind, we come together for rebuilding, and for recognizing long, loyal service." Someone in the back cheered. The King beckoned to the Chief Records Keeper, who stepped forward. She held aloft a sheet of vellum covered with dense quilling and emblazoned with a large disc of red wax, alike in color to her robes. "Behold," Dalock said, "the granting document for the House of Jinil, Dalock King's Friend. My colors, and the symbols of myself and my Queen, the sword and the book, will forever be the emblems of your house, and in them shall be preserved the memory and the spirit of my reign."

. The Records Keeper stepped aside as the King beckoned to his Second. "I call forward Jinil, King's Second, to be Acta Sua, head of his house." The new Lord stepped toward the King as the King's Page Bafnil handed his ruler a scabbarded sword. "I present this blade to you, Lord Jinil, at the founding of your house. May it be faithful to you and your heirs."

Jinil accepted the sword, though he drooped for a moment as though it weighed more than he expected. Then the Acta Sua spoke. "Thank you, my Lord King, for your kindness and trust these many years. May my house honor and serve yours as long as The Powers see fit for my line to continue."

Marna watched her son, who smiled broadly at Saril as the two older men embraced.

"For your Lady," Dalock continued, and he reached to receive a bronze-chased book box from Bafnil. The Queen squinted to catch a better glimpse of the present, for Dalock had studiously avoided telling her anything about the bestowal objects. Her greatest curiosity was what he thought suitable for the little one in her arms.

Bright garnets gleamed along the edges of the bronze sheeting Saralya's box, and an *S*-shaped arrangement of copper-colored pearls glistened in the center. "A token in recognition of your love of reading, and your loyal service to my Lady Queen as her Reader. Inside is an illuminated copy of poetry by Jasbad, a favorite of both Lady and Lord." Marna nodded with approval, knowing her friend would treasure the bestowal.

Never one to relish public attention, Lady Saralya bowed to accept the box, her deep brown eyes on her slipper-clad feet. "Thank you, my Lord King." Dalock's gaze fell to his wife, his eyes warm as he ascertained her favor with his granting.

Turning to Jinil's eldest child: "Lord Saril, for you, a sword alike to your Lord father's." The young man tilted his short black curls forward in deference to the King. Saril's voice was glad and distinct, as full of self-assurance as one born to a Lordship. "I will treasure this blade above all others, my Lord, and keep it as an heirloom of my house."

Dalock grinned, patting the young man's shoulder.

"Young Lord Marnil, your Sword Earning is yet to come, so for you, a scabbarded long knife wrought by the renowned knifesmiths of Kaymif, in the colors of your house."

Marnil raised his brown hands to accept the red wire hilted knife and bent his knee, his dark eyes steady and serious, betraying a hint of his mother's introversion. Yet when Marnil spoke, it was as though inspired by a distant vision. Perhaps The Powers whispered in his ear, or he had spent more time than even his parents reading the Legend scrolls beloved by Eskalinders, for their lilt and language flowed from his tongue. "My Lord Dalock King, bestower of my house, I pledge that my house and my heirs will remain forever loyal to the line of the Strange Kings, through whatever may come, from now until the end of this world."

All the adult members of his house, and the Queen as well, turned to gaze at him in surprise at this prophetic pronouncement, for had anyone wagered which of Jinil's sons might say such a thing, all bets surely would have favored Saril.

"Then my line," began the King, "will have the best of care and the most loyal of friends." Lord Marnil lowered his eyes and a smile curved his lips.

An odd sensation tingled across Marna's forehead, perhaps a harbinger that indeed, their houses were entwined in a way that only The Powers perceived; someday, her line would call upon his. She felt calmer, and her earlier anxiety about the storm's devastation quieted. Perhaps The Powers were not at war, and all would be as well and as good, just as the last line of Legend scrolls always foretold.

Jinilya squeaked, reminding everyone of her presence. Dalock gazed at her. "What to give the little Lady Jinilya at the founding of her house?" The Queen glanced to the King's Page, whose eyes were as big as a bread bowl, as though he had forgotten something very, very important. Then she saw her husband grinning at the babe. "Ah, what do I have here?" Reaching into his sleeve, Dalock drew forth a curious item. A small bronze box shaped like an open book with a tiny long sword laid across the pages. The King held the hilt of the miniature sword between his fingertips and shook it, causing a clacking sound.

Marna queried, "Is it a rattle?"

"Aye, and when she outgrows its first use, it can be fitted with a pin to be a brooch." He smiled at Saralya. "Do not worry, the blade is rounded and blunted. No sharp edges!"

The babe reached a cautious hand from her swaddles to grasp the rounded blade. A tentative shake brought forth a serious knit of her tiny brow. Another jiggle, strong enough to jingle the bits inside, elicited a toothless smile and an attempt at a giggle. Dalock grinned, a soft, fond expression in his eyes that Marna had not seen since their son was a wee babe. "She is a swift learner." He tenderly squeezed his wife's arm, whilst gesturing to the assembly. "To the House of Jinil, Dalock King's Friend. Hail!"

"Hail!" called the people. Dalich, standing at the forefront of the gathering, raised one hand in the Eskalind salute as the others did, but his other hand touched the slight lump in his tunic, which she supposed was the locket she had sent him with Damina's portrait. His gray eyes shone bright. "To Lord Jinil!"

Fresh cheers to each of the newly ennobled members of the family, and the stomping of feet, followed. Then Kermon threaded swiftly through the crowd, leaping forward and up the few stairs to embrace his blood cousin Lady Saralya and his caysin Lord Jinil.

King's Son clomped forward, up to Marnil and his brother, as Saril quizzed, "What a fine speech, brother! Did you quote one of the Loremasters? Which one?"

"I…don't know. I don't think so." Marnil felt confused and oddly cold.

Saril chided, "Come, we are nobles now, use Noble Speech."

Marnil's brow knit at the correction. "I said, 'I do not know.'"

King's Son thumped Marnil on the arm and grinned at his brother. "My Lords!"

"Well met, King's Son!" Saril laughed, and the young men embraced.

"Friend!" called King's Son, breaking from his brother to hug Marnil tightly.

Marnil saw Saril's smile dim slightly. He replied, "I thank you, my Lord."

King's Son beamed at the brothers. "Show me your new blades!" They each obliged, unsheathing the weapons, and the trio fussed over their fineness. "Marnil, think on it," Dalich said. "My father must have had your knife made while we were in Kaymif. I wager he has been planning this granting a long time. That was over four months ago."

"I thought that too," interjected Saril. "My Lord, we should go to the feast straightaway, as tomorrow we two depart with our Lords for the northern borders, to assist with the rebuilding there." Marnil wondered why his brother was recounting what they already knew. Saril glanced at him. "And you, Marnil, will travel with Mother to see to the redecoration of our estate." Jinil's eldest grinned broadly. "Everything to be redone in Dalock King's colors, the colors of our house."

Marnil wanted to protest that he too should be allowed to journey with the men, rather than watch Mother fuss over wall hangings and furnishings. But he would not give his brother the satisfaction of watching him beg, for that was surely why he was being goaded in such an obvious manner.

King's Son spoke, his gray eyes kind and sincere. "We will miss you then, Lord Marnil."

"And I will miss you, my Lord. But now we are together and should celebrate." With that, he roped an arm around his Lord and led him through the crowd to the Great Hall, pleased that for once, he had outmaneuvered his brother.

Dalich closed his book with such force a breeze swept his hair. "I was reading this same volume the last time I spoke with her. Ah, Damina." The young man tossed the book onto his bed and reached up to stroke the locket concealed under his collar, glaring at the stone walls of his lonely chamber. "I had no opportunity to speak alone with Mother before journeying northward with Father. It is already Third Month, and we are home, I must discover where Damina lives. Now!" He leapt to his feet. "Tonight I will find out; nothing will stop me." He tromped his way to the rebuilt Scriptorium.

Scriptors worked at orderly rows of candlelit desks within the Scriptorium, even at this late hour. Their tunics and cloaks bore a brown emblem of an open book, with a red quill across it. Their identical uniforms and downcast eyes rendered them identical, a homogeneous grid of humanity.

The Chief Scriptor rose from her desk, which overlooked the others, and greeted him. "My Lord Cousin." Palika's smock was embroidered with the device of her office: an open book, red, with a bronze-threaded quill crossing it. The embroidery glimmered in the candles' flicker.

"Is my mother here?" Dalich glanced at the Queen's large table. The inkwell was covered, thus he knew the answer before his cousin spoke.

"No, she retired but half an hour ago." Palika regarded him with ever-serious blue eyes. "Are you well?" How concerned she sounded, the vertical worry wrinkle in her forehead deepening as she studied him.

Palika should take a lover, Dalich thought. He smirked. Perhaps then she would be less uptight. "Of course I am fine. Just searching for Mother. 'Night." He turned and left, quickening his pace as he entered the royal corridor. Orange torchlight shone clear and brilliant in the hallway. At the bottom of the King's and Queen's stairways, he queried the Guards. "Are my parents above?"

"They are, my Lord," King's Guard Trevil replied.

King's Son suppressed a groan that both were present, but then considered: if he first told his father that he must speak with Mother, he risked less chance of interruption. Dalich climbed the stairs to the left. At the top, the Guard outside the King's door stepped aside to allow him to knock. Hearing no answer, Dalich opened the door. "Father?" he called, pacing into the room, which was lit with many candles. Parchment maps and letters littered the King's quilling desk. The garderobe door was closed. Dalich shut the main door, went to the connecting door, and opened it. Only a few candles, just enough to navigate the room by, illuminated the darkness of the Queen's chamber. The scent of sweet herbs perfumed the air.

"Just a moment, Dalock," Mother said. Her back to him, she wore a soft-looking sleeping robe that hinted at transparence.

"It is Dalich." He suddenly wanted to be anywhere but where his feet were planted.

"Oh, Son, you surprised me." Mother reached to a nearby chair for a thicker robe. She turned to face him, fiddling clumsily with the sash.

"I was hoping to talk to you alone, Mother," he began, still standing in the doorway.

"Now is not the time, Dalich."

"But please, it is important." He entered her chamber, closing the door behind him and creasing his forehead as though in pain. "Just a moment, Mother?" She never resisted his pleas when he was hurt.

She sighed. "Sit by the fire." The Queen gathered a long taper, illuminating more candles. The room brightened enough that one could read a document quilled during Trelich King's time—red letters upon orange parchment.

His eyes traveled to the couch before the fireplace. Two chalices and a carved clearstone decanter, full of crimson wine, rested on a small table. A twinge of jealousy filled Dalich's heart. He wished he were the one entertaining a sweetheart. He sat where she bid, just as he heard the door connecting the Queen's chamber to the King's swing open.

"Hullo, Mmmarna," purred his father.

King's Son's face flushed, fearing his father might be as underdressed as the Queen had been. But Mother went swiftly to Father's side. After a moment of feverish whispering and overlapping murmurs, the King's door thumped closed, and Dalich's Queen and mother returned to sit by his side. "Now, what does my son wish to talk about?"

Dalich glanced at the King's door. "Dalock will not interrupt us again." A firm finality tinged her voice, as though she were issuing a decree to a borderland ambassador.

Her son inhaled slowly, hoping it would calm him. Then he reached to his neck, pulling forth the fine chain that lay hidden under his tunic. The locket slipped over his collar to dangle before his chest.

"Ah," his mother said. "What do you think of it?"

Dalich could not help smiling. "It is beautiful. *She* is beautiful, is she not?"

Mother's large cheeks rose with a grin. "I am told it is a fair likeness. I am glad you like it."

"Thank you, Mother, you give me hope." He fingered the carved metal.

She inclined toward him. "My son, I know it has been difficult for you, being separated from Damina."

Dalich nodded, not certain how to proceed. Now that he had this opportunity, all thoughts fled his head. After a long pause, he ventured, timid as a Page new to service, "When can I meet her?"

"Do you want to meet her?"

"Of course! I want to meet with her, I want to join with her, I want to . . ." He stopped. Her expression was pained as though she had spilled a full bottle of ink over a just completed letter.   "What is it, Mother?"

"She is not of age yet." Her gray eyes observed him intently.

"Oh," he said, his voice flat with realization. He released the locket. "I thought she would be older . . . as you are to Father. Soon, then?"

She said nothing.

"Not soon?" His mother shook her head. "Oh." The young man sucked in a long breath, flicking his fingers upon his belt buckle. "I . . ." Suddenly, Dalich's heart swelled with certainty. "But The Powers will us to be together. I am King's Son. Father can arrange it, yes?"

She said nothing.

Resolutely he hammered, "I have earned my sword, I am of age. What difference does it make if she is a bit younger?"

Her gray eyes hardened, and he felt a vexing Apprentice under her gaze. Yet it was not her eyes but her words that undid him. "Damina is nine years old."

"What?"

He thought of the girls that age in King's Halls. All the things he had imagined doing with Damina suddenly sickened him, and a terrible gripping sensation seized his gut. His throat tightened, thick and dry. "How did I not realize that when we spoke together? Or when I looked at her portrait?" Dalich whispered, not realizing the thoughts spilled from his mouth. Then, as though The Powers held a scroll before him with all his prior ideas and emotions writ upon it, he knew. He had wanted her to be his age, to be his companion and equal—wanted her to be how he imagined her to be. Not how she truly was. "I have been a fool."

His mother reached, embracing him. "I am sorry, my dear boy." Her words were soft near his ear. "I wish it were not so." She had not comforted him like this since he was young, maybe even Damina's age. His arms spanned his mother's back now, strong enough to lift her. He felt the thinness of her sleeping robe through the thicker fabric. He wanted his wife. He pulled away.

"She will wait for you." Mother's voice warmed as she reached to stroke the soft hair of his new beard.

"Seven years?" King's Son snorted. "But will I wait for her? Do I want to wait for her?" Dalich's voice was low and brooding.

"Only you can answer that." The Queen withdrew her hand, straightening her long robe where it draped between them.

"I am a man, and would act as a man."

"That is your prerogative. I am sure many women have shown you their feet; nothing prevents you from enjoying their favors." The Queen's lips formed a smile, but her eyes lacked any mirth.

"You do not like that we can have lovers when we are of age. Do you wish we were Humikslanders?"

"I am well aware that the customs of my birthland differ from those of Eskalind. As I make my home here with you and your father, I abide by the laws and traditions of this land. Our land."

King's Son crossed his arms. "Saril has a new lover. Marnil kissed a girl." He paused, searching for more examples to annoy her. "I caught a stable hand doing more than kissing with one of your Apprentice Librarians!"

"That is enough gossip, Dalich." Her cheeks flushed, and she again adjusted the velvet folds of her robe. "You may find a lover if you wish. I will not trouble you about it. But," and she fixed him with a raised eyebrow, "the woman you *join* with must be a woman of Gift. That is the way of Eskalind's Kings, and Damina's Gift is clear and certain."

"There are other Gifts. Father's mother saw The Powers. I read it in her chronicles."

"Ah, you have been reading and absorbing the histories of your ancestors." Her air was that of a victor triumphing after a long-fought conquest.

Dalich shook his hands, grumbling, "Perhaps one of the pretty serving maids is without a lover." Standing, he glanced at the royal bed. "Give Father my love." Exiting through her main door, he swung it shut hard behind him, and stomped down the stone stairs loud as his boots allowed to sulk in the dark of his lonely chamber. He set a plan: tomorrow he would attach himself to Lord Jinil's family and journey with them to their new estate's seat, where he could enjoy the companionship of his friends. He wanted nothing more than to be rid of King's Halls.

Chapter Eighteen—A Gift Revealed

The sky overhead shone brilliant blue as a warm, Summer-like breeze wafted over the crimson blankets spread upon the grass. The Acta Sua of the House of Jinil, Dalock King's Friend, reclined on wide, shaded chestnut cushions, stretching his hands overhead. "Thank The Powers, at last an afternoon free of decisions and duties." Lord Jinil rolled to his side, watching Saralya make faces at their babe. Wee Jinilya lay on her back, feet wiggling as she giggled in appreciation of her mother's antics. Behind them, their newly granted, stone-faced home rested on a knoll, overlooking an ordered garden that stretched into the lawn where they lounged. Beyond the lawn, a cluster of trees marked the beginning of their forest, and beyond that lay their fields and crops. In the near distance, their sons thwacked wooden swords at one another while King's Son shouted encouragement.

"Faster footwork, Marnil! Your opponent is taller than you: be swifter than his reach!"

King's Second smiled, murmuring, "Thank The Powers my sons and I get along well. If only the same were true for King's Son and his father. I hope this holiday away from King's Halls will do him well."

"Jinil, look!" Saralya lifted their daughter to him. "Her eyes—they have changed from brown to your green!"

He reached for his daughter. Jinilya yawned as her father tried to survey her face. "Jinilya, let me see." The little one half opened her eyes in an imperious squint. "She is teasing me."

"No, it is simply her nap time."

"Da, da, da," said the babe.

"Ah! There, yes. You are right, they appear green. Or perhaps it is some trick of the light."

"Thank The Powers one of our children inherited your gorgeous eyes," his wife said with a fond smile.

"If the rest of her resembles you, we will have to build a stout wall to keep out the young men until her sixteenth Naming Day." Saralya laughed, whilst the youngest Lady's little eyelids drooped closed. "Ah, Daughter, I understand how you feel. I never used to be this tired." King's Second gestured at his sons. "*They* never seem to tire."

The couple watched as King's Son skirted around their sons. "Bend your arm, Saril!"

Marnil screamed, *"Hee-YAH!"* He hefted his practice blade at his brother. Saril blocked the blow, which rang with a deafening crack.

Saralya turned away. "Thank The Powers they are not using steel."

"King's Son and Saril have earned their swords; they might if they wished."

"Not without protective clothing." Marnil pulled his tunic off, his skinny torso gleaming with sweat. "And supervision." Their youngest son charged his brother.

Jinil raised a hand. "Calm down, boys. You frighten your Lady mother."

His eldest replied, "Your pardon, Father." Saril bowed low.

The Acta Sua made a dismissive gesture. "You need not bow when we are on holiday at our own estate."

Marnil cried, "But we love and respect you!" He mimicked his brother's bow, then whispered something to the others. The trio laughed, then all three bowed at once. "Hail, Lord Jinil!" they called, like a chorus of eager traveling players.

Jinil grumbled to his wife. "Now they are being cheeky."

"They mean well." She brushed a strand of Jinilya's black hair away from the babe's dimpled cheek.

"They are up to something." The Acta Sua waved a hand to acknowledge their deference. They saluted him with their swords. He shook his head, chuckling. Saril slapped Marnil on the back, and the brothers resumed their swordplay.

"Pff," snored the babe.

Her mother mused, "It is unseasonably hot today; one would think it were Seventh Month rather than Fourth. Much too warm in the sun for the babe. I will bring her inside."

"No no, let me. I will nap too, in the library, I think."

"As you wish, my Lord."

"Oh, nonsense." Jinil stood, kissed his wife's head, then carried his wee daughter into the house.

———

Saralya sat a moment watching the young men. "They are not really boys any more," she observed quietly. "Well, Marnil is. Too thin, like an outerland orphan. You would think he never ate." Gazing at them, she felt she could see the men they would become as they matured—tall like their sire, lean limbed but strong. Lords of the Strange Kingdom. A twinge of regret that her parents could never have seen her beautiful family threatened to plummet her mood. She shifted her concentration to her eldest. "My wise one." The Lady smiled. "Most like his father. Hard to believe he has a lover. Hmm, I could be a grandmother soon, if The Powers will it." She reached for a toy wooden horse, still wet from her daughter's gums. "My sweet little girl, why did you come to us so late?" She laughed. "The Powers *did* will that." The Queen's Reader gazed back to her sons and their friend. "I would have them all be glad, if I could."

Standing, Lady Saralya called, "My Lord! Boys! I am going inside; do not stay out in the hot sun too long."

Saril replied, "If it gets hotter, we will go into the shade of the trees, Mother."

"Or continue undressing," joked Marnil, as Dalich doffed his crimson tunic onto the bright green grass.

"Very well." She waved goodbye as she followed her husband's path to the house.

———

"Here we go," Marnil breathed to his compatriots. The youths drew closer together.

"Wait a moment, brother." Saril poked the grass with his blunted wooden sword tip as though trying to make a grasshopper jump.

"You have done this before?" Dalich whispered, trying to contain his enthusiasm.

Saril nodded, and his brother pointed at Dalich's neck. "When did you get that necklace?"

He had forgotten to hide the locket when he stripped off his tunic. "Um, not too long ago. It was a present."

Jinil's eldest pursed his lips. "Present from an Innkeeper's daughter?"

Dalich gaped, and Marnil barked, "Shh!" All three watched the last swoosh of Saralya's red dress as the Lady entered the house.

"Now!" Saril commanded. The trio charged into the nearby forest.

"This way!" Marnil called. Dalich and Saril scrambled through the underbrush after him. In his excitement, Dalich ignored the leaves and twigs scraping his bare arms and sides.

The trio entered a clearing. Sunlight filtered through the lacy leaves of the trees as a cool breeze shifted the branches. The place felt larger than it appeared; it seemed that even while Dalich observed it, it receded from him. King's Son felt a strange shimmer in the air as if it breathed on its own. He fought the urge to shudder; yet he was not afraid, only wondering.

"I hid them over here." Marnil bounded to a large rock. He pulled away loose twigs gathered to one side of the smoothed stone, uncovering a brown cloth bundle. It rattled like metal as he unwrapped it.

"Real swords!" Dalich exhaled. "Where did you get them?"

Marnil grinned as he handed a blade to his brother. "Our Armourer does not keep a close tally."

Saril frowned as he accepted his blade. "Yet we always return them, right, Brother?"

"We did not the first time, and they got rained on and rusty. That made a lot of work." He whistled. "My Lord, choose one, and at last we can all spar together for real!"

King's Son grinned, happy the three were together alone, free to do as they pleased. He had always felt for Marnil. Being younger than him and Saril, the lad missed out on so much. Dalich balanced a blade in his hand. "I will use this one."

"Good!" Marnil stood, sword in hand. "Come, my Lord, match me!"

They circled one another in the glen as Saril darted out of their way.

Marnil tried to bellow, but his voice broke, sounding more like a panicked squawk. Dalich laughed. Saril teased, "You make a ferocious warrior, Brother."

"Quiet or I will have you both at once!" Marnil squinted at King's Son, which might have been an attempt to appear vicious but instead made him resemble a Scriptor weary from work.

"Brother, you are all posturing, no style," Saril mocked, draping himself against a tree.

Marnil jeered. "I hope that tree has thorns."

"Good one, Marnil!" Dalich laughed, then thrust his blade toward his friend.

The skinny youth parried, pushing away. "You caught me off guard!"

"With a compliment?" Dalich held his sword at the ready.

Saril interjected, "King's Son is the one who should be wary of compliments."

"Especially from you two," Dalich cut a quick glance at his older friend, who grinned.

Saril's eyes widened as he shouted, "Watch out!"

Dalich turned to find Marnil charging him. He jumped aside, blocking the blow with his sword, but in his surprise at the sudden attack, he did not turn the blade. The sharp steel caught the youngster, tearing into his bare right arm. Marnil cried out, dropping his sword and swooning to the ground. King's Son bent to him as Saril rushed to their side. Dalich turned the injured youth's forearm to assess the wound. Blood pulsed thick over white bone. King's Son swore. "By The Powers!"

"Don't tell Father," Marnil moaned. "Please don't tell . . ."

Saril yanked his own tunic over his head. "Wrap it around his arm!"

Dalich tried. "It is too thick!"

The younger boy whispered, "We can't tell Father!" Sweat beaded on Marnil's forehead; his breathing ran ragged.

Saril yanked the bundled cloth from Marnil's arm and grabbed his brother's sword. He sliced the fabric repeatedly, then tore a thin strip from the lining. Flinging the sword away, he cinched the cloth in a tight tourniquet on his brother's upper arm. "Come, talk to us, Marnil. Show us your fine tongue like at the granting ceremony!"

"I am sorry I charged you, my Lord," whimpered Marnil. "The Powers punish me."

"No no, forgive me for harming you," Dalich answered.

He looked at Saril, who barked, "Elevate his head!" King's Son held the limp youth in his arms as Saril tore more strips and bandaged the cut. A rapidly darkening stain spread across the brown fabric as it swelled, then dripped blood.

"I . . ." Marnil strained, eyes rolling in his head. The youth's brown skin tightened in pain, the color drained, pale against his dark curls. For a moment, Dalich thought the light in the glade seemed brighter. He felt keenly aware of everything—the breeze, the sunshine, even . . . was it true? A hum in the rocks…

"You will get better," King's Son promised. He closed his eyes tight and inhaled deeply, hugging Marnil, hoping with all his will. *I wish I had not cut him. He should be healed. Please heal him.* He exhaled slowly, unshuttering his eyes.

"Thank The Powers. The bleeding seems to have stopped at last," Saril reported. "That is good news, huh, Marnil?"

The younger brother blinked. "I think I can walk. I feel better. Much better. Let me." Dalich released him and the youth stood.

"The bandages!" Saril cried. "The stains are … disappearing!"

Dalich and Marnil peered at the cloths, which indeed were desaturating to their original shade. "It is true," King's Son breathed.

"I told you I felt better." Jinil's youngest son harrumphed as the other two stood.

Dalich shook his head. "Saril, help me remove the wrappings from his arm." The older pair tore the pristine bandages away to reveal a smooth, brown-skinned arm with nary a scar.

"By The Powers!" Saril murmured, eyes brimming with wonder. He looked at King's Son. "You have the Gift of healing."

"No, I just thought it …"

"My Lord, that is a great Gift." Saril's voice was husky with astonishment.

"Get this tight thing off my arm; it hurts," Marnil complained, trying to loosen the tourniquet. Dalich retrieved the small knife scabbarded to his belt, carefully sawing the knot till it frayed loose. Jinil's younger son groaned with relief. "That hurt more than the cut." He rubbed the red mark encircling his upper arm.

"Brother, do you not realize what just happened? King's Son healed you just by thinking about it."

"I know!" snapped Marnil. "I feel stupid, and grateful, and …" He gaped at Dalich, tears rimming his brown eyes. "I want to go home!" the youth cried, sounding much younger than his fifteen years.

"I will return the swords." Saril gathered the metal back into the bundle.

Dalich asked, "But Saril, how do we explain your shredded tunic?"

"By telling the truth to my father."

Marnil protested, "We cannot tell Father! I will get in trouble for using a real sword without the Swordmaster here."

Saril glared at his sibling. "Would you hide King's Son's Gift? Think of how many people he can heal at home, and on the battlefield."

"If it works again," Dalich interjected, though his words were smothered by Marnil's cry, "But you have already earned your sword, and I have not. I will be punished worse than you."

Lord Saril's dark eyes flashed with constrained anger. "Do not be as selfish as a Havadran. If we are punished, we deserve it for disobeying our custom." The eldest son of Jinil turned to King's Son, lowering his gaze. "We cannot conceal your Gift, my Lord. If The Powers will it to be sustainable, the suffering your healing could alleviate amongst our people would be unaccountably great. That is my counsel."

Dalich pondered a moment, recalling when he first called Saril his Counselor, before the Records Keeper when they were seeing to the rebuilding of King's Market. As a boy, he had thought of them each in their father's roles, and now as they grew older, he saw it coming to pass. It comforted him. "Saril is right. We will tell the truth and submit to our punishment like men. This may delay your Sword Earning, Marnil, and for that I am sorry, but we should not have done this in the first place. It would be worse to conceal what happened."

Marnil turned away. Dalich knew it was a harsh thing to say to his friend, but it would likely be the outcome of the afternoon's events. He would be King one day, and the King of Eskalind must be forthright and just. That was Saril's meaning. Dalich would embrace it with all his being to be worthy of such a charge.

Saril patted his brother on the shoulder. "With any luck, there will be another battle soon, right, Marnil? Then you can earn your sword." He finished wrapping the sack of blades, knotted the cloth closed, and hoisted it over his back.

Dalich felt a hand on his arm. He turned to face Marnil, who, with a quick glance at his brother's back, mouthed, "Thank you." His raised eyebrows made his eyes appear large as a babe's. The sincerity and trust in his expression spoke to Dalich's heart. Maybe he could be a leader of men, a respected man, a good ruler like his father. He acknowledged Marnil's gratitude with a nod, placing an arm around his young friend.

Thus the trio departed the glade where King's Son first realized his healing Gift.

Marna sat at her quilling desk in the Queen's Chamber, reaching for a fresh sheet of brown papyrus just as the King opened the door connecting their quarters.

"How fares my husband?" The Scholars' Mistress gazed at her inkwell as she prepared to dip her quill. Sunlight glinted on the bronze vessel, casting reflections onto her wrist. She still preferred to quill by sunlight rather than candle flame when she could, though her anxiety about The Powers' intentions had diminished. Still, Marna labored to improve and broaden the Scholars' reach. One never knew when a fresh crisis might present itself. This was true regardless of one's status, but Marna was aware that being royal made it likely she would be called upon to design a course of action. Especially since the blank scroll of Treya Queen had warned her to prepare.

Dalock stood in their doorway, saying nothing. "Daaalock?" Marna called, drawing out his name.

His voice unrecognizable, as though uttered from far away across a cavern, he said, "Jinil is dead."

"What? How?" Her voice was pinched with shock.

Her husband came into the room, pace leaden, and sank into the nearest chair, rubbing his knuckles on his forehead. "Saralya found him in their library. She heard the babe crying. Jinil was holding her, having a nap. He never woke up."

"Oh no."

"At least he had a peaceful end."

"Aye," Marna agreed, feeling numb. She thought of her poor friend, widowed with a babe in arms. She stood and stepped to her husband's side, placing a hand on his shoulder. They stayed silent awhile, both staring not at what stood before them, but at an undefined point ahead where their thoughts might collect. "But he was a healthy man!" she said at last, squeezing his shoulder through the soft linen of his tunic.

"Most would account Jinil's a long life."

"A long life? He was but fifty and four. Five?" The Queen was suddenly keenly aware that a mere ten years separated the King and his Second, his friend.

"Most would account his a long life."

"But my father still lives, and he is nearly eighty!"

"He is not from this land, my dear."

The Queen glanced down to her husband, that old familiar fear rising through her body: the sense that she was an outsider, unfamiliar with the ways of Eskalind, which by The Powers' strange plan, she ruled with her husband. "What would you say is considered a long life here?"

"Anything over fifty, I think," Dalock replied, brown eyes steady ahead.

"Surely you cannot mean that! Why, think of Lady Lasta, and Chamberlain Mardril, and even Lasta's sister, Cook. They all lived well past fifty." Marna pursed her lips, trying to recall their exact ages when they died. "Well past."

"They were exceptions, my dear. My parents never saw fifty."

"But your father was killed in battle, and your mother died of grief."

The King sighed heavily; she wished she had spoken of his parents' death in more empathetic tones. Quietly, he said, "All too often in Eskalind, one spouse dies just after the other."

Marna brought a hand to her lips. "Oh! Do you think … Saralya?"

Her husband stood swiftly to place his arms around her. Marna gratefully accepted his embrace, whimpering against his shoulder, "How I hope not! Poor wee Jinilya!" She leaned against the fabric draping his shoulder, keenly aware of his warmth.

"I would not want to live without you, Marna," her beloved whispered hoarsely.

"I … would have you as long as I am able." Not for the first time she choked back telling him that she knew, somehow knew, ever since she founded the Scholars, how much time she had left. And it was well past fifty. She glanced at her hand as the vision again rose before her …

That same hand, lying upon a crimson coverlet, the knuckles bony knobs, the skin slack as crinkled fabric, with dull brown spots and ropy veins. Warm evening light and muted shadows angling across the bed, traveling to the wall beyond as the sun set and her eyes dimmed forever.

If only she knew how much time Dalock had left.

She lay her hand upon his back, hugging tightly. If her Scholars worked for better diplomacy and information, her husband and son would not see battle soon. By her stratagems she would not be a widow for a long, long time.

"Marna," Dalock began, pulling back to gaze at her. "I must tell you," he continued, "something else that Saralya wrote, about our son." The Queen lifted her head, stepping away slightly. They released one another. "Dalich accidentally cut Marnil's arm, deeply, but he healed the wound. As if it had never happened."

"How could he heal him? Dalich has never shown any interest in herbcraft."

"Merely with his thought."

She pressed a hand to her face, speechless.

"Marna, it is a great Gift from The Powers."

The former Humikslander nodded, a knot in her gut. "Yes, The Powers have richly Gifted our son." Yet somehow it did not seem important now. "Oh Dalock, I am shocked about Jinil, and worried about Saralya, and about you … how this loss will affect you," she corrected, leaning forward to grasp his arm. He clasped her hand.

"I must make you some of my broth." The Queen smiled weakly. Since their earliest courtship, the efficacy of her chicken broth to heal and soothe him was legendary. "That will help … us . . . feel better." She resolved to cook broth for him every day.

———

Dalich marked his seventeenth Naming Day at King's Halls in the tradition established on the fifth anniversary of his Naming Day and birth: a feast of Queen's Recipe chicken, all the more delicious for being prepared by the hands of his mother. Yet the occasion was dampened by the recent loss of Saril's father. Dalich's closest companion was left responsible for many duties as his mother, Lady Saralya, plunged into grief and secluded herself from all save her small daughter.

The Lords and Ladies of King's Halls toasted the young man's health, and Dalich, new sword at his side, thanked them whilst his parents watched. He felt a strange sadness, as though he had expected more, as though something was missing.

He glanced at Saril. His childhood comrade smiled, but the depths of his eyes revealed his loss. Dalich found himself envying the goodwill and trust Saril and Jinil had enjoyed whilst the elder still lived, which carried forward in the son's mourning his lost father.

Upon his return to King's Halls, King's Son's days had resumed the usual boyhood activities of tutors, studies, and weapons practice, whilst Saril lived the life of a man, taking pleasure in the companionship of his latest lover. While the thought of taking a lover had once thrilled him, Dalich found that he turned away, suddenly fraught, whenever a young woman showed him her feet. Even the hint of a woman's shoe peeking from her hemline sent his attention elsewhere, as though The Powers themselves demanded his notice.

Thus, when Dalock King suggested, later that evening in private quarters, that his son test his new healing Gift across the land, Dalich gladly followed his father's command. His mother requested that he first revisit her Lady Reader Saralya at her estate, and while hesitant to intrude upon the Lady's seclusion, he went. While perhaps not completely released of the sadness that weighed on her days, Lady Saralya now read to her little daughter with the same lightness Dalich recalled from his own childhood, and watching this gladdened his heart. But when a visiting young Lady from a neighboring estate surprised Dalich with her bare toes, King's Son turned away as if she were of no more interest than a wall decoration. The Heir of Eskalind spent that year traveling Eskalind from town to town, estate to estate, unfailingly healing those in need with his Gift. An ever-fattening letter pouch followed his progress, and later, multiple letter pouches, as Swift Riders brought requests for healing from across the land. All of these requests The Powers allowed him to grant—even from a distance, as long as the patient was within Eskalind's borders. The people marveled at his remarkable Gift, and thanked The Powers for their benevolence, but the young man found the work slipping into routine. Only when he healed a person in his presence did he experience any sense of pride in the action.

More unjoined women bared their unclad feet to him, but despite his words with his mother, he still lacked enthusiasm for their charms, contenting himself publicly with the glad-faced thanks of the cured. Yet when he sat alone in his tent at night, or in the chamber apportioned to royal visitors in a noble household, or in yet another inn unpopulated by an Innkeeper's daughter named Damina, that gratitude weighed on his heart. Staring at the candles, he would think, *I restore people to health only so they are led to fresh disappointments.*

Still, he hoped for a chance encounter with Damina, thinking that perhaps if he met her, even though she was but a young girl, he would know, truly know, she was meant for him. Alas, he did not find her.

In the Fifth Month of 2906, the Heir of Eskalind returned to King's

Halls for his eighteenth Naming Day, eager to see his friends and family. And, of course, to enjoy his favorite meal of Queen's Recipe Roast Chicken. Instead, he arrived to news that Saril had departed for his first Apprentice Ambassadorship just days before his arrival, and Marnil, fresh from earning his sword, was away in the farthest part of the country, training with the army.

"But, Father, could you not have delayed their departures until after my Naming Day? I wanted to see them."

"It could not be helped," the King explained, though it was not much of an explanation. The Lord of Eskalind turned away. Dalich stared hard at his father's back, but his mother reached for her son and drew him close. She related, in hushed tones, that the Ambassadors' tiles had been drawn, and Saril's name came up first, whilst Marnil's company followed a schedule dictated by supplies and myriad other things . . . Dalich stopped listening. At last she squeezed his arm, saying, "Your father would be breaking our custom to grant them a stay. We must be fair and equitable in our dealings, especially with those closest to us."

"Yes, fine, I understand. But why cannot Father tell me that?" Her gray eyes were sympathetic, but King's Son shrugged her away. "First he denies me Damina, now he denies me my fondest companions." He stomped to his tiny chamber to continue waiting for time to pass.

Chapter Twenty—A Long Affair Settled

"Hullo, Favik!" Damina called from above, her black-braided head, bobbing with excitement, peeking out of a window on the middle floor of her father's inn.

The Queensman waved as he walked toward the stone building, thinking the eleven-year-old must have grown a great deal since he saw her last, as she seemed much taller. Then he saw her jump down and realized she must have been standing on a table. Damina disappeared from sight as Favik chuckled at his misinterpretation of the scene.

Opening the front door of the Lamorda Meadows Inn, he entered the main room, which served both for reception and as a common dining area. At present it was oddly quiet, devoid of either customers or staff, empty chairs neatly tucked under each table and sturdy, unoccupied pillows in a lonely ring around the hearth where a Story Teller would stand to recite the Legends of the land. Rapid footfalls thumped the ceiling until Damina appeared at the top of the long stairs and rushed to greet him.

He smiled and stepped back. It was a game they played, but she had forgotten. Halfway down the straight stairway, she paused, violet eyes bright with sudden remembrance. "Is it my turn or yours?"

Favik pointed to his temple, replying gently, "Think."

The black-haired girl nodded. "It's yours."

"Then I call for a King's Halls greeting this time."

She came forward, this time at a stately pace. "Who is who?"

"I will be the King, and you, a Lady."

Stepping softly down the stairs, she lowered her eyes, approached, and executed a perfect curtsey, daintily pinching her house smock to lift its hem counter to her bow so the fabric never brushed the oak floor. "My Lord King."

"My Lady." She raised her eyes to his grin. "Very good, Damina."

She tittered and dropped hold of her skirt, bouncing on the pads of her feet. "Guess what? We had a guest rent the whole inn for a week!"

"One guest leased the entire inn?"

"No, not one guest, two! Two Nordakspeople. Nobles!" She stopped bouncing to lean on his arm. "They're a husband and wife, and she has a necklace of ice stones that is the most beautiful thing I've ever seen." She clasped her dainty hands before her chin as though she would faint with delight.

A door creaked open on the far side of the room. "Ah, Queensman."

"Deenofts? A surprise to find you here."

Damina piped in. "He's our new tutor."

The Havadran corrected as he walked toward them, "*Your* new tutor. Your sisters are of age now, so I have you"—he raised his eyebrows in an expression of mock horror—"all to myself. The Powers help me!" He knit his hands together as though beseeching Them in desperate need. Damina giggled, playfully slapping his arm with both hands. The short-nosed man resumed a courtier's serious reserve, clasping his hands behind his back. "Now, my charge, before our lessons begin today, are all your household chores done?"

"Oh! No! I've not finished tidying the guests' room." She turned to dash off, caught herself, and curtseyed to Favik. "My Lord."

"My Lady." He bowed slightly. She grinned, then rushed up the stairs to the guest quarters.

Deenofts regarded him skeptically, his brown eyes narrowed. "Did someone neglect to send me an invitation to an ennoblement ceremony?"

The Queensman shook his head, speaking softly. "Do we have any business to discuss while we have this likely-brief moment alone?"

The other Scholar spoke in a similar tone. "None save this—the guests from Nordak? It is a certain *former* Eskalind noblewoman and her *second* husband."

"Lady Nalya, truly? What are they doing here?"

"Torturing the locals." Deenofts glanced about the room. "She treats Gamin and his family as if they were indentured servants. I haven't seen anything like it outside my homeland. The poor man went with Yamina to the merchants to refill the larder. The cupboard must teem with food more suitable to these Nordakspeople's *expensive* tastes." His upper lip rose in a sneer.

"Did the guests say where they journey next?"

"To Gergelt. They travel through Eskalind from Eastlant to avoid passage through Havadra. A strategy for which I could muster approval if the outcome had not included gracing this particular establishment with their patronage." One corner of his lips edged wryly upward for a brief moment, then the Havadran turned serious again. "Ah, I must," and the man touched Favik's sleeve to draw him closer, "also report that your young Lady"—he glanced in the direction Damina had departed—"has a sister who has shown me her feet, twice."

"Let me guess. Pamina?"

"Well it certainly was not the dark-haired twin." Deenofts closed his eyes tightly. "By The Powers, I wish I could erase the memory of Pamina's foot baring. She would not listen to me when I told her she was not my type. At all." The Havadran opened his brown eyes as though startled by a revelation, then squinted. "Has she done the same to you?"

"No, not me, but Onath, when he tutored the girls."

"Onath? Well then I am truly flattered I suit her rather unorthodox tastes. Must be my exotic Havadranness that attracted her." Rather than show pleasure at his own joke, the Scholar continued, "But Pamina has just come of age, since I arrived."

"Indeed."

Deenofts pursed his thin lips, his eyes large again under his prominent brows. "Oh my. I pity her father."

The former Humikslander chuckled, partly at the situation and partly at Deenofts' animated expressions. While the Havadran could be histrionic at times, he also possessed remarkable self-awareness and self-control, reigning in the theatrics as circumstances demanded. The Queensman wondered if the man's exaggerated personality compensated for the ridicule and scrutiny Havadrans encountered outside their homeland. For if most saw in Deenofts a typical Havadran, a synonym for "one who must not be trusted," Favik, for his part, saw his closest link to a nation he longed to return to, for even the slimmest chance to see his lost love. *Melande.*

The clomping of horse hooves and clatter of wheels on the cobbled drive outside caused both men to turn their heads. "Gamin returns?" asked Favik.

"Too light a rig. It's one of the Nordakspeople. They came with two carriages." Deenofts rushed to the bottom step and made a quick glance out the window. He called up the stairs, "Damina, she's back!"

A muffled shout of "Coming!" followed by what sounded like small pebbles pinging across the wooden floor. "Oh no!"

"Everything all right?"

After a pause, "Yes!"

"Do you need help?"

"*No!*"

Deenofts turned to Favik. "This is a matter worth investigating." He reached in his pocket, pulling forth a slim book. "Here, sit down and read this. Pretend you are a casual traveler who stopped for a meal."

"Why?"

"That woman had a fit yesterday when a merchant came in to inquire about a room. This," he wiggled the volume, "may be a useful prop."

Favik shrugged but accepted the book. The Havadran swiftly mounted the stairs. The Queensman seated himself at the first table, facing the front door, which was flung open just as he flipped to a page midway through the volume, as though he held a talisman that triggered an invisible door-opening mechanism.

The former Eskalind Lady Nalya stepped into the room, eyes immediately on Favik. A timid, woman attendant lingered outside. "What are you doing here?"

"Waiting for someone who can provide me with the bill of fare. I don't suppose that would be you?" He smiled indulgently, eyes traveling purposefully to admire her shimmering ice stone necklace, draped above ample cleavage. Nalya still possessed an enviable figure, and a nearly line-less countenance, despite being close in age to his Lady, who would celebrate her forty-eighth Naming Day soon.

"I am renting this entire lodging house."

"I would ask, respectfully, should that hinder a weary traveler from enjoying a meal?"

Her blue eyes darted over his attire. "Who are you?"

He rose. The Queensman knew this former Lady bore no love for his own Lady, or for his Lord for rescinding her estate, but he recalled Marna Queen telling him once that Nalya's father had been an Eskalind Ambassador. He sought to show his authority but betray no hint of his closeness to the Queen, or to Damina and her family. "I am Favik, former Ambassador of Eskalind to many lands, freshly departed from King's Halls." The blond man dipped his head slightly, lifting an eyebrow to invite her to introduce herself.

"You seem glad to have departed King's Halls." Her statement reminded him of a saying from Ambassador's school. *Speculation reveals more about the speaker than the subject.* The door to the kitchen banged open, and Pamina entered, her gaze pivoting about the room in the automatic manner of a proprietress assessing the needs of her establishment. The young woman spied Favik, and before she could utter a greeting, Nalya said, "Girl, see to it this man has a meal."

Gamin's oldest daughter peered at the woman, rosebud lips tightening with a restrained retort. Nalya turned with a swish of her spotless white cloak and marched up the stairs to her rooms. Her maidservant at last crossed the front door's threshold, closing the door and tiptoeing behind her charge. A flutter of footsteps sounded above. Pamina asked, "What's going on up there?"

"I'm not certain." A door banged closed, and then Damina, followed by Deenofts, zipped into the main room from the kitchen, breathless. The Havadran Scholar's brown eyes darted about the room. The girl's usually smooth forehead was creased and tense. "What is going on?" demanded Pamina, in a tone worthy of Nalya.

Deenofts pulled forth a stool and sat heavily, like a man expecting a tribunal. "There was a small accident upstairs."

Damina began sobbing. "I'm sorry! I didn't mean to! They just spilled out ..."

"Now, my charge, do not wail and carry on. It is a small matter."

Pamina crossed her arms, glaring at the pair. "Must I ask again what happened?"

"Your sister was tidying the guests' room, and she knocked over a small black velvet pouch, which contained several ice stones. The jewels spilled onto the floor. I found her picking them up."

Damina squeaked, "I think we got them all."

Favik asked, "How many?"

The Havadran held up his hands to mimic counting out stones. "I counted fifteen, twice, and placed them back in the bag, on the dressing table. We heard someone coming up the stairs, and assuming—correctly, I must point out—that it was the guest, we made a mad dash down the back stairs to the kitchen."

Pamina uncrossed her arms, pointing at the ceiling. "That woman left a bag of ice stones sitting openly on the dressing table?" She shook her head. "I don't like it. I've had a bad feeling about her the minute she set foot—" A woman screamed upstairs. All necks swiveled to the ceiling, then to the front door as it opened. A light-haired, light-bearded man wearing a fur-trimmed cloak entered.

"Was that my wife?" he asked, an odd apprehension in his voice, just as Nalya tromped into view at the top of the stairs, one hand holding aloft a small black item. "Nalya, are you well?"

"Someone has been snooping in my possessions," she announced, pronouncing the syllables individually as she came down each step. "Is this common etiquette in Eskalind these days?" A sob escaped Damina's lips. "Was it you?" Nalya accused, gliding toward the group. Her husband looked away, leaning both hands on an ivory walking stick.

Damina's tear-stained eyes pled with the woman. "I knocked the pouch over by accident when I was tidying your room. The stones came out, but I put them back. I'm sorry!" The girl glanced to the Nordaksman. "I'm very sorry!"

"Husband, can you believe this story?"

He asked, a bit wearily, "Did you count the stones earlier, Nalya?"

"There were fifteen stones." The former noblewoman untied the drawstring, drizzling the jewels one by one onto the nearest table. Deenofts and Favik watched carefully as she shook the empty bag. "See? Now there are only fourteen." She glared at Damina. "I suppose you thought a week's stay and meals are worth one small jewel?"

Pamina interrupted. "My sister is not a thief."

Deenofts tapped his chin. "Odd that there are only fourteen stones, when I distinctly counted fifteen not a few moments ago." His eyebrows lifted high above his brow as he regarded the woman.

Nalya's bottom lip lowered as she hissed, "So it was you, Havadran!"

"I believe," began the so-addressed Scholar, "that if you disagree with my assertion, we should send for a Records Keeper to assess the situation and pass judgment."

"A Havadran calling for a Records Keeper? This must be a first." Nalya raised her chin high. "I do not have time to wait for one to be summoned."

Pamina countered, "You *were* to stay here three more days."

"And I do not trust your Havadran manservant would linger for the judgment. This man"— Nalya gestured to Favik—"is an Eskalind Ambassador."

"I am a former Ambassador," he corrected.

"It is of no matter. You have the training, yes?"

"I do."

"In my father's time, Eskalind Ambassadors could serve the same duties as Records Keepers and render verdict." She smiled sweetly at Favik. "Is that still true?"

"It is."

"Then you will serve as Records Keeper for this trial."

As she seemed to have forgotten that part of the legal proceedings for an impromptu trial was agreement by all involved, Favik replied, "If all parties are willing."

Everyone but Deenofts nodded or assented. The Queensman pressed his fellow Scholar. "And you?"

After a moment, the Havadran waved a hand, as though swatting a fly. "Yes yes, I am willing."

"Then I stand in judgment of this incident, and my pronouncement shall be law, as agreed by all present. Everyone find a chair and sit." Even Nalya complied, though she allowed her chair to scrape loudly across the floor as she dragged it forth. Favik stood before the assembly, raising himself on his toes as was the custom for Records Keepers passing judgment. "We have all heard a different account of what happened. The girl admits to knocking over the bag of jewels and returning them to the purse. The Havadran admits to opening the purse and counting fifteen stones."

"Twice," Deenofts added. "I counted five, three times, and again, I counted three, five times. That is fifteen by both counts."

Favik continued, "Fifteen stones, he says. The woman returns to her rented rooms to find her bag of fifteen ice stones tampered with." The Queensman glanced at Nalya, noting her self-satisfied expression. "She brings forth the bag, and in the presence of present assembly, fourteen stones are counted." He waved a hand toward the glimmering clear jewels, then arranged them into five neat rows of three stones per row, but for the last row, where only two gems sparkled side by side, casting tiny rainbows onto the table. "I affirm a count of fourteen." Reaching for the bag, Favik shook it over the table, then laid it flat and ran the edge of his hand across the length of the pouch. "Fourteen and no more."

Nalya spoke. "Then it is settled."

"Not quite," began the Queensman. "The heart of the matter is this: Were there fifteen stones in the purse when the girl disturbed them? When the Havadran counted them? When the woman found them?"

Nalya scoffed. "There were fourteen when I found them!"

"This argument is difficult to solve without more evidence, so I will call into question the character of each involved. Fortunately, I am well versed in this topic." It was his chance to smile at the former Eskalinder.

"What?" she said.

"This girl, Damina, Gamin's daughter, I have known for three years. While she does have a fondness for pretty fabrics and fine things, she has also proved herself respectful of the property of others, as has her family. Not a single complaint against this establishment has been filed with the Records Keepers since her father purchased this inn, years before her birth. I personally have looked into this matter." He nodded slightly to Pamina, as the eldest representative of Gamin's family present. Her arms were again folded before her bosom, her hands twitching as though they would rather be tightening around the Nordakswoman's neck.

Nalya spoke, "Then it was clearly the Havadran."

"His character I can speak for as well, having known him also for three years and finding him to be a man of great integrity, knowledge, and, dare I say in his presence, wit."

"He is from Havadra! There is no such thing as integrity there."

Deenofts bared his teeth in a smile. "That is why I prefer to spend the bulk of my days here, in Eskalind."

"Lastly," said Favik. "Nalya of Nordak."

"How do you know my name?"

"You are the former Lady Nalya of Eskalind, are you not?"

Her husband spoke. "What do you mean, *former* Lady?"

She said nothing, so the Queensman continued. "She left her estate underfunded and in disrepair to finance her travels abroad, whilst the people tending her lands were left in a low condition."

Pamina muttered, "Why am I not surprised?"

The former Ambassador continued. "Ignoble behavior to be certain, which could be corrected, but the reason Dalock King rescinded her title was that she re-joined after being widowed."

Damina's hand shot over her mouth, while the Nordaksman said, "What of it? I myself have been joined four times."

The young girl gaped at the man as though he had grown an extra head. Even Pamina raised her eyebrows, and Favik said, "Good man, that is not the custom of this land. Citizens of Eskalind join once and once only; it is a well-known law amongst Eskalinders. Some would say it is what makes an Eskalinder an Eskalinder."

Deenofts brightened. "Why, even I, a native-born Havadran, know of this custom."

"So, Wife, you are no longer a noble of Eskalind? Then what does that make me, besides a fool for believing you?"

Nalya stood and approached Favik, eyes radiating hate. He lowered his heels and stepped back. When she came closer still, he reached for his short knife but did not draw it. Deenofts stood, shouting at Gamin's daughters, "Go to the kitchen!" Pamina grabbed her sister's arm and the pair scurried away.

Nalya, stopping her pursuit of Favik, glowered. "You have ruined my life."

"I believe that was your own doing."

"The Powers curse you!"

"That, They have done already."

She opened her mouth but said nothing. A step at the top of the stairs squeaked, and she turned to see what it was. Favik glanced also and saw Nalya's maid apprehensively peeking down. Nalya's living husband stood, pacing to the stairs. "Symeea," he called to the attendant, "pack my things. I depart at once."

"You cannot go!" begged Nalya, suddenly mincing after him.

"Watch me." The Nordaksman marched up the stairs, tapping his walking stick along the way in staccato bursts. His wife trailed him, pleading.

Deenofts drew his lips into an *O*, exhaling slowly. "Well played, Queensman."

"That is quite a compliment."

"It is. Especially coming from"—he paused—"a Havadran."

They chuckled warily as all manner of commotion was heard above: the scraping of trunks on the floor, arguing, wailing, the pitter-patter of the maid's feet as she darted down the stairs, carrying small parcels through the front door and out to the stables, then rushing back into the inn. This pattern repeated, the size of her burden growing with each departure. She called the two carriage drivers to assist.

Meanwhile, the crying upstairs turned to angry, accusatory shouts. The Nordaksman departed alone, with a glance at Favik. "Here," and he lobbed something small toward the Queensman, who caught it. It was an ice stone identical to the fourteen still resting on the table. "She will claim the rest, but I told her this one I am giving to you. I found it in her bodice, this time." With that he made for one of the carriages, and the driver led it away. Pamina and Damina came from the kitchen to view the activity.

Not long thereafter, Nalya too quit the building, but not without first laying hold of the fourteen jewels. As her carriage trundled away, Deenofts leaned close to Favik. "Your final retort to her was most convincing."

"Oh?"

"About The Powers having already cursed you."

"Ah. An old Ambassador's trick, deflating an insult by accepting it as a given."

Deenofts tsked. "Perhaps my people could benefit from Eskalind's Ambassador training."

Favik laughed, but his attention reverted to the drive as a light wagon came into view.

Damina shouted, "Father and Yamina are back!"

Her sister grumbled, "I hope they didn't buy all the fancy food the Nordakspeople demanded. How will we ever pay for it now?"

Favik held aloft the jewel. "I think one ice stone will more than cover the expense."

"You had it all along?"

Deenofts chuckled. "The Nordaksman gave it to him before departing. It seems this was not the first time his wife claimed to have a jewel stolen."

Pamina rolled her eyes. "Why am I not surprised?"

Dalock entered the King's Library hoping to find his wife in her Library chamber. Many scholars were making advantage of the bright light of the sunny day to pursue their research. The great room echoed with the creaking of chairs, the rattle of scroll knobs, the soft whoosh of rapidly flipped pages, and the occasional whisper. *Perhaps Marna will have a good idea for Dalich's Naming Day present. Hard to believe he is almost nineteen. 2907 already. Where does the time go?*

He spied a dark-skinned Guerish man reading alone in one corner. The outlander reminded the King of Saralya's cousin, who had come to Jinil's family's ennobling ceremony. So many memories of his lost friend, his Halls echoed with them. Yet everyone went about his or her duties as though Jinil had never existed. Dalock felt weary.

He glanced at the nearest long table, where two men stood sorting envelopes while a third poured a letter pouch onto the table. "What is all this?"

The men bowed. "Letters for King's Son, my Lord," the shorter man explained. His crimson-colored tunic bore the emblem of a Librarian: an open book, embroidered in brown above the Lord of Eskalind's emblem. "From people seeking healing." He culled envelopes from the pile and added them to a carefully constructed but teetering stack on the far end of the table.

Dalock gestured to that orderly pile. "All these are for Dalich?"

"Yes, my Lord." A young woman carrying a woven basket, the open-scroll device of an Apprentice Librarian embroidered in brown on her red cape, came toward them. She bowed to the King, then briskly filled her wicker container with envelopes for King's Son. The Apprentice departed as another Apprentice Librarian entered the Library. He also carried an empty handled basket and replenished it as the woman had done.

The Librarian turned away from the table to add an envelope to a small pile of about half a dozen on the table behind him. The King pointed. "Hand me those."

"If you wish, my Lord, but would you rather a servant delivered them to the Queen?"

"What?" Dalock stopped midreach. He squinted, the *M* and *Q* on the facing sides of the envelopes coming into focus. "I will deliver them." As he scooped the envelopes into his arms, a few fluttered from his grasp.

"Will you require a basket, my Lord?"

"Of course," the King said, none too pleasantly. Another Apprentice Librarian entered the room with an empty basket tucked under her arm against her red cape, and the Librarian directed her to give it to their Lord. She retrieved the envelopes from the floor and helped him fill the container. He turned to leave.

"Oh, my Lord? Do you want your messages?"

"There *are* some for *me*?"

"Yes, my Lord. Here you are, my Lord," the short man replied, giving his ruler three thick, sealed letters.

Dalock accepted the smooth envelopes, smug as though collecting a wager no one had expected him to win. *Well, at least mine are thicker than theirs.*

———

Marna sat at her desk in her Library chamber. Sunlight glimmered through the high, multipaned windows to her right, while on her left, stacks of books and shelves of scrolls towered to the ceiling. A few tables and chairs lay scattered about the room. Empty baskets teetered next to the fireplace behind her, which served more for burning read messages than for warmth.

A man entered, carrying a basket. She called, "Please bring it here." The man walked the length of the ovoid room and stood before her desk as she dipped her quill in crimson ink. Her eyes intent on her work, she wondered why the man did not deposit the carrier and depart. "I thank you. You may go."

The servant spoke. "Hullo, Marna."

"Oh, Dalock!" She gazed at him with an apologetic smile. "Thank you, dear." She stood, accepting the basket from her husband, careful to place it atop Favik's latest report concerning Damina's education.

"Oh no, these are mine." The King grabbed three bulging envelopes from the pile in the container and clutched them to his chest like a child protecting a favorite toy.

"You received some weighty correspondence." Marna gave her husband a maternal smile and straightened her walnut-colored smock as she came around her desk.

"It seems you and Dalich keep the parchment and papyrus merchants happy."

She thought she heard a hint of a jest in Dalock's tone. "In his case, the scribes for hire as well," she replied, glad to see his mood lightening. "Come," the Queen offered, touching the red velvet encircling his sleeve lightly and leading him to a spacious window seat. "Do you know, I sleep here sometimes when you journey beyond our Halls. It is far easier than traipsing up all those stairs." She laughed lightly. "I will call for some broth."

"No, Marna, I would rather sit and talk." He lowered himself onto the crimson cushions, scooting aside a tassel the color of dark honey. "With you." His brown eyes were focused, serious, and a bit weary. She sat by his side, conscious that she was giving him her full attention for once.

"Marna, it is no wonder Dalich is always in a morose mood. All he does is sit in his quarters and read letters. He is a young man, he should be active, out and about. Doing something." Her husband shook his head. "Is he really healing that many people just by thinking about it?"

"Many of those letters are not requests; they are thanks."

"How do you know this?"

"He told me." The slight hitch in her husband's breath told her that their son's confiding solely in her injured his father's feelings. "But only once. Dalich is difficult to talk with these days. It is just his age, I hope."

"Hmm." The Strange King looked about the room with the impatience of one uncertain where to settle his eyes. "When I was his age, I was already King. I was grieving for my parents, yet trying to enjoy my life. Between battles." He glanced at her. "Well, I am glad he spoke with you, at least once, on this matter. All I ever have from him are grunts."

Dalock gestured to the thin metal sheets that lay scattered on a nearby table, alongside thin steel rods with sharp points. "What are those for?"

"An idea of mine."

He folded his arms.

"I wondered if one might be able to cut deep into metal and make letters, or drawings. I thought to apply ink to the incisions, then press the metal sheet against parchment or tissue to make exact copies. It would save the Copyists much tedious work. But so far it has only generated an inky mess."

"Ah, my scholarly wife; she never stops thinking and inventing." The corners of his lopsided lips rose slightly, but the skin about his eyes did not crinkle. "Hmm, perhaps that is what Dalich needs."

"A scholarly wife?" The Queen pondered the direction this conversation was heading.

"Well, that might help too, but that is in The Powers' hands. Though I think a wife would cheer him. Or at least a lover." He unfolded his arms and placed a hand on her thigh. "No, Dalich should go on another tour. Healing along the way, of course, but a diplomatic mission to one of the borderlands would be good for him. Change of scenery. Why, he could go to Eastlant and visit Saril there, hmm? Those young men have always gotten along well. What say you, Marna?"

She could not hide her frown. "I find your idea sound, but perhaps not Eastlant."

Her husband leaned back into the crimson cushions, hands upon the soft upholstery. She spoke succinctly to make her point. "I think it important that Saril establish himself as his own man on his first Apprentice Ambassadorship. If Dalich visits, Saril will be viewed in light of his relationship to King's Son and treated differently, perhaps receiving attention that should be reserved for your Ambassador."

"Wise. Then, Humiksland. He could pay our respects at King Humik's court, visit your sister's family along the way, meet your father at long last, see his forge in Castleton."

He looked eager and pleased with his plan, but again Marna frowned, this time at the mention of her homeland. Before he could pat her leg and make his final pronouncement on the suitability of his scheme, she interrupted. "Dearest, I would rather he did not go there. Werna's letters are full of complaints that she is still not a grandmother, that three of her children have abandoned her for Eskalind, and how she needs yet more servants and coin. And she never breathes a word of thanks for all—"

"How about Amkland." The terse tone made this clearly a statement rather than a question. He folded his arms again, shoulders high.

She raised an eyebrow. "Ah, you know, the Amkish king has several eligible daughters." She gave the bronze threading edging his sleeve a playful tug. "Is my Strange King playing matchmaker?"

"Amkland, then. The King has decided!" He stood.

"Dalock, you *are* matchmaking!" She rose to her feet, amazed.

"Of course not!" He grinned mischievously, clearly delighted to surprise her. "But the visit may do him good. I sense it is important for him to go soon." He looked at her, brown eyes intense with certainty. "We will tell him just before his Naming Day feast; it will make him happy."

"Then Amkland." Marna glanced away, pretending to relent.

"You have no objections?"

She reached to stroke the last remaining patch of brown in his gray beard. "Perhaps, along the way, he will meet a Bladesmith's daughter." She gazed fondly into his warm eyes.

"Aye." He grinned and pulled her close to purr in her ear. "Mmmarna."

She laughed, pleased with his contentment. "*Now* will you have some broth?"

———————

"Who would have ever thought an Ambassador's letter would bring good news?" Dalock's Queen laid the Amkish parchment on her dining table. "Especially after the last one. What sad tidings that was—our poor son must have been quite disappointed to find his healing Gift has no effect outside our borders."

"Aye. But he handled it well, thank The Powers. Yet while I am pleased to hear Dalich's behavior at the Amkland king's halls is exemplary, it would be better news if he were sending home wagonloads of fat chickens," grumbled the King. He batted the untouched basket of bread away and dipped a finger into one of the many bronze sauce bowls crowding the dining table. "A chicken plague! Whoever heard of such a thing?" He licked his finger and frowned.

"I recall there are pestilences that only kill cows in some of the outerlands," his wife replied.

"But never in Eskalind! What is happening? In 2904 we had those terrible windstorms, then just this year, it rains during the day, followed by flooding throughout the land—and now no hope for Queen's Recipe chicken until The Powers know when!" He rubbed his eyes. "Eskalind is supposed to be protected by The Powers, yet in the past three years, we have had horrible catastrophes." The King tapped a thumb on the table.

"I have a theory," Marna began, running her fingers along the bottom of the parchment before her. Over two decades of living together had taught him that this gesture meant a lengthy postulation would follow. He shifted his gaze to her window. A gentle breeze rustled the crimson curtains, twirling a honey-brown tassel on its silken cord, almost like a beckoning finger.

Despite his lack of encouragement, she continued, as he knew she would. "It seems that every time Dalich leaves our borders, tragic or strange events occur."

The King grunted, a signal that he listened unenthusiastically, but something inexplicable in the distance beyond the stone-framed window cut through his ennui. "Marna, look!" He pointed to a muddy green cloud that hovered above the horizon. A pillar of black smoke ascended from the ground, widening as it reached the cloud.

His wife swore. "By The Powers!"

"What is it?" he asked, mouth hanging open in awe. The pillar grew larger and advanced across bare fields toward King's Halls.

"Could it be …." Marna sputtered. She turned to him, eyes wide with panic, speaking so fast he barely understood. "It is coming this way! I— we must get out of the tower, Dalock!"

He stood stock-still, an odd sensation trickling through his veins. "It is a warning, Marna. From The Powers."

She seized his arm, yanking vigorously. "We must get out of the tower!"

Despite her pleas, he paced to the window, bellowing, "I will send for King's Son to return home!"

As soon as he spoke, the black pillar lifted from the ground, diminishing into the murky cloud, which dissipated against a sky that faded from gray to blue in a blink.

"Dalock?" his wife said, her voice smaller than when she had sobbed on his shoulder after he arrived unlooked-for at her sister's farm, over two decades ago.

"Marna, my dear, I think you need to quill our son and tell him—"

"To come home," she whispered. "The Powers want him home. Now we understand." The Queen squeezed his arm and went to her desk to quill, pulling her chair forward with a squeak. "I should have realized it when his healing Gift did not work beyond our border." Sitting, she flipped to a blank papyrus and waited a moment, then composed her letter.

He glanced at his wife, sitting in the broad sunlight, the garnet necklace he had given her when they first joined glistening on her neck, her only adornment. He recalled his mother sitting there, using that same desk as a dressing table, her jewelry arrayed for her daily selection, the soft glimmer of golden braids of necklaces reflecting sunlight onto her pale face.

———

"Dalock, love," Treya Queen had called to her boy, who was cavorting by the window. "Do be mindful of the ledge." He watched one of her Ladies pin a tapered onyx peg into Mother's blond hair; fluted gold beads jingled on its end. She regarded herself in an ebony-framed mirror.

His attention turned to the clear blue sky, then the brown earth below, rushing toward him as he fell, the screams of his mother and her attendants drowned by his own. Yet he had survived the long fall, landing upon a pile of soft, fluffy hay that no one recalled piling against the royals' tower. Protected by The Powers, uncrushed and unbruised. Now only his lopsided face remained as a reminder of that day.

———

Forty-one years later, Dalock King leaned against the same high tower window, eyes again on the vastness of blue above. "I thank you for your Gifts and protection," he whispered, "and for my wife and son." He turned to watch his Queen as she quilled.

Marna marched through the main aisle of the King's Library toward her chamber door at the far left end of the long hall. She nodded at each of the outerland Scholars along the way. *Well done, Favik and Saralya. Their correspondence has been fruitful.* As per her instructions, three Apprentice Librarians waited at her door.

Using the key belted with a bronze chain around her waist, she undid the great lock, allowing entry into her private chamber to the two young men and one woman. Closing the thick door behind her, she walked to her desk, the Apprentices following like dutiful ducklings. She sat to survey the young people standing expectantly before her.

"Your next research duty is to *independently* draw up a list of all the misfortunes and oddities that have befallen this land during the last eleven Kings' reigns, from Dalock back to Narmlich," the Queen commanded. "Search the chronicles and compile a list of every plague, storm, call to arms, every daytime it rained, and so forth. Present it to me in chronological order. By next week."

"Yes, my Lady." They bowed.

Marna dismissed them, and set to her own task. "Eleven reigns of

Kings ought to keep them busy, and unmindful of my true intentions." She went to a window seat and lifted the crimson cushion to access the secret storage underneath. Bending, with an "Umpf!" the Queen retrieved the small chest that contained her journals, hauling it to her desk and unlocking it.

"Now I will assemble my own list. When did Dalich first leave our borders? He was quite young . . ."

Dalock pondered the four lists his wife laid before him as they sat on the couch by his hearth. When she first entered his chamber, he had been certain that her visit was solely to monitor his broth consumption. A half-full ewer of said liquid rested on the table behind him, its contents the final dregs that remained since the last chicken in Eskalind perished, but the actual reason for her visit weighed too heavily for him to consider refilling his cup.

"There can be no doubt." The Lord of Eskalind dropped the papyrus sheets next to his empty bronze bowl. "Every time Dalich has crossed our border, calamities have befallen our land."

"No one must know," Marna cautioned.

"What a strange Gift this is." He rubbed the rough hairs of his beard, coarser with each passing year. "The Strange Kings are meant to protect, yet how will Dalich ever lead an army if he cannot leave our borders?"

"We must have better diplomacy, to guard against wars." Marna rose as though practicing a speech and paced behind the couch. "And information."

Dalock shook his head. "The Ambassadors do their work the best they can, since the time of the first Kings. What more can be done?"

"Leave that to me," his wife said from behind him.

He turned to glance over his shoulder at her.

"Husband, what if I were to tell you that there is a group of people, knowledgeable people, who possess a loyalty above that of King and country?"

"What are you saying, Marna?" He studied her closely.

"That there are those from the borderlands and the outerlands who are willing to provide us with useful news."

The King twisted with a groan to face the fireplace again. "We cannot trust spies or traitors."

"Perhaps in their own lands they might be called that, but what if they were loyal to us?"

"Why would such people be loyal to us?" The Lord of the Strange Kingdom did not hide his sneer.

"Because we represent peace, peace means stability, and only under stable governance can certain things flourish." The Queen lowered her voice. "Such as the pursuit of knowledge."

Dalock twisted to face her again as he caught her meaning. "You would enlist scholars as spies?"

"I would not call them spies." His wife came round the couch to sit by his side, and he followed her with his gaze.

"Marna, think on what you say!" He leaned toward her. "Think of how this would be perceived by those in the other lands. Eskalind is meant to protect, to be honorable, to be above the petty foibles and wasteful intrigues of the outerlands. How would it look if one of these people were discovered?"

"It will look as it has always looked. Men and women going about their boring, scholarly interests. Who pays attention to them? They are visible and invisible at the same time, intelligent and discreet. What could be more perfect?" How firm she looked, just as one would expect from a Queen.

He began, "Eskalind, and *we ourselves*, are entrusted by The Powers to be more principled than all other nations. Spies . . ." Dalock shook his head. "We must think on this more."

"My husband, the man of action, needs to think?"

He leaned away. "Do not jest with me on this matter." The King crossed his arms before him.

"Dalock, these scholars come to our Library, they come directly to me, elated to have an opportunity to study without fear of a battle erupting on their doorstep." His wife's voice rose. "They crave peace, and would be willing to work for it. For us."

He shook his head. "Perhaps they are working for someone else. How can they be trusted?"

"I know as soon as I meet them. I can tell." He lowered his brows. "Call it my Gift," Marna said.

"Hmm. Now my wife has the Gift of Guerish Merchant Masters!"

Her voice was even. "Dalock, the evidence is clear, and so is our course of action."

"I will think on it."

How she watched him. "You told me you have wondered if the role of our Kingdom was the best path, if Eskalind should march to war to stop quarrels in other lands." He glared. Marna leaned close. "If the Scholar system works, our people will not have to give their lives to keep the Outer Peace. Our son could use his unique Gifts to heal in *our* land. People would come to Eskalind to be cured; that would be profitable for the merchants and Innkeepers, and thus for us. And our son would never have the need to face battle again."

The King growled, feeling pushed into a corner. "I cannot believe that even if it worked, it would work all the time."

"Of course no plan is foolproof. But think of all the lives and effort that would be saved if it worked *most* of the time."

Dalock watched the fire. "How shall we tell Dalich he cannot leave?"

"Start with the story of the Second King." From her tone and the swiftness of her response, he knew she had rehearsed this. "How he wanted to expand the borders set by his father."

"Till he joined with his wife and knew that death in battle was a possibility if she got with child?" Dalock shook his head, not for the first time thinking the tale of Heedlock King his least favorite. "That seems a dangerous topic with our son. I think he still pines for that girl."

She leaned away, resting a hand on her hip. "Then perhaps that girl is meant to be his wife."

The King was uncertain which topic irritated him more: Scholars as spies or Marna's continued insistence that The Powers willed for Dalich to join with a girl who distracted him from battle practice. He scowled.

"Now, do not glower at me so! Our son has waited years already. If your man was right about her age, it will be another four years till she is eligible to join, and who knows what will happen in the meantime? Oh, you are out of broth."

The Queen picked up his empty bowl, went to his dining table, and poured the still steaming liquid from the thick-glazed ewer. "I think it would hearten him to recall the tale of Heedlock King, how his will bowed to that of The Powers. Sometimes one needs to be reminded that there are larger things in the world than oneself." Marna smiled and brought the bowl to her husband, the rich, satisfying scent wafting seductively in the air. His pulse slowed and he felt calmer, as though something in his thoughts changed and he realized that yes, everything would be well and good, like in the last line of a Legend scroll.

Dalock received the brimming bowl with a sigh. "The first shipment of chickens is set to arrive when?"

"Tomorrow, with Dalich. And there are new Cooks starting today, as the current ones are nearly done with their term of service."

"When are you teaching them how to make your roast chicken?" He sipped from the deep cup, contentment melting into his bones. Perhaps his wife was right.

Marna raised an eyebrow. "If we are in agreement, as soon as the chickens are here. After we greet our son, of course."

"Mmm, then I eagerly await dinner tomorrow." He drained the bowl and placed it on the table. "But I do not look forward to conversing with our young man about his new Gift." He closed his eyes.

Dalich King's Son returned from Amkland with dozens of hens and a few very happy roosters. The attentions paid him by the three pretty and of-age Amkish princesses had been enjoyable, while their obvious rivalry for his hand amused him. Still, none of them had truly captured his heart, and clearly, none of them exhibited a hint of the Gifts required of the future Strange King's Queen. He would never admit to anyone, not even Saril, that the work of strategizing his interactions with the young women, and choosing his words carefully so as not to lend favor to one more than the others, had made fine use of his mind and concealed the chasm in his heart, for a while.

His correspondence with the blue-eyed Kaymif princess also helped to ease his mind. Kostaza wrote well, and often, despite her duties as regent for her young brother the king, which had distracted her so when he last saw her. Dalich could not pretend, even to himself, that her attentions displeased him, but he still felt his heart rested with another. Yet the temptation presented itself to reroute his return home through Kaymif to visit. Then an urgent letter arrived from his parents, exhorting him to cross into Eskalind as quickly as possible.

After the homecoming ceremony at the borders, he stopped briefly at each inn along the way, ostensibly to see if anyone needed healing, but—thinking of two things at once—also to see if he might find Damina. While he could simply ask his mother where she was, as he was certain she knew, he now considered the matter best left in the hands of The Powers. He did not want to reveal to his mother that he still desired to find Damina. If he was meant to find her, then he would. After all, she was still a child—but perhaps if he happened to meet the girl in person, their thought speaking might return, or he would sense that she was genuinely meant for him and thus settle the matter. In truth, he missed Damina's conversation in his mind, missed the connectedness to another person. But if that was The Powers' Will, then he must suffer, for a time.

Unexpectedly, he encountered Lord Marnil on leave at a tavern along the way. This surprise reunion cheered him, as did Marnil's journeying with him to court, where Dalich's parents greeted him with concerned tenderness that immediately made their son suspicious. When they later drew him into the Queen's private quarters, their faces grave, his heart pounded with a sudden terror that some awful fate had befallen his hoped-for love.

After a lengthy homily about the Second King bowing to the Will of The Powers, during which his heart nearly stopped with anticipation, and some discussion about an idea of his mother's, during which his mind forayed into a calculus of horrible events that might have happened to his intended, they finally divulged their news. The discovery of another of his Gifts did not seem as terrible to him as it did to them.

His mother leaned toward his seat in the chair by her couch. "Dalich, this means you must not cross our border. Ever."

"Yes, Mother." He flicked the bronze clasp of his belt and silently thanked The Powers for sparing him a truly awful surprise.

His father spoke next. "You will not be able to lead the army beyond the border wall."

"And no one must know." Dalich echoed their earlier phrase in the serious voice his mother used.

The King and Queen looked at one another.

"It is fine." Their son forced a smile. "Not what I expected, but fine. I thank you for your counsel. If that is all for now, I will go see Marnil." Realizing that they might think he did not desire their company, even after his long absence, he amended his last statement. "He must depart tomorrow to return to his company, and I do not know when our duties will coincide again," he added, letting a hint of regret into his voice. His time at the Amkish court had served him well.

After a nod from Mother, Father said, "If you wish, Son."

———

After their grown child closed the door to the Queen's Chambers, Dalock said, "Well, that went far better than expected." He exhaled. "Perhaps Dalich has matured more than we give him credit for."

"Hmm." The Queen's tone was skeptical. "Or he has matured *less* than we expected." She arranged her skirt smoothly over her knees and gazed at the fire in the hearth. She parted her lips as if to speak, then closed them. Her gaze hardened and she looked away.

"I wonder what Dalich did expect?" Dalock placed his arm around her back and stroked the soft fabric of her low-bodiced gown, silently thanking The Powers that she had not worn a smock for Dalich's homecoming feast.

"We may never know. But I wager when he thinks on it longer than a moment, he will realize what is lost to him." His wife shook her head, shifting forward in her seat. "We must comfort him when that time comes, Dalock." Marna then settled back against his arm.

"I think I could use a little comfort myself."

"Oh?" His beloved raised a slow eyebrow, an inviting light in her eyes.

"My ... arm," he choked. "You are ... crushing it."

A couple weeks shy of his son's twenty-second Naming Day, Dalock strolled alone on the grand terrace of his Halls, tracing a finger along the carved stone patterns of King's Flowers decorating the columns that held aloft the balconies. The King inhaled deeply, catching the rich scent of roses in the late Spring air. He paused and thought back to when he held his newborn son aloft in this very place, asking The Powers to Gift his heir. "More than twenty years have passed." He gazed at the vacant spot where Jinil stood that long-ago day. "And my father before me, fifty years."

"Father?"

His son called from under the shadowed arches of the colonnade across the terrace.

"You are returned! Come!" Dalock waved to the young man, happy to stay in the present moment. Dalich marched forward as formally as an outerland ambassador, but when he reached his father, his composure melted and the men embraced. When they broke apart, the King still clasped his son's elbows. "How fares my Gifted son?"

"Well, and no one at King's Market can say any less." The pride in his eyes was unmistakable.

"How many this time?"

"Well into the hundreds. Many came from across the border."

"Hmm." Dalock leaned back and stroked the thick hair covering his crooked chin. "This old man was right to send you to the markets to heal. Or did your mother suggest that?"

Dalich grinned, his beard fuller than his father remembered. "Father, all these visitors bring a great amount of trade for the merchants. The Records Keepers report record business. And the Innkeepers too."

"And that is good for the King, his family, and his people." Dalock bent close to his heir's ear. "It will not surprise you, your mother has plans to establish new schools and Scriptoria."

"She wrote me that you are to go on a diplomatic mission soon." Though King's Son's countenance remained pleasant, his good mood seemed to diminish.

"Yes, trouble in Kursak; their alliance with Nordak weakens." He looked to the balustrade and began walking toward it, Dalich at his elbow. "I hope I can talk some sense into the two of them. But I am sorry I will miss your Naming Day celebration, again."

"You know I will miss you, Father. But we will have many, many days—two whole weeks—together before you go." His face mimicked false innocence, and in a light voice Dalich asked, "Will you forgive me if I eat your portion of roast chicken at the feast?"

"I will not begrudge you that!" The older royal laughed. "I am afraid I do not need it." He patted his round belly, a bit embarrassed by its size. "I have missed our sparring and riding, as you can see." They walked together along the balustrade, coming to a bench overlooking the courtyard. Below, members of Dalich's party unpacked their wagons and horses. The King and his heir sat side by side.

"Father, I had news from Saril along the way. He said you want him back from his Ambassadorship in Eastlant in a month, and then he will be sent to Havadra."

"Ah yes. I will miss seeing him before he leaves on his next posting."

Dalock sighed. "I am certain his father would have been pleased with his accomplishments. Havadra will be a difficult posting, yet I am confident Saril will manage." He tapped his son's knee. "You know, when I drew Saril's tile at the same time as Havadra, I found it difficult to believe The Powers had guided my hand to send such a young man to serve as Ambassador there." Dalock silently considered how well Favik had served when he suddenly became Havadran Ambassador during his Apprenticeship, but kept the thought to himself. "Yet I bend again to the Will of The Powers and believe it will prove to be for the best." He pretended to watch the activity in the courtyard, but every ounce of his notice studied his son.

"Of course, Father." If there was a hint of disgruntlement in his voice, only The Powers could discern it.

"Marna will be delighted to hear you are safely returned home. Now, where do you think she is?"

"The Library."

"I know something you do not," the King teased.

King's Son, in a poor imitation of his mother's signature gesture, tried to raise an eyebrow.

Dalock grinned. "Lady Saralya is visiting. With Jinilya," he added, knowing that the image of that little five-year-old tempest scurrying through the Queen's prized Library would lead his son to one conclusion.

"Queen's Chambers," the two men said in unison, and father and son enjoyed a deep chuckle together.

———

Days later, Marna's husband called from the door that connected their chambers. "Are you engaged, Marna?" She sat at her desk, polished bronze candelabras at each elbow gleaming with lit candles illuminating her task.

"This letter will occupy me another few minutes." The Queen rested her quill in the inkwell a moment and rubbed the indentation in her index finger with her thumb. "Sit by the fire and have some wine." She heard her husband pour a glass for himself. Retrieving her quill, she scratched a few more lines upon the papyrus sheet. *At least I revised the last chapter of my herb book in time for the scribes to make copies for Dalock to give out at the Kursak court. Only a few more days till he leaves.* The thought surfaced that before he left, she should tell him of her warning that The Powers warred amongst themselves. Yet it had been years since the admonishment, and even Treya Queen, decades before, had known of it. Perhaps The Powers' disagreements followed a less-swift timeline than she had feared. She looked at the candle flames but felt nothing but calm.

From the door to the King's room came another familiar voice. "Father?"

"We are in here, Dalich," the Queen replied. "At this rate I will never finish."

"I am sorry to interrupt you, Mother." Marna did not stir from her work.

"Have a seat by me, young man." Dalich slid next to his father.

"Have my cup if you wish," Marna offered. "I can always"—wine tinkled into an empty goblet—"call for another."

"Well this is pleasant," Dalock commented. "A quiet evening with my family in private quarters." They sat in silence a moment, the only sound the raspy scratch of Marna's quill. The King cleared his throat. "Are you nearly done yet, my dear?"

"Not with all these interruptions." She heard him sigh and settle into the couch.

Dalock touched his son's arm. "How do you find the wine, Dalich? Have you developed a taste for it yet?"

The young man nodded, then sank into the cushions, his dark brown locks sliding before his eyes. Dalock recognized this behavior, though he had not seen it from his son since the lad earned his sword. He cleared his throat, realizing as he did that he had done so once already. "Is there something on your mind?"

Dalich paused, entwining his long fingers around his chalice. "Do you ever find it a burden to be King?"

"Why do you ask?"

Dalich looked at him, colorless eyes so akin to his mother's, the King felt as though his wife herself looked at him. "Father, do you always answer a question with a question?"

"Do you?" He laughed. Dalich grinned and sipped his wine. "No no, Son. I enjoy ruling our land. The only time I feel burdened is when my duties remove me from time better spent with you and your mother." Dalich nodded. The King looked at his wife to gauge her reaction. Marna kept quilling, so he continued, draping an arm across the couch. "Otherwise, my duties make use of everything I enjoy: using my mind, strategizing, protecting our land, leading our people." His son's expression wilted.

"But you will be a King of different Gifts." He placed a hand on the young man's knee. "A great Healer. Like your mother."

The Queen reached for a new sheet of light brown papyrus to begin another page of her letter.

"Father, I want to go on this mission with you."

The Queen interrupted. "You know that is out of the question." Both men glanced at her.

Dalich looked back to his father, leaned toward him. "I do not want to be seen as weak," he confided in a quiet voice, "because I cannot leave our borders."

"No one knows you cannot leave but us. And you are not weak, my son. Here, stand up. Wrestle me." The King stood, placing his chalice on the short table before them, and rolled his red-velvet tunic sleeves to his elbows. Dalich looked at him with surprise. "Come on!" The older man beckoned, stepping away from the couch toward the middle of the room.

Dalich chuckled and rose to his feet. "All right, Father." King's Son grinned and removed his caramel-colored doublet, pitching it on a nearby chair as his father circled him.

From behind her desk, the Queen intoned, "Do not trouble my furniture with your antics."

"Let us go to my chamber," said the King in a conspiratorial tone. They left the Queen to her business.

———

Marna looked at the sheet before her. "By The Powers, will this ink ever dry? There has to be a better way. Hmm. I said that with scrolls too, did I not?" She reached for the bellpull and gave it a sharp yank. "At least using bells for signals was a good idea."

Her Guard opened her public door. "Send for Favik Queensman." He nodded, closing the door. She blew on the ink, blew again, waiting. Touching it with wary fingers. "Finally."

Hearty male laughter came through the open door to Dalock's chamber.

She folded the papyrus, which wanted to curl. Eventually it yielded, and Marna stuffed it in an envelope, then dripped crimson candle wax over the closure. The pooling wax's glossy sheen slowly altered to a dull finish. Turning her sole ring, she impressed her seal into the congealing liquid.

The main door opened and Favik entered.

"My Lady."

She looked at him and noted beads of sweat above his upper lip, hiding in his blond beard. His sun-kissed face betrayed a bit of a blush, and the faint scent of green herbs peppered the air.

All evidence pointed to her man recently enjoying the close company of his current lover, the Cook. The Queen raised an eyebrow. "I hope I did not interrupt anything," she said in coy tones.

"Of course not, my Lady." Favik folded his hands before him. A series of short grunts came from the King's chamber. Her man's demeanor did not change.

"Tonight all my men are behaving like … men," Marna said, placing the sealed letter into her man's scarlet-gloved hand. He clutched it with his short fingers whilst she quietly commanded, "Deliver this to Lord Radil in the north. Personally, into his hands."

"As you wish, my Lady," he said. "Is that all?"

A great growl came from the King's chamber, followed by young laughter.

She regarded Favik, neither one of them acknowledging the suggestive sounds.

"If you need finish any business here in King's Halls, please do so before you leave."

Favik nodded. "Thank you, my Lady."

"I yield! Father, I yield!" Dalich's muffled pleas reached their ears.

The Queensman bowed and went to the main door. He reached for the doorknob.

"Favik," Marna said in a sharp tone, as she rose from her seat.

"My Lady?" He turned back.

"Have fun," she whispered, no longer concealing her mirth.

He grinned, and his gray eyes shone with amusement, the dark blue encircling the pale iris lending his look a keen joviality. "Likewise, my Lady." The Queen smiled. He bowed again and left the room.

"Ha ha! Now I have you!" shouted Dalich.

"Would that we could stay like this. A moment when they are all happy!" She went to Dalock's chamber. On the woven brown carpet her son sat atop her husband, pinning him to the floor. The King's face shone, crimson as his tunic, as he struggled to regain the advantage over his son.

"Gentlemen," the Queen said with warmth, "is this what you call a quiet evening with your family?"

Favik made for the Queen's Library chamber, conscious of his every step. Not since his time as an Ambassador to Havadra had he been so keenly aware of the separation between his actions, appearance, and feelings. Anyone noticing him pass would think, *Here is a man on ordinary business.* Would that were the case at this moment.

He nodded at the Apprentice Librarian stationed at the receiving desk by the Queen's door. She was an umber-haired woman who once showed him her bare feet. At the time, he enjoyed the affections of one of the Cooks, and he had gently refused her. As in so much of his life, he kept secrets well, and his affair with the Cook went unnoticed by most—including this woman, who glared at him now.

"I must see the Queen."

"Something urgent?" She twisted a strand of hair around her finger and turned her attention to the volume on the table before her.

"Announce me," the Queensman ordered.

She glanced up.

Favik fixed her with a no-nonsense stare.

Her chair groaned as she pushed it back. "Well, all right, then," she huffed. The Apprentice went to the crimson bellpull by the Queen's door and gave it a tug. She crossed her arms as she awaited the Queen's acknowledgment: a bell without a clapper, dangling from its brown silken cord, swaying in answer to her call.

In a way, her theatrics provided a distraction from the miserable duty he was about to perform. *I would spare my Lady the pain if I could, but to bear its first hearing in private will offer more solace than the public spectacle it will surely be.* They both stared at the bronze bell. The young woman tapped her leather soles on the stone floor. At last the bell swung in response. She opened the door and announced him; he followed her into the room. She turned and left, closing the door with a pronounced thud.

Marna Queen sat at her desk, a scroll unrolled before her. The scent of burnt parchment hung in the air and the dying fire behind her tinted her gray tresses the slight red they once had been. The candelabras close to her desk flickered as he walked toward her.

"How many times must I tell that girl the bell signals?" she muttered. "Had I known it was you— Well, never mind now. So, what news, Favik?" She asked as she always did, her gray eyes on the words before her.

"My Lady," he greeted her, his voice calm as he considered this last single moment of normalcy. But she looked up at him, and her gaze narrowed as she realized that no ordinary errand brought him before her.

Falling to one knee and bowing his head, he began, "My Lady, it grieves me to tell you . . ." He looked to her, and he lost his courtier's restraint, eyes welling as he spoke the words. "My Lord Dalock King has died."

"No," she said, as clearly as if refusing an unwelcome invitation.

"My Lady, your forgiveness—how I wish it were otherwise—but the news is certain. A party from the Kursak king's seat rides at this moment to these Halls to impart the news."

She turned from him and faced the last embers in her fireplace. After a moment she asked, "How?"

"In his sleep, my Lady, at the Kursak court."

"A peaceful end?"

"Yes, my Lady. There is no hint of foul play," he said gently. "The Kursak king is sending his deepest—"

"Like Jinil," she whispered.

"My Lady?"

"He was but fifty." Then she stood and railed at the hearth: "He should have brought more broth with him. I told him. Over and over I told him!"

Favik heard the anguish in her voice; he gazed at her desk. The carved wood bore her initials and the dead King's, conjoined in fanciful designs with their emblems, his swords and her books.

At long last she asked, "Does my son know?"

"No, my Lady. The news was relayed to me through our confidential means. I rushed to tell you, ahead of the official party."

"No one else at King's Halls knows?"

"No one, only the Scholars from whom the message came."

"When will the Kursak messenger arrive?"

"An hour, maybe two, my Lady." He raised his gaze to her face.

She said nothing for a moment, then asked, in a voice quiet and far away, "Will you sit with me till they come?"

This was why he treasured her, for the moments when she would show she valued him more as a confidant, or as a dutiful son, than a servant.

"Anything you wish, my Lady," he replied, rising to his feet. She held an unsteady arm to him. The gesture reminded him of a blind man he saw once in the outerlands, searching for his misplaced support. Favik came to his Lady's side and with compassion led her to the window seat. There they sat, mostly in silence, with an occasional question from his Lady, asking about other matters both great and small, till the bell rang again.

"Dalich," she whispered. "Now comes the test." She looked at Favik. "I hoped that Damina would be of age before he became Lord of the land."

"Soon, my Lady," he encouraged her. "These six years have passed swiftly. The final year will seem a blink."

Frantic pounding sounded on the door.

"Oh, that stupid girl!" King's Mother fumed. "She will never make a Scholar. Ring the response bell, Favik."

He nodded and went to the bell as the Apprentice's muffled shouts—"My Lady!"—came from the door. He yanked on the bell and the door opened instantly. The Apprentice tumbled into the room, her cheeks red and her eyes wide. A Page followed her.

"Well?" Marna asked sharply, no hint of the grief she bore in her tone. "What is all this fuss about?"

The Apprentice looked to Favik, unspeakable horror, concern, and sympathy evident on her face, and he saw a mirror of the emotions he had concealed when he realized he must relate the sad news to his Lady.

"Go on," he encouraged her, with a gentle nod.

The young woman looked to her Lady through misting eyes. Then she spoke, and forever after recalled that moment when she, before all others, delivered the sad news to she who was once Marna Queen.

Dalich King stood on the terrace overlooking an ever-growing assembly of his father's, no, *his* court. Guards and groomsmen, Ladies and maidservants slowly filtered toward the open area, streaming through the graceful archways to cluster in whispering groups, sad eyes upon their new Lord.

By his side, his mother spoke not a word, processing the news so calmly one could believe she had expected it. Before him, the Kursak messenger prostrated himself, the embroidered hem of his robes trembling slightly. Never had Dalich seen a messenger quaver so. Never had he received news as awful as this. Numbness flooded his veins. He sought to steady his breathing.

"Rise," he commanded, his first word as acknowledged ruler of Eskalind. "Bring the message to King Kursak that I will meet my father's bier at the border, in three weeks' time."

"I will, Lord of Eskalind." The man regained his feet, eyes on the new

King's shoes. He made the Kursak gesture of respect, left hand held open before the face, palm facing the mouth, bowing the head to touch the forehead to the fingers.

Soft and cool, the King breathed, "The Powers help Kursak if my father's death was the result of ill-doing." He nodded briskly at the man. The messenger departed, shoulders low, certainly aware of the glowers following his back.

His mother touched his velvet-clad arm, and rather than solace, he felt stung by a keen annoyance. "The traditions, I know," Dalich muttered. She withdrew her hand, her eyes steeled, but the hint of a tear glimmered in her gaze.

His faith in himself sank: his first act as Lord of the land had been to upset the bereaved widow. Dalich strove to make amends by showing strength before the mournful assembly. A few Bakers, their faces glistening and flushed from tending the ovens, hugged one another through quiet sobs. The new King announced in a firm voice, "As follows our custom, I choose now my emblem and colors."

Dalich paused, his next utterance hanging in uncertainty. A stillness fell upon the gathered people awaiting his pronouncement; no one moved. His father's banners languished upon their poles, defeated, spent.

"Today begins my Kingship." He glanced to the bench where he and his father had sat, only a few weeks ago, when he returned home from healing at the markets. His throat caught as an inner tingle of weakness shivered his breast. Touching the concealed locket of Damina under his collar, Dalich looked to the banners again.

For a brief moment a vision stirred of his own colors waving there— bold, proud.

"I, Dalich King, by the Will of The Powers, choose as my colors black and violet, and my emblem shall be…" His eyes darted about the crowd. An Apprentice Librarian stood on the far side of the terrace, his thick hands clutching a long-handled basket, laden with notes requesting Dalich's healing. "My emblem shall be symbolic of my healing, of the letters sent to me requesting healing."

The people of King's Halls responded with curious looks, then the smatterings of a sober cheer: "Hail, Dalich King!" and "To the black and violet!" Some stamped their feet, building a slow rhythm that energized the assembly. Others called out, "May The Powers protect our new King!"

But King's Mother murmured, "Violet will be expensive."

Under his breath, Dalich drew toward her ear. "It is what I choose."

"And I know why you choose such." The widow's gray gaze skimmed the crowd.

"She will be my wife," the young Lord ground through his teeth.

"*I* have always thought it a strong possibility." His mother continued regarding the crowd, perhaps distancing herself from grief by studying the assortment of faces. Dalich turned his head away, just catching her side glance at Favik, standing amongst the nearest courtiers. The man's face bore an expression of such tender sympathy, it seared Dalich to his core. He felt pitied, chastised, and more alone than ever before. Mother had another to comfort her, whilst he had only the walls and furnishings of his new chamber. All the years he had favored her over his beloved father became a recounting of regrets.

In a quiet murmur he spoke. "I will build my father a magnificent monument that all will admire." Several Ladies dabbed their eyes with crimson handkerchiefs. Lady Dara openly wept, her dark head bowed. A brazier near her elbow seemed the only cheerful element upon the terrace, its bright flames dancing in the bronze bowl as though it were pleased with current circumstances.

Seeing the many familiar faces saddened first prompted Dalich's sympathies; then the numbness in his blood seeped deeper into his being. Saying to no one in particular, "I must see to the preparations for the funeral journey," he departed his mother's side, the crowd parting for his passage as though glad to lose him from their sight.

———

"Dalich, an Ambassador's letter has been awaiting your attention for hours!" King's Mother nagged her son from the connecting doorway between the royals' rooms, waving the pages in her hand hard enough to disturb the King's candelabras' bright flames.

"Can you not see that I am busy?" Her late-night intrusion surprised him, but Dalich did not raise his gaze from the sketches upon his desk. The candles' light gave a compelling glimmer to the ink. "It seems I must remember to always lock the door between our chambers."

She plodded toward his desk. "Your father's tomb can wait; urgent messages cannot." She plopped the letter atop the Builder's plans.

Dalich swept the letter aside and leaned back in his chair, fingers flicking the upholstery nails. Mother answered his stare with her own. How odd she looked dressed in black, his color. One would think after these last months he would have grown used to it. Then he noticed golden cake crumbs on her smock.

"*This* is how I mourn, Mother," he began. "How I choose to—"

"Do not think to outshow me in grief." She arched a gray eyebrow and planted her hands on the table. "There is much to do as King, and as King's Mother, that is not of one's choosing." With a quick motion she turned and left, the candles sputtering in her wake. He reached to where he had brushed the letter aside, and found it was no longer there.

"She would do my work for me?" he growled. "Fine. Let her. All I am needed for is healing, healing, and healing."

Someone pulled the blankets away from Damina's head. "Are you going to lie abed all day, Sister?" Pamina's voice was tinged with icy sweetness. She held the covers in one hand, pressed against her hip, brown eyes daring Damina to retrieve them.

Pamina's head nearly touched the ceiling of the room the two sisters shared with Pamina's twin, Yamina. The attic space, furnished, and nearly filled, with their bed and a chest of drawers, had served as the sisters' bedroom as long as Damina could remember.

The green laces on Pamina's bodice hung loose, like her tousled dark blond tresses.

"At least I am tired from working, not from lying with a different man every night," Damina groaned, lifting an arm to shield her eyes from the sunlight coming through the small window. "You're supposed to have only one lover at a time, and wait to see if you are with child. Like Yamina does." She sighed. "Then you would know you were meant to be with him, like Mother and Father."

"Oh come now, only six more months till you're of age, and then you'll have no need to be jealous! Mmm, perhaps The Powers will grant you a bosom like mine by then." She laughed. "Oh, speaking of men, you missed the King passing by."

"What?" Damina shot out of bed. "When?"

"He must be the most handsome man I've ever laid eyes upon," Pamina answered languidly. "Mmm, mmm."

Damina fell to her knees to ransack the chest of drawers, tossing garments onto the bed, searching for her best skirt, or at the very least the bodice with the prettiest embroidery.

"Ha! Damina, you are too late. It was a few hours ago." Her eldest sister smiled as she wilted against their bed.

"By The Powers!" Damina wailed.

"Damina! If Father heard you say . . ."

"Why did you not come wake me?"

"Because I was outside watching! And then I was meeting with Durmil."

"I could have guessed," Damina said, glancing at the dangling laces of Pamina's bodice.

Her sister smirked, probably glad that she had noticed, and rethreaded the laces. "It isn't my fault you slept in this morning."

"I was up all night caring for the motherless foal!" Much as she wanted to cry, she would not before Pamina, who would never relent in her teasing. "I would have thought Yamina, at least, would have come for me."

"Why am I not surprised? Oh, Yamina, the dutiful one you can always count on," Pamina sneered, tossing the blankets onto the bed, over Damina's clothes. "Well, she missed him too," she said, just as the door opened.

"Missed who?" Yamina asked as she entered their bedroom. She wore a deep brown shawl over her head that blended with her hair. She looked at her sisters, her plain features distressed.

"Pamina saw the King pass by a few hours ago and did not wake me."

"The King? Oh my goodness!" Yamina's wrap slipped to her shoulders as she reached to place a comforting arm around her youngest sister's slender shoulders. She glanced at her twin. "You know she wanted to see him! Why didn't you wake her?"

"Why do I have to do everything?" Pamina grumbled as she flopped onto the bed, which complained with a loud creak. She stared at the ceiling. "Why didn't you wake her?"

"If I'd known he was coming, I would have." Yamina gazed at Damina, her brown eyes wide with sympathy. "The guests from Thislin were talking last night about the King's Progress staying at a nearby estate, then coming this way, but they thought it would be a few more days yet. Poor dear." Damina embraced her, trying to stifle a whimper.

Pamina taunted, "Well, what were *you* doing that was so important you missed the King?"

"Caring for the foal, after Damina went to bed," came the soft reply.

Damina broke their hug to give her sister a worried look.

"He seems stronger," Yamina reassured her with a kind smile. She looked prettier when she smiled. "He drank more milk. But I think he likes you best. I came to see if I could bring him one of your things, a shawl or blanket. The scent might comfort him."

"Oh, do spare me your love talk," Pamina pulled a pillow over her head.

Chapter Twenty-Six—Naming Day Present

"He will not be coming home for his twenty-third Naming Day," Marna huffed. She was reading her son's latest letter in her private chamber in the Library. "I hoped the lure of my roast chicken would hasten his return." She turned her gaze to the bright sunshine pouring through the tall window at her side. Favik stood nearby, patient as always, though he looked like an outlander to her now, clad in her son's colors. Everything in her home seemed strange as King's Halls transitioned from good-natured brown and crimson to morose black and violet. At least it gave the seamstresses and craftsmen much work. King's Mother almost caught herself smiling at this practical attempt to cheer herself.

"My Lady, has my Lord said when he will come back?"

She knew Favik sought to engage her in conversation to keep her mind from sad thoughts. Would that she had something glad to talk about.

"He will return after he completes Dalock's tomb." The words felt as dry as a bitter lie in her mouth, even though nearly a year had passed. "He sent more plans. Again." Marna glanced at the stack of rolled parchments on her desk, each tied with a sable ribbon from which hung an amethyst-colored seal. "But, it gives him something constructive to occupy his mind with. For that I should be thankful."

"Damina will celebrate her sixteenth Naming Day soon."

"Yes, 2911—the long-awaited date arrives. Though Dalich shows no interest, nor has he even asked me anything about her since he discovered her age…" Marna shook her head. "He once was quite earnest, but now seems…removed." She looked to Favik, who nodded gently. "Still, I want you to bring her a present from me." The former Queen of Eskalind rose and walked across the gleaming, uncovered wood floor, squinting from the brightness. "I must decide which pattern and color of carpet I want soon, I am told." She went to a dusky gray metal chest, its surface chased in carved *D*'s, sitting atop a table. She placed a hand on the casket. "Favik, sometimes I wonder if all the decorating decisions one must make for a new reign are designed simply to keep one occupied."

"Perhaps for some, but my Lady always finds a way to keep herself useful."

Marna smiled at his comment and lifted the heavy iron lid. She reached inside and retrieved the sole contents: a delicate, soft, violet-colored scarf. "Purest Mavoldian linen. With velvet trim." She tilted the fabric in the light so Favik could admire its quality and texture.

Her man's odd gray eyes were curious. "To cover a book?"

"Oh, of course I will give her a book too, but I thought to give her something frivolous that any young woman would enjoy." Her voice grew wistful. "Dalock gave me a fine brocaded cloak once. He thought I would enjoy it. Ha." She stroked the fabric. "I thought it too fine and locked it away after wearing it once. The moths have probably had their way with it, and now I cannot wear his colors. Well, were it red, I could, to honor First King, but no, 'twas brown." Catching herself teetering toward distraction, she continued, "I should have worn it and enjoyed it at the time. Then again, I never was one for fine garments and jewelry." She glanced at the garnet bead necklace Dalock had given her, now worn twisted around her wrist, hidden under her sable-colored sleeves. King's Mother found herself drawn to wearing this small reminder of her beloved husband. At odd moments she still felt a foreigner in her adopted homeland, despite all the years. "Now that Damina is of age and no longer my secret charge, I may never give her anything again. From my Scholars' reports, it seems she might enjoy this scarf above all other presents."

Her man walked toward her, and she placed the scarf in his black gloves.

"Give this to her last," she commanded. "And may The Powers' plans for her, and for my son, be revealed soon."

———

Favik stood in the doorway of the family quarters of the inn, watching Damina model his Lady's final present before her family. Her sister Yamina clapped her hands in appreciation as Damina twirled toward him, the deep violet cloth draped around her arms.

"It is beautiful, Favik!" the young woman cried, as her father called for more ale. Yamina went to fill his cup while their brother, Haril, reached amongst the platters of bread, sauces, fruit, and sweetmeats crowding the table to retrieve his flute. Damina glided toward Favik, eyes bright and a keen match to the hue of her scarf. A wreath of Lamorda, its small purple flowers bright and fresh, crowned the ebony braids encircling her head. "You will tell King's Mother I love it?" she breathed, touching his leather sleeve.

"I will, but know that my Lady is a great admirer of your quilling."

She laughed. "I will quill her a note too!" The young woman glanced at her family, gathered round the table. Haril began playing a song, and Yamina sang along. After a verse, Pamina added her voice to theirs, watching Favik with an intent gaze.

"Do you think," Damina asked, leaning toward his ear, her fair forehead wrinkling with concern, "that the King . . ." Her eyes widened, and she seemed more an anxious child than a woman. "That he will come see me?"

"That I do not know," he said, as gently as he could. For a moment, she seemed to diminish, and she parted her lips as if to speak.

"To Damina!" cried her barrel-shaped father, interrupting his older children's song as though the room had been silent and demanded an utterance from him. He raised his cup. "It's 2911 and my little girl is a full woman of sixteen," Gamin moaned. "Oh, Damina, my youngest! What will become of your poor old father?"

"Please, Father," Pamina interjected. "Your four children are all still at home. None of us have left you yet, except when Haril went for his army service."

The large man broke into red-faced sobs. Damina rushed to hug him whilst Yamina did the same. But Pamina strolled to Favik, latched onto his arm, and towed him toward the kitchen.

"Why am I not surprised? Oh, never mind him. At occasions such as this, Father becomes an ale sponge. Next he will pine for Mother."

Gamin wailed behind them, "Oh, Damina, if only your mother were here, how proud she would be!"

Favik glanced back to the crowded room. "You have seen this before."

"An oft-repeated performance." They entered the warm kitchen. "That, and Haril's flute needs more practice." Pamina let go of his arm to lean against a chopping block, a bundle of fresh rosemary hanging near her honey-colored hair. Gamin's eldest daughter placed her hands behind her, looking toward a stack of bowls awaiting washing. "I think he still blames himself for letting Mother tend the horse that ran away. It was not his fault she fell chasing after it and birthed my sister unattended. Mother always loved horses, I am told." Pamina inhaled deeply, her bodice rising with her breath. She glanced at him. "What about you?"

"What about me?"

"What do you love, Favik?" Pamina's brown eyes watched him with acute interest.

"Many things." His response left the door open for a flirtation in which he had minimal interest. At least, he had thought he had minimal interest. The young woman was rather compelling in close quarters.

"Women?" She kept his gaze, lowering her chin. When he did not answer, she reached to a nearby saucepan and ran a finger around the rim. Pamina licked the fluid from her finger. "Well, Damina is the beauty in the family." She slunk closer to him. "But she reserves herself for the King, it seems." She smiled. "I could … reserve myself for you …" Something clopped hollowly onto the floor. "Oh, I think my shoe just fell off! Would you get it for me?"

"Are you wearing … stockings?"

"Not in this Summer-like weather. But that is not the only reason." The Innkeeper's eldest daughter eyed him with anticipation, wet lips lifting, certain of her victory.

"Then … I think not."

Her brown eyes narrowed. "Is it because you prefer King's Mother's bed?"

Any attraction he might have felt for her vanished like a flame doused in water. "That," Favik began, wearing his best stern Ambassador's face, "was rude."

"Mmm?" Pamina watched him with a brisk tilt of her head. "If you think you prefer older women, I can change your mind."

At this Favik smiled, his strategy coming into focus. "If you think this conversation is going to end with you in my arms, you are mistaken."

"I would prefer it ended in bed."

"And I would prefer it to end," Favik said. He adjourned to the family room.

"Well, that did not go as planned." Pamina crossed her arms over her bosom. "Perhaps that guest from Kaymif is lonely tonight. Maybe that would make Favik jealous." She leaned to sniff the bundle of rosemary near her face, its purple flowers fragrant. "Now that my lovely little sister is of age, I may have a hard time finding any men for myself. Thank The Powers I live in an inn!"

"The Acta Sua of this house will see you now." The manservant bowed slightly, holding open the red lacquered door. Favik walked into the oval-shaped library. Scrolls upon scrolls towered to the ceiling, cradled in graceful wooden shelves that mimicked the room's curve. Lady Saralya approached from the far end and stopped, laying both hands upon the top of a red-damasked chair that Favik recalled seeing last in Dalock King's chamber.

She greeted him with the title he retained for their Scholarly ventures: "Welcome to my *new* quarters, Queensman."

He wondered if her emphasis hinted that she would not be returning to court. "Thank you Lady Reader. I must say, I am impressed by the multitude of volumes in your collection."

"Ah yes. You already know my dear husband bore a great fondness for scroll collecting and organizing, but did you know my father was a scroll merchant? It is truly a family trait." She gripped the chair back tighter. "Jinil's love of reading was well known, and on every presenting occasion he gained more volumes. Many of these," she gestured with a graceful hand, "are second and even third copies."

Her voice was a bit tentative, as though she was embarrassed by the luxury of the situation. Favik merely nodded, scanning the variety of scroll knobs. One pair, at about knee level, caught his eye, the finials smoothly tapered ivory fishhooks. Before he could inquire about the unique design, she continued, in a quieter voice, "While we have this moment alone, do we have any Scholarly business to conduct, Queensman?" The Lady held her palms together.

"I have no news. I collected a few unopened letters to be delivered to our Lady, but that is all."

"I have one of my own. Here, come." She led him toward the desk at one narrowed end of the room and opened a small cylindrical box made of a shiny red material akin to the surface of the library door. She handed a small sealed envelope to him, and he stowed it in the pocket lining his sleeve. She pointed to her box. "Would you believe, when we were granted this house, the shelves in this room were coated with a blue lacquer similar to this. Thank The Powers I was able to have it scraped off and removed. As you can see, the wood is a beautiful natural brown shade, more suitable to my house, in the colors of Dalock King."

The door creaked open, and Lord Saril entered, with his young sister trailing behind him. "Do not traipse behind me like a duckling, Jinilya. It was you who insisted we intrude." The near seven-year-old cast her eyes to the carpeted floor. "I heard Favik was visiting," the young man said, with his knowing smile. "Someone here told me." The girl dashed to her mother for a quick hug, then bounded back into the room, her red dress billowing behind her, completely ignoring Favik.

Saralya crossed her arms. "Jinilya, mind your manners and greet our guest."

"Hullo, Favik." The youngster ran her small hands over the scroll knobs at her hip level, the back of her black-braided head facing him.

"I told you, Mother," began Saril, "she only acts in this manner around him. I am gone a year at my posting, and nothing has changed."

Saralya shook her head. "I am sorry, Favik. She normally is a very good girl."

"I'm certain she is."

The child squeaked loudly, backing away from the stacks, but one of the scrolls followed her. The fabric of her skirt had caught upon one of the knobs of the hook-handled scroll, and the handscroll withdrew itself from the shelf, unwinding as Jinilya yanked her skirt to loose it. As the cylinders clattered to the floor, one unrolled to its full length toward the door. The young Lady stared wide-eyed at the script-covered parchment.

Her mother marched toward her. "No more visits to the library for you, Daughter. That scroll is irreplaceable, and if there is any damage to it, you will have a very plain Naming Day!"

Jinilya did not move, or heed her mother's words; she simply gaped at the parchment, her expression transforming from shock and surprise to puzzlement, as though the manuscript itself communed with her.

"Is she all right?" asked Favik.

"Mother . . . Mama . . ." Jinilya began wailing, a long, lonely cry, and Saralya's demeanor changed entirely as she raced to comfort her youngest child. The girl flung herself into her mother's arms, sobbing cries of heart-wrenching pain.

"What is wrong?" Saril shouted over the din as the two men approached the Ladies.

Saralya said nothing but tried to peel her weeping daughter away from her bosom. "Dear, what happened? Here, look at me."

Jinilya clung to her. "I saw it! I saw it!"

Saralya looked to the men and rocked the girl. "What do you think you saw?"

"People . . . people hurting each other. Mama!"

Saralya gazed away, her lips set in a hard line. Saril placed a comforting arm around the pair. "Little sister, whatever you think you saw, it was not real. Now see, Mother and I are here for you." He patted her back. "And see, your favorite is here too."

His mother replied brusquely, "Now is not the time for teasing, Saril."

Pulling away from her grown son, she gathered her daughter into her arms, the child's long legs flopping awkwardly, and made for the exit. Favik dashed forward and opened the door for the pair. Saralya's dark eyes were glassy and distant as she passed him, her child squeezed tight against her chest and sobbing. He wished he had offered to carry the girl, but the tightness of his Lady Reader's face convinced him that any offers of help would have been declined. As he watched Saralya struggle with her burden along the hallway, he considered whether she might now accept his assistance. He made to follow her just as the same manservant who had ushered him into the library stepped from an alcove and held out his arms to his Lady. She shook her head.

Favik turned to face the room. Lord Saril sat on the floor with his chin held high, leaning back on his hands, appraising Favik. "I am sorry for my sister's outburst. I do hope whatever business you had with my mother was completed, as she will likely be occupied for a long while."

"Will your sister be all right?"

"I hope so, but I have little experience with children." His countenance did not change, but his tone sounded slightly more pointed—an Ambassador probing for more information than was freely given. The young man made no move to stand or collect the handscroll strewn across the floor. "Do close the door, would you? I had hoped to talk to you in private, as one former Ambassador to Havadra to another, and it seems The Powers have presented us this opportunity."

Favik said nothing, but closed the door. Saril stood and gazed down at the parchment. "I will leave the scroll there for my mother to collect, so she can appraise it for any child-inflicted damage. She will judge if there will be any subsequent diminishment of Naming Day presents." Ambassador Saril craned his neck closer to the sheet. "An odd script?"

"'Tis Thislin, but upside down from your perspective."

"All those superfluous dots make the letters run together from this angle."

Favik felt a glimmer of pride at recognizing the style of quilling, but as he frequently communicated with Scholar Onath of Thislin, he had the advantage over Lord Saril from constant familiarity with Thislin script. He paced toward his host, scanning the lines along the way. One row caught his eye in its entirety.

My Soldiers' blades did blush, lusting for the blood still wet in our enemies' veins, soon to be cut from its safe circuits to smoke upon the thirsty earth.

He recognized the text as Baavnif's infamously graphic description of the Battle of Delant. The thought flashed that the child had read the text, or somehow grasped its meaning. On his first reading of the story—not long after earning his sword, on a dare from another Apprentice Ambassador—the gore-laden imagery of the tale had produced nightmares for weeks. If the young girl had read that, he worried about her welfare. Though for a child that young to be competent at reading, not to mention reading Thislin script, would be remarkable. Especially as she had viewed it bottom-side up.

Oblivious to these revelations, Saril called him to a seat, and Favik followed the Lord's bidding, mindful to compose his face into a neutral expression. He had always found Jinil's elder son a bit slippery, and he kept his Ambassador's guardedness at the ready with the young man.

Settling into a chair opposite, Saril laced his hands together. "Did my mother share our family news?"

"We had very little opportunity to speak."

"I will interpret that as a no. Well, my brother Marnil has got his lover with child. They just found out yesterday. The joining ceremony will be the day after tomorrow, and I will miss the formal joining reception in a few months, as I must hasten to my next posting, in Mavold."

"My congratulations on the increase of your house."

"Yes, we will be growing both in population and in property. My soon-to-be saister is Lady Athla of the House of Buloft, Mavlock King's

Friend, one of the estates bordering ours. As she is the sole child of her generation, her lands will become ours when her parents die." He let just enough regret seep into his tone to sound rueful.

Favik nearly grinned at the performance. "You are freshly returned from your Ambassadorship in Havadra?"

"Do I sound like a Havadran?" Saril laughed. "Yes, a very long year it was. How that place does warp and shift one's thinking. I thank The Powers to be back in the cleansing and pure Willed air of Eskalind." The young Ambassador leaned back and smiled in what he no doubt regarded as a charming manner. "I knew *you* would understand, Favik. You were there, what, just over eleven years ago? How long did you serve, one, two years?"

"Nearly two. A very long nearly two years."

"I was grateful to return as well." Again Lord Saril's dark eyes watched with an extra measure of caution. "I am sorry, did you not say you were glad to return?"

"I didn't say; rather, I implied." He gazed evenly at the young Lord.

"I see. Well, I for one am pleased to be home with my family." He smiled again, and Favik felt the insinuation that he did not possess a family. "I did have some odd interactions while I was there. You do recall the general?"

"General Yirlofts, of course."

"He has been in power for such a length of time, upon my first meeting with him, he listed all the men who had served as Ambassadors from Eskalind during his tenure: Saril, Havnil, Kanil, Kinakil, Favil," the slightest of pauses, "Hornil, Vanip."

"So that listing was a test to see if you would correct his error?"

"Which I did, reminding him that Favil was correctly Favik. He merely smiled, and we spoke no more of it. Then later, not long before I departed for Eskalind and home, would you believe the general found enough favor with me to introduce me to his brood?"

Favik's blood chilled at the possibility that Saril had seen Melande, then he realized the young Lord likely meant the general's grandsons. The thought of Melande mothering children with her husband was something he preferred not to think on. He offered an impartial, "That is highly … unusual."

"Well, I do not mean the women in his family. The Powers only know if he has any, but he must—or at least he must *have* had women in the family at one time."

King' Mother's man tried not to tense at the thought that his lost beloved might no longer be alive, but surely it was a possibility. It had been indeed just over eleven years since he had seen her. How he wished he could go to her, though a part of him wondered if, after all this time, part of Melande's enduring allure had been her unattainability.

Saril was still talking. "The general presented a grandson to me."

Attempting to keep his emotions at a distance, Favik used his logical sense to wonder why Saril wanted to impart this information to him, other than to boast of his closeness to the general. He decided the best line of questioning would be to switch from the personal to the political. "Do you think the general is grooming this grandson to follow in his footsteps?"

"Perhaps, but the child is not much older than my sister. The general would have to remain in power for many more years for a boy of ten to successfully succeed him."

Something in that last sentence vied in for prominence—for attention, for action—in Favik's thoughts, yet faced with a mind trained in the same techniques as his own, King's Mother's man unconsciously switched to an Eskalind Ambassador's best tactic: the fact that he enjoyed the challenge of matching wits, knowing he was being played, and finding a method that would trump his opponent. There was no established formula for success; the solution relied on training and instinct. A specific, cultivated instinct born from that training.

He switched to a personal tack. "The general is known for anticipating, and planning, well into the future. Perhaps," he tilted his head, "he seeks to join his grandson with your sister."

Saril leaned back slightly, his brown eyes lit with a concentrated spark. "Hmm, I can imagine it now, my green-eyed sister joined to a gray-eyed Havadran. Gray-eyed for the most part, though there is a bit of blue about the edges of his irises. Very distinctive."

How the young Lord watched him, and all Favik could see or feel was that scrutiny; all his thought was upon it, watching the other man watch him. A pair of mounting, niggling thoughts trembled and contested within him for primacy, but the weight of his observation squelched them as he counted the hairs in the young man's beard, calculated the size of the red jewelstone stud in his left earlobe, estimated his own pulse rate as he pressed his wrist into the arm of the chair. "Then they would make a remarkable pair."

Something in Saril seemed to yield. "Well, former Ambassador, enough of foreign issues. Have you seen our Lord Dalich King recently?"

"I have."

"Is he well?

"I believe so."

"I am heartened to hear it." Saril nodded his black locks as though he had made a decision. "I found it odd that when the King sent his formal command for my reposting to Mavold, his missive insisted that prior to journeying to my new Ambassadorship, I should visit solely my estate and not travel north to his Halls."

"Traveling north and then back to Mavold would add weeks to your stay in Eskalind. He must require your presence in Mavold sooner rather than later. He may also be considering that you had not seen your family in some time."

"I have not seen the King in some time either. Not since he was King's Son." His tone sounded wounded, but Favik would offer no sympathy.

"My Lord Saril, your pardon, but unless you have more news or business with me, *I* must hasten to King's Halls. King's Mother expects me."

Saril raised his head sharply. "Yes, of course. I will not delay you.

Fare well. And give my fond regards to Lady Marna, and especially to her son." The Lord stood.

Favik rose to his feet and bowed. "I will. Please give my fondest wishes to your Lady mother and Lady sister, and congratulations to Lord Marnil and his betrothed." Turning, he went to the door, opened it, and exited into the main hallway, smug with victory at having defeated whatever ploy Saril had played at with his talk of the Havadran general. The same manservant he had seen before called for his horse and saw a packet of bread and cheeses bestowed upon the visitor. The man gave his Lady's regrets for her absence at Favik's departure.

Accepting the victuals, the former Ambassador marched from the house. For a brief moment he studied the small, red-limbed tree planted just inside the apex of the horseshoe-shaped drive. It was no taller than Jinilya and centered within a wide circle of tea-colored stone, indicating that ambitions ran high for its future growth and girth. Only when Favik climbed onto the horse and the methodical, hollow clomping of hooves sounded on the rusty red gravel path did clear thought come as he realized what Saril had told him. The two thoughts he had somehow managed to separate twinned in his mind.

If Melande had mothered a gray-eyed son ten years ago, the boy was not her husband's, but Favik's.

Chapter Twenty-Eight—Breakage, Revelations

"Oh, not again!" Damina wailed as her quill nib crunched and shattered. Shards of milky, translucent quill rocked atop the papyrus, atop the only letters yet quilled: *My Lord Dal—*

"What's the matter, Sister?" Yamina came toward her and placed the tray of dirty mugs she carried on the table. A spoon clattered inside one of the ceramic cups. She sat by Damina's side.

"Oh, Yamina, this is the third time it has happened. I try to quill the King, and my quill breaks. Or the ink bottle is dry, though I shook it before and it sounded full and wet." She covered her face with her hands, cheeks hot against her palms.

Yamina smoothed a hand over the top of her sister's black hair, down to her thin shoulder. "Why are you quilling him?"

"Because it has been over two months since I came of age, and he hasn't come for me. I thought he would. I told him I would wait. Why doesn't he come?" Gamin's youngest daughter lowered her hands to the table and pouted at her sister, wanting to cry. Frustration rang in her veins like a metal bell struck hard with a hammer.

Her sister's lips puckered slightly, but her brown eyes were serious and kind. "The King is a very busy man—he has a lot to do. Many people seek his healing, and he meets with ambassadors from the outerlands to hold the peace. Just think of all the things he must do to keep our land prosperous and in The Powers' favor. It must be a very hard, difficult job."

Damina shrank in her seat, feeling selfish. Her violet eyes scanned the empty common room. "I know," she whispered. "I just thought, maybe he would send a note, at least. He has scribes who work for him, doesn't he? It wouldn't be that much to send a small, quick note?" She rubbed a palm on the table. "I just hoped he would come. It's Summer already." She noted the wilting sprig of Lamorda in a rosy-colored vase. Once again, she had forgotten to change the water. To The Powers, she could do nothing right!

"When I try to quill him, something always goes wrong. Maybe I should just show my feet to the first handsome young man who comes in the front door."

Her sister grinned, nudging her. "If Pamina doesn't intercept him first." They both giggled, eyes darting about to see if their sister was in hearing range, but the large room was quiet and vacant. Yamina asked, "Do you want me to quill the King on your behalf?"

"No, I want him to see my quilling. I worked very hard improving it so it would be pretty when we corresponded." Damina sat straight and reached for the dish tray. "Let me help you with the dishes. Looks like the Amkish guests drank a lot in their room again."

"Every night!" whispered Yamina as the pair stood. Damina grasped the wooden tray as her sister pulled the two heaviest mugs off it.

"But Damina, I could lighten your load by quilling him." She smiled.

The younger sister lifted the tray. "Thank you, but I will try again, and if it doesn't work or I don't hear from him by the first day of Autumn, I will allow my eyes to roam and my feet to show!" She laughed, even though her words troubled her.

Favik entered Marna's chamber to find his Lady at her desk. Gray light from the windows told of the foggy morning outside. "What news,

Favik?" Marna said, looking up from the letter she quilled. "You are back sooner than expected." She dipped the tip of her black feathered quill in the ebony inkwell and continued to write.

"As 2911 draws to a close, I bring letters from Lord Radil and other Scholars." He retrieved a few sealed envelopes from the pouch he clasped in his hand, and placed them on her desk.

She touched them and withdrew her hand. "They are cold."

"Yes, my Lady, it is a true winter morning, even for the Strange Kingdom."

Marna smiled. "But not like the snow we used to have in Humiksland."

Her man nodded in agreement. "I made opportunity to stop at Damina's inn before arriving at King's Halls."

"So close and yet so far from my son. Well, what do you have to report?"

He said nothing. The only sound was the grating scratches of her quill.

After a moment, King's Mother spoke. "That is a long pause. It must be bad news."

"I am not certain what to make of it."

"Then report, and I will make of it what I will."

"I believe Damina has a lover."

The Bladesmith's Daughter did not pause. "Believe?"

"I am nearly certain."

"Well, that is her prerogative. She is of age, has been since Spring. She may do what she will." Marna inked her quill. "As my son has not even asked me where he can find her, I cannot say that I blame her." She sighed, glancing away from the page before her. "Would that he would wake from this eternal languorous mood that troubles him. He is more morose now than before he completed that . . . building." She pictured the long aisle of her husband's tomb, lined with tall windows, which led to Dalock's bronze effigy resting atop the sarcophagus chased with designs depicting scenes from his life. Next to it, her empty casket, the lid bearing her likeness leaning against a nearby wall.

Perhaps he wishes I were in it. She ground her quill into the purple parchment.

"My Lady, what if Damina got with child by another—what would happen?"

"You know the beliefs of this land; then she would be meant to join with the father of her child."

"My Lady, what if the King came to her during that time and wanted to join with her?"

"She would tell him if she were with child."

"What if she did not know?"

Marna looked up at her man, surprised by his insistence on this scenario. She could see in his blue-rimmed gray irises that he withheld something. She knew him too well. "Let us sit together."

Favik walked to the hearth and sat on the couch before the warming flames.

King's Mother followed him and sat by his side, smoothing her black smock. They sat an awkward moment. "I want to relate something about my family that I never told my husband, or any other Eskalinder." She inhaled. "My sister, Werna, and I are half sisters. Her father was a nobleman who got my mother with child. My father joined with her in exchange for being made armorer to King Hudik." She turned toward him. "For that reason, I have always found it hard to believe as Eskalinders do, that The Powers show men and women their only mates." She kept her voice low. "What do you believe?"

Favik looked at her, and she discerned an inner struggle roiling within him.

"Favik, I would have your true answer." Then Marna calmed her tone, aiming to sound more confiding than authoritative. "For just between us."

He searched her face with soft, thoughtful eyes that she felt said he readied to tell her a secret.

"My Lady, I do not believe it either."

"I thought so. And yet you serve the Strange Kingdom."

"I serve you, my Lady."

She smiled. "Our higher ideal, you mean."

"As you wish, yes."

"But why is it you do not believe in The Powers' providence in this matter?"

"It has not been my experience." He folded his hands in his lap.

"Your meaning?" The Lady of Eskalind studied his face, aware that he knew she examined him.

In a flat tone he replied, "I have a child, and his mother joined with another."

"Truly?" She raised her eyebrows. "You have done it at last, Favik. You have surprised me."

"Would that it were not so, my Lady." He rubbed his stubby fingers with his thumbs.

"Is it Lord Radil's boy? Is that why you offered to watch the north?"

He looked at the fire, his eyes distant and glassy, as though he did not hear her.

"Favik," her voice softened, "forgive me. That was terrible. It is none of my affair."

He leaned forward, covering his face with his thick hands. "It is not Amril. I have never… seen my son. I never will."

"Oh, Favik." She touched his arm with maternal concern.

"I am sorry. I would not break before you, my Lady." His face was shielded under his hands.

"My dear Favik." She gathered him into her arms, where he soundlessly shuddered on her shoulder as she patted his back. She closed her eyes and rocked him a long while, her thoughts returning to when they had first met, when he was just an orphaned boy. When he told her about his father's fate. He had hid tears from her even then, close as he was to the grief.

He has endured many losses. She held his head against her shoulder. *His mother died birthing him, his father in battle, and now his child who he has never met. How I hoped he would find a wife to equal him and know some measure of joy.*

A subtle creaking jarred her thoughts. She opened her eyes to see the young King glowering from his doorway, gray eyes accusing, a bright contrast to his dark hair and attire. He turned and left, slamming the thick door behind him.

Favik bolted from her arms. "My Lady?" His eyes were rimmed red.

"It was just my son. I will go to him in a moment. Are you all right?"

He nodded. "I hope I have caused you no trouble, my Lady." He wiped the corner of his eye on his black sleeve, the cool Ambassador's demeanor returning as swiftly as a wind-pushed cloud blocks the sun. "Forgive me."

"There is nothing to forgive," Marna soothed, patting his arm.

He paused a moment, expression softening. "I have never wanted anything more than … to be your faithful servant." His voice shivered with sincerity, just as when he was her Page and unexpectedly, wholeheartedly, pledged his service to her.

Marna stood. "You are that and more," she said, and leaned toward his face. "You are as dear to me as family."

He closed his eyes and smiled. "Thank you, my Lady."

She kissed his forehead. "Now I will discover what Dalich needs. I will see you tomorrow."

Favik opened his eyes, then stood and bowed. He departed her chamber.

Marna crossed the room to the King's door, pausing before she opened it and muttering, "Why is my son not more like Favik? Dalich is rash, and judgmental, prone to fits of despair. He is ungrateful and angry, and yet has had everything he needed his entire life."

She closed her eyes. "Except for Damina. And his father. And—" She leaned her head on the thick wooden door. "I cannot, I will not, be like a foolish mother who loves one child over another. Each is his own man, with his own qualities, and experiences that have shaped him. I know this." She sighed. "I would not wish Favik's hardships on anyone, let alone the son of my body. Dalich has had troubles enough."

She opened her eyes and stood straight. "Courage, Marna." She entered the room that once belonged to her husband, now held by their son.

Parchments littered every horizontal surface and obscured all but the velvet-tasseled pillows at the head of the bed. A few black candles flickered in their iron holders, but their flames did little to dispel the gray gloom that felt thick in the air. She found her son with his velvet-clad back to her, facing the wall.

Dalich turned toward her, gray eyes narrowed. "How long has he been your lover?" His voice was pierced with anger.

His words and venom shocked her. "You cannot possibly believe—"

"What I see with my own eyes?"

"You saw nothing but one person comforting another." Marna kept her voice calm and steady, aiming to win him by reason.

"Is that what you call it? A lover's embrace is mere comfort?"

"Dalich. I have known Favik since he was an orphaned peasant boy. If you could have seen how uncared for, how thin he was—"

"Now you play the part of mother! Which is it? Comforter? Or mother? Or lover?"

Wearily, sadly, she shook her head. "Son—"

"Yes, Dalich. Son of Marna and The Powers only know who!"

Marna gaped at his accusation. All reason left her as she sputtered. "How dare you speak to me in that manner! You … ridiculous boy!"

"I am no boy! I am King."

King's Mother's voice was cool and mean. "Then behave as such." Her hands on her waist, she regarded the young man. "If your father could hear you now, he would … not be proud."

He scowled. "If my father saw you holding that man like that, he would challenge you, just as I am."

"No." Marna strode to her door. "He would have understood." She walked through the doorway and yanked her door shut with a satisfying thud. A moment later, the hollow sound of Dalich's door banging closed, then the scraping of the bolt thrown through the latch.

It would be months before she saw him again.

Lady Saralya gazed out a long window to the grassy field outside her home, then turned her eyes to the drying brownish ink staining the nib of the red-feathered quill in her hand. Marna King's Mother had presented her with dozens of similarly colored plumes, no longer of use in the King's household. The death of Dalock King had led to an exodus of household goods and furnishings decorated in his colors and carved with his symbols. From King's Halls to her own they came in wagonloads, while violet and sable furnishings created for Dalock's son's rule began to eclipse the red and brown. Many a tradesman and crafter labored long to fulfill new orders. The process would consume years.

She tapped the nib against the papyrus and read words from her own hand, but quilled in the less fluid script she used for Scholarly business.

My Dearest Lady,
It is strange to write of this matter, for what I write I hope to say in person one day.
I swear to The Powers my daughter possesses a unique talent. She can read any written script or code presented to her, as long as it was written with clear intent. I tested her with all manner of

quilling and content suitable for a child her age, and she told me
the meaning of each with merely a glance. I further examined her
by creating missals of nonsensical characters, and still, if I had
quilled them with a firm message in mind, she can reproduce that
message in words.
My Lady, her Gift will be useful to our cause, yet as her mother,
I do not wish to expose her to any text that may be traumatic
or harmful to her delicate young mind. She has found scrolls I
would have hid from her eyes, and torturous nightmares are the
aftermath. I now keep those volumes under lock and key.
May The Powers reveal to me when she has the strength and
maturity of mind to weather this distress, but if They claim me
before then, I trust that They will show you when the time is right.
I am entrusting no one else with this knowledge, not even any
member of my family.
With grateful affection,
Your Lady

The Acta Sua of the House of Jinil, Dalock King's Friend did not sign her name, for she hoped her lack of specifics would save Jinilya from any harm that might come were the note to fall into the wrong hands. Folding the papyrus sheet, she sealed it with the innocuous seal of a traveling scribe, most useful for Scholars' correspondences, red waxed and devoid of impression. Saralya slipped the letter into an envelope, which she had a servant address to Marna, Queen of Eskalind, using her Lady's old title so that the missive appeared to have been written in the reign of Dalock King. Into the red-lacquered pyx that her sons knew contained her important papers it went. She hoped its seals need never be broken.

Dalich King dropped the last healing note to the floor. How many he had read today, only The Powers knew. How many people he had truly healed, well, that was Their privilege to know as well. Not that it mattered.

Nothing left to do, he paced to his unmade, empty bed and lowered his posterior to the floor, encountering a cushion of papyrus letters. Eyes closed, he leaned against the bedsheets cascading over the mattress and rubbed his head against the fabric. The scratching motion almost felt good.

A shuffling by the main door announced the arrival of yet another letter basket full of healing requests that awaited his attention. Dalich considered calling for the Guard to bring the basket inside, but that would upset the expected routine, in which the King procured baskets only when he wished.

No, he would wait. Let the baskets crowd the landing until they rose into stacks, the basket bearers whispering, wondering if their Lord was all right, if they should knock on the door, trouble his concentration. It would not be the first time.

Let them wait. Since The Powers had cursed him with this interminable separation from Damina, all must suffer.

"By The Powers, he must leave his quarters at some point," Marna muttered, plodding through the corridor that led to the royals' tower. A line of Apprentice Librarians stepped aside at her passage and bowed. Each held a basket woven of dark twigs and filled with envelopes for the King. "He must make plans for his Naming Day celebration next month."

A Guard, his wide face beaded with sweat, came down the stairs bearing a stack of empty baskets. "My Lady," he puffed with a bow.

"Many letters today?"

"More than many, my Lady."

Marna acknowledged his words with a nod and trod up the stairs to her chamber, silently cursing the pains in her knees and wishing she might discover some herbcraft that would alleviate her woe. She paused at the midpoint and regarded the sunlit stone steps looming before her.

"Who goes there?" called the Guard at the top.

"She who was once Queen." How she longed for another to acquire that title and be her son's wife.

The Guard came toward her, rounding the curved passageway. "Are you well, my Lady?" It was Trevil.

"Of course," she said sharply, but to herself she listed her complaints. *As fine as one can expect when my son hides in his quarters, leaving me to rule in his name, make excuses for him, and manage the Scholars, Ambassadors, and whatnot against whatever onslaughts The Powers have planned for us.* Marna accepted Trevil's arm as he led her to her door. "Ah, I thank you."

Dalock's Queen plodded into the dim light of her chamber. The ebony-colored curtains hung heavily from their rods; shadows obscured furniture as ponderous as her mood. "Please call for some cakes for me, Trevil." He departed and shut the door while she drew the curtains open.

"I could send for Damina," King's Mother mused, "but I would not want her to meet him in this mood. And what if she still has that lover?

Enough time has passed, she could have taken five lovers!" With a groan, she settled at her desk.

"The Kaymif princess still quills him, and he replies to her letters, so she must hold his interest. I could send for her. No, she could not come; she is still regent to her young brother. How old is he now? He was six when Dalich was sixteen, seven, eight years ago, so he must be about fourteen now. Only two more years before he is a man, or is it older in Kaymif? I need a quicker solution."

She stared at the walls she knew not how long. Her Page Fornil entered and presented her with a plate of small buttery yellow cakes. "Here," and she pointed. He placed it by her elbow.

"Do you wish some bread and sauces too, my Lady?" the lad asked. "I have a plate ready. The King refused his again."

"Just the cakes," Marna replied, wondering when Dalich ate last. She reached for a moist treat, considering that perhaps her son would not resist cakes if she were to bake them. King's Mother pushed the soft sweet into her mouth, grateful—and not for the first time—that it was not Eskalinder custom to make their food into the King's colors.

Fornil bowed, then departed.

"I could send for his friends Saril or Marnil," she deliberated. "Dalich missed Marnil's joining reception, too busy staying in his room healing people." She sighed. "Now Marnil has a son, Saralya is a grandmother. Life goes on."

Her quills lay flat on the table, ready to be of use. The gray light in the room momentarily gave way to a warm ray of sunshine, and the ribbed texture of the black feathers emerged in the slanting light. "If only there was a way to heal Dalich." She stroked the nearest feather. The yellow glow faded.

"What if someone wrote and asked for the King to be healed?" She withdrew her hand. "No, he would not do it. But what if . . ." She stood. "What if a mother wrote, asking for her son to be cured, describing his symptoms and not mentioning his name until the very last . . ." She reached for the bellpull, yanking the purple beaded cord. "Cleverly quilled, so Dalich does not realize it addresses his ailment till he has begun healing himself." A smile formed on her lips for the first time in months.

Her Page reentered her room. Before Fornil could speak, Marna ordered, "Bring me one of the baskets that is full of letters for the King."

"Yes, my Lady," the boy said, brown eyes wide and curious. He ran to do her bidding, nearly tripping on the carpet on his way out.

"Careful, Fornil!" Marna shook her head. "I must disguise my quilling, and use the plain papyrus that the Scholars' messages sometimes require. Black ink will suffice, it is common enough." She pushed the cake platter away and sat at her quilling table. "When the letter is complete, I will mix it with the others, and roast him some chicken to aid his recovery. Then I will wait."

———

Marna awoke early the next morning to find a quilled message from Favik. Damina had broken with her lover, after she knew she was not with child. Despite the months that had gone by, the young woman had stayed with the same man the entire time. Sitting up sleepily in bed, King's Mother smiled as she read of Damina's hope to meet with Dalich, if Marna would deign to arrange it. The Powers knew she most certainly would.

Before she could act, a noise sounded that she had never been so glad to hear since Dalock died—the opening creak of the door that adjoined the royals' chambers.

"Mother?" came a thin voice.

Instantly fully awake, she rose, placing Favik's letter aside.

"Dalich?" she called softly as she approached the door.

"Come in, Mother." She heard him step back into his room.

She crossed the threshold into the darkness of her son's closed-curtain room. The candles were stubs; faint gray light meekly attempted to penetrate the draperies. Her eyes adjusting to the gloom, Marna saw stacks upon stacks of papyrus and the occasional parchment sheet, interleaved with torn envelopes teetering in piles or scattered upon every surface, even across the floor, surely ankle deep. She turned to the main door, barely discerning her son's form standing in the murk. "Let me see you," she said gently, raising an encouraging hand as though he were again a wee child making his first steps.

Dalich traipsed toward her. Clad in a thick, sable-colored sleeping robe, his head was topped with a close-fitting cap. Either he had shorn away his hair or it nestled inside the head covering. Dark circles under his eyes, his shoulders drooping as if an invisible weight pulled him low. In his hand, he held the letter she had quilled, asking for healing for her son. He would not raise his eyes to her.

She noticed a strand of hair protruding from his cap. "Your hair?" Dalich dropped the letter and removed his cap. Graying locks tumbled around his neck. "My poor, dear son!" Marna said, placing a hand on his cool cheek. He grasped her hand, squeezing its warmth, and wept. She gently pulled him into her arms and stroked his head.

"I am no King." Dalich clung to her.

"But you are," she replied, her voice thick despite wanting to keep it light. "The evidence is all around you. See?"

"What do you mean?" He raised his head.

"All these letters," she began, scanning the room as he broke their embrace. The bed overflowed with enough missives to conceal its use as a place of rest. "From people needing healing. And *you* have healed them. Only a King of great Gifts can do such a thing. But Dalich, there is another Gift that you have."

The young man's gray eyes gained a flicker of interest.

"Damina," she said.

He lowered his head. "No, that future is gone."

She touched his arm. "It is not. Listen to me. She is of age now—"

"No, it is still a long while off, not until 2913."

Marna shook her head. "You have the years confused; it is 2912 now, the Fourth Month, and she is of age." Not certain he comprehended her meaning, she pressed, "Listen to me, dear son. She is of age, now, and wants to meet with you."

"But how do you know this?"

She raised an eyebrow. "Am I not your mother?"

Dalich's face relaxed as though he might smile. Then a fresh worry must have presented itself, for he turned and glanced over his chamber. "Would she have me, as I am now?"

"As you are, and as you will be."

"Mother, forgive me. I had no hope." Her son closed his eyes and whispered, "It was … as though The Powers forsook me, considered me unworthy. I could sense their … disapproval. It made me numb." His words curled around her heart, her fear growing that indeed The Powers were forsaking them, forsaking Eskalind. Yet here he stood, the Healer King, seemingly recovered of his own ills, confessing his experience in an utterance of purest trust.

"Come, let us cast away this gloom! First we will make some light in this room. I think these letters will start a nice fire. Then," she squeezed his arm, "we will call for roast chicken."

"Your roast chicken?" His voice lifted with hope, eyes open and bright.

At this, Marna grinned broadly. "I prepared it last night."

A month passed as King's Mother nursed her son back to health on a diet of roast chicken, hearty broth, fresh air, and plentiful sunshine. Despite her earlier misgivings, she arranged a leave of absence from the army for Marnil, though he had scarcely returned to duty after the birth and Naming of his son, Kaloft. His wife, Athla, and the new babe came from their estate, accompanied by Lady Saralya, Jinilya, and a trio of nursemaids.

To Marna's relief and delight, it seemed that even The Powers aided her plans, for Dalich drew the Ambassadors' tiles, and Lord Saril's name and Eskalind were drawn together. When her son announced he would name Saril his Second, she cringed, thinking the young Lord too inexperienced for the position; not wanting to risk the hint of discord, she stayed silent on the matter.

The King delighted in these reunions. "I cannot believe how much Jinilya has grown," he laughed to his mother and her friend as he crawled on all fours, giving the leggy girl piggyback rides on the expansive violet rug in his chamber.

Marna glanced at Saralya. "Well, it has been two years since you saw her last," she said, instantly wishing she had stifled the edge in her voice. But Dalich seemed unoffended, chuckling as young Lady Jinilya commanded her steed to gallop faster.

"He will make a good father," Saralya whispered to her Lady.

Marna rejoiced, glad to see her son at last cheerful and relaxed before those who were close as family to him.

"Will you be my father?" Jinilya asked the King, her green eyes betraying no sense of the absence her question revealed. Marna's Reader looked away.

"I thought I was your stallion," Dalich teased. He neighed loudly and the seven-year-old squealed in delight.

But there was one meeting she would postpone as long as she could, for she believed Dalich should not see Favik until she deemed him fully recovered.

Some days later, she gathered with other members of King's Halls to watch the young King spar with Saril on the terrace. Dalich fought with determination, grace, and strength, earning cheers and stamping feet from his people, but his mother at last saw Dalock's good-naturedness surfacing in their son's demeanor.

"You have learned much on your journeys, my Second." The King smoothed a sweaty strand of hair behind his ear. "Even my Mavoldian Swordmaster did not have such flair."

His mother stiffened, worried this talk of borderlands he would never visit would lead to a morose mood.

"All I learned, I will show you, my Lord," replied Jinil's eldest with characteristic diplomacy. Saril demonstrated his technique while Dalich watched with interest, and then the King repeated the action. No hint of impending gloom shadowed his movements or demeanor.

"At last," Marna murmured, "perhaps the time has come." By her side, young Page Fornil tried to mimic his Lord's arm movements and nearly crashed into a pillar. She shook her head. "With practice, dear Fornil."

"Yes, my Lady." He grinned sheepishly, his pride the only injured party of the day.

Later that evening, after making arrangements, Marna called on her son in his quarters, only to find the young King and Marnil playing at chess. Saril sipped a goblet of wine and kidded with them, just as he had when they were boys.

She called from the doorway, "I did not mean to trouble you, gentlemen." Marnil and Saril stood and bowed. "I know this is your last night together before Marnil must depart. I will come back later."

"Mother, come in. Please, share wine with us." Dalich sounded as though he truly meant it.

She shook her head. "Perhaps another time, I thank you." She closed his door and returned to her quarters, leaving her connecting door open, and settled to read on the new velvet daybed by the window. Another creation of Lady Dara, the couch was upholstered with diamond-shaped purple and black velvet fabric studded with onyx buttons.

"Mother, are you asleep?"

"I must have been." Her book lay upturned on her lap and she yawned.

"Is it too late to talk?"

"No no, come here." She sat up and motioned Dalich to her side.

The young King sat by her. In the gleam of the candlelight his mother saw hints of red highlights in the locks that were still dark. *Like Dalock's.* She gazed at him. "I was just thinking of your father." A tear welled in her eye.

"I think of him often."

She reached for his long-fingered hands. "I know I was not always the most attentive wife," Marna began, glancing at the garnet beads at her wrist. "But I did love him. We had many happy years together."

Dalich looked at their hands.

"So you still think of Damina?" she whispered.

"All the time." He raised his eyes to hers. "But I would not disappoint her. Do you think I am well enough to see her now?"

"I do."

"How shall I find her?" His voice carried a sense that he knew she knew where to find Damina.

"You will have a guide who knows the way," Marna said. "Do you want to meet him?"

"Of course."

"Then wait a moment." King's Mother stood and went to her desk, grasping the polished beads of the bellpull and giving them two hearty jerks. She paused a moment and pulled three times.

Dalich sat on his mother's daybed, willing himself to steady his breathing as he contemplated who might be the fortunate person who knew the way to Damina.

The main door creaked open. He jumped to his feet. Favik entered the room at a slow pace. *Not you,* Dalich thought, though he was certain his face broadcast it as clear as shouting.

"My Lord." Favik's voice was quiet and even as he bowed. He kept his eyes to the floor.

Dalich looked at his mother. She came toward him, touching his arm. "There was no one else I would entrust on a mission as important as educating your wife."

"Your meaning?" Dalich asked, his throat tightening. "What type of education?"

"I would not have her come to the throne as unschooled as I was when I joined with your father," began King's Mother, gray eyes gazing into his. "Do you recall that I could not even read when I came to Eskalind? The very night your connection with Damina was broken, I sent Favik to the tavern where your father's men found her. Favik arranged to have tutors brought to her, so Damina might enjoy learning suitable to her possible future station. All this time I have kept her in my thought and attention. For you, my son. I could not have done it without Favik's assistance." She drew close to his ear. "He can lead you to her."

Dalich regarded the man before him. Last time he saw the man, Favik was in his mother's arms. The King wondered if he was close with Damina as well. "Where is she?" He paced toward him.

"It is but three hours' ride," Favik replied in a reassuring voice.

"Three hours?" Dalich turned to his mother. "All these years she has been this close? The Powers must not have wanted me to find her."

"My son, I have thought that as well."

The Lord of Eskalind nodded, then stepped closer to the former Humikslander, standing as straight as he could. "Look at me." His mother's man raised his eyes to his King. Dalich stared into those blue-gray windows, seeking treachery. But Favik met his gaze with thoughtful and steady calm.

"Tell the groomsmen I will ride Haanip. We will leave in the dark," Dalich commanded. "I would be there at sunrise. You are dismissed."

"My Lord." Favik made a careful backward nod of his head so he would not bump foreheads with the King. He departed from his Lady's chamber.

Dalich turned toward his mother, scrutinizing her pleased expression. "Call for my barber, valet, and a bath!"

His mother stepped toward him, thick arms unfolding to embrace him. "Dalich, will you bring back my daighter from your journey?"

"I will, Mother," he said into her ear. "I will." He felt a calm envelop him such as he had not known in a long, long time.

Damina woke earlier than her sisters, the sound of Pamina's shuddering snores troubling her from sleep. "Would that you bedded elsewhere," the young woman murmured, though most nights she got her wish. Despite the late night spent cleaning the inn's common room after unusually boisterous clientele, she found she was no longer tired. A walk in the fields before chores would be pleasant, and afford her the rare opportunity to be alone with her thoughts.

Damina rose slowly, pondering her dull gray shawl, draped on the peg designated for her clothes on the back of the door. She never wore the scarf King's Mother had given her, despite owning it for over a year. Deciding it was no use to keep it hidden away like a forgotten treasure, she slipped from bed and trod quietly to the chest of drawers. Kneeling before the lowest drawer, she pulled the handle toward her. The sisters' garments lay folded in neat rows, thanks to Yamina's fastidious tidying.

Even in the dingy morning light, she could discern the scarf's rich, beautiful color. The young woman stroked the soft velvet trim, imagining how wonderful it would be to wear an entire dress made of the cloth. Damina lost herself in a daydream for a moment. But there would never be an occasion to dress in such finery at the inn.

Behind her, Pamina said something in her sleep that sounded like, "More." Damina rolled her eyes, gathered her fine scarf, and tiptoed from the room.

Draping the plum-colored fabric over her shoulders and head, she made for the fields behind the inn. The grass shimmered, echoing the blue-gray light. The Innkeeper's youngest daughter looked back to see her home reflecting the sky's color. From the kitchen window came the orange glow of candles and the hearth as the Cook set about the day's bread making.

"I should go help her." Damina started back, but saw a man with a slight limp come from the stables, making for the kitchen. "Ah, Cook will not want me to disturb her when her lover is visiting." The young woman turned, walking toward the open land again.

"Everyone has a lover," she whispered, traipsing her fingertips over the small purple flowers of the Lamorda stalks. "Except me. I did, though." She shook her head. "Do other women like their lovers so rough?" The thought hit her hard as a blow.

"Why did King's Son never come to me?" She stifled a sob. "Would he have been gentle? Oh, what does it matter." She gazed at the grass, the dull morning light warming as the sun rose closer to the horizon. "I'll feel better if I walk faster."

Damina followed that inclination until she was running through the wafting green blades of Lamorda. Stretching out, the long scarf fluttered against her bare arms as she pounded the earth, not knowing she sought to diminish the surge of emotions plaguing her heart.

Faster and faster she ran, till she felt free of thought, the world but colors passing by, greens and the deep blues of shadows, the sky purpling at dawn.

She laughed, not knowing why, and sank to her bottom to rest, to breathe for a moment. But the place she sat felt familiar, a grassy hollow large enough for a person to lie in, a jagged rock on its edge. Damina thought she heard a horse neigh in the distance, and one word came to her lips, as though someone had told her to say it.

"Mother."

Then she knew where she was: the place her mother fell while chasing a horse, and where she, before her time, came into the world and first drew breath.

Shivering, she pulled the violet cloth over her head again, staring at the place awhile, lost in wishing for a way to change the past. Then a voice said, "Damina." She stood and turned to face a man, richly dressed in blacks: velvet, linen, leather. His gray eyes held a familiar light, as though she knew him, as though he offered comfort, peace, love.

He held out a hand to her.

Dalich saw her before anyone else. He had turned his head and noticed a spot of shadowed purple against the sunrise-lit green field. Spurring his steed, he made for it, breaking away from his men, leaving his banner fluttering behind as he changed course. Perhaps The Powers whispered to him in that moment. Now she stood before him, more beautiful than any painter could portray, black hair braided and encircling her head, eyes the color of her violet scarf, lips parted as if to speak, and best of all, her pale hand reaching to accept his.

"King's Son," she said aloud, as they touched.

"Now it is King," he said, or thought he said.

"Dalich King," her voice said, but her mouth moved only to form a smile, not words. *"It came back!"* she thought, and he knew her mind as clearly as if she had shouted.

"Oh, Damina!" He gathered her into his arms, about to melt with joy. *"How I missed you."*

Favik watched the King embrace Damina, glad laughter ringing between them. The mounted group halted alongside the former Ambassador and grinned, nodding approvingly. King's Mother's man figured that his Lord must have recognized the sable-haired woman from his locket, but how Dalich King had spotted the young beauty from such a distance was a mystery.

The couple now faced one another. They did not appear to be speaking, for their mouths did not move, yet Damina's face told many things, as if she were conveying a troubling tale. The young King nodded, tracing a gentle finger around her ear. She lowered her gaze, tears sparkling on her cheeks. Favik could not fathom why they were quarreling this quickly after meeting. The King knelt before Damina, his head raised toward the young woman.

"Ambassador, what is happening?" The Guard closest asked.

"I think they are speaking."

"But they are not saying anything."

Favik smiled. "It is her Gift."

The man gaped, watching as Damina wiped her eyes and nodded to the King, who stood.

"By The Powers, this is the strangest thing I have ever seen," murmured the other man alongside Favik.

At last Dalich King turned to his company. "Favik," he summoned, his voice glad as though calling to a beloved companion.

"My Lord?"

"I want you to perform the ceremony. Come, join us," he commanded, his gaze and smile alike to the beaming young woman at his side.

"As you wish, my Lord."

Favik dismounted, tossing his reins to the nearest Guardsman, who whispered, "Here? Our King is going to join in a field?"

Favik raised his eyebrows at the man. "Witness the Legend," he said softly, then turned and walked through the grass to the grinning couple. He wished his Lady could see them, could participate in this long anticipated moment. Smiling, he began.

"My Lord Dalich King, my Lady Damina King's Betrothed."

Damina's eyes widened and she giggled.

———

After the words were spoken, the King stated his desire to spend the day walking alone with his bride. "We will stay tonight at my faither's inn, and journey to my Halls tomorrow," the bridegroom declared, gray eyes never leaving his wife's.

Favik acknowledged this with a nod, a bow, and a contained smile, certain that neither half of the newly joined couple noted his actions. He sent one of his company with word to Marna King's Mother of their joyful news so King's Halls could prepare for their homecoming, and another to alert Damina's family to be ready to receive their newest member.

The second man returned with a basket of food, assembled by Yamina for the King's men, and the promise of a fine meal later that evening.

When the delighted family gathered for the joining feast that night, Damina's father called, "A toast to our King and his bride!" Apparently standing on the floor was not enough, and he lumbered up onto his chair, helped by Yamina, who steadied him as he raised his mug. "My Lord the King, my new sain, may The Powers send you many sons!"

"I thank you, but I only need one," Dalich replied, with a surprisingly shy gaze at his bride.

"Oh, who would have thought my youngest would be first to join?" the King's faither crowed. "It seems just yesterday we celebrated her sixteenth Naming Day!" Yamina assisted him off of the chair.

Pamina, sitting across from Favik with her arms folded below her chest, briefly gazed at the ceiling. When she caught him looking at her, she lifted her arms slightly, giving her bosom a boost to its swell. Favik stifled a guffaw as Gamin swallowed more ale. The large man's nose and cheeks reddened as he bent forward and sobbed, "If only my dear wife were here to see this!"

"Father," Yamina calmed, placing an arm around his expansive back.

"No no, I must be a good host. Hospitality, hospitality." Gamin recovered, standing straight again and wiping his mouth with his hand. "My Lord," he boomed to the young King, who occupied the Innkeeper's usual seat at the head of the table, "tonight we have prepared our finest chamber for you and my beautiful … daughter." This reference caused him to break into renewed sobs, which sent even the bride running to comfort him.

"He is a very emotional man," one of Dalich's men commented as the new Queen helped her father from his chair.

"He loves his children," the King countered, in a stern voice that contained command and admiration.

"Your pardon, my Lord," the man stammered. The King nodded, slightly.

Damina looked at her husband as her father settled into his seat.

"We must get him to bed," she said. *"Sleep is the best remedy when he falls into this mood."*

His gray eyes watched her, kind and sympathetic, and she heard his thoughts: *"Will you come to me outside when you have him to bed?"*

She smiled in reply and turned to Yamina, who was already whispering to their father that it was time to seek his pillow.

"Damina." His voice came into her thoughts again. She turned back to face her husband, still not certain how to respond to his presence both in her mind and in the same room. *"Remember, my heart, I am not like other men."*

"I know."

"Oh, Father!" Yamina cried as their inebriated parent swayed on his feet. Damina whirled to help. "Haril!" she called to her brother, who dashed over to assist with the heavy man. The three siblings led their father from the crowded family dining room. The Queen glanced over her shoulder for one last look at her husband, just in time to see Pamina leaning toward one of Dalich's men.

"More ale?" she asked sweetly, stroking the skin of his bare arm. Damina shook her head.

King's Mother's response to the news of his joining was to send well wishes and a wagon to gather Damina's things for the journey to King's Halls, along with half a dozen Guards to escort the new couple. These men arrived just as the family's feast ended. Dalich commanded four of the six to bring torches outside into the night to await his bride.

The King felt weary and excited all at once on this day that saw the fruition of all his long years of waiting for his wife. Yet he tempered his eagerness with the knowledge Damina had shared with him earlier as they wandered the fields together, seemingly silent to any observers, yet full of discussing the years since their last contact. It did not bother him that she had taken a lover; it bothered him that her lover had misused her. He must work to undo a careless man's harm. Tonight marked the beginning of that undoing, and the revelation of another of his Gifts.

"Bring your shawl," he told his wife in his thoughts. Thus, Damina emerged from the doorway with the purple linen wrapped about her shoulders, its velvet trim shimmering in the torchlight. Her hair was so dark, the purple Lamorda sprigs crowning her head looked to be floating free of any attachment. It pleased him she could still hear his thoughts even when she was beyond his sight, and he thanked The Powers for restoring their Gift intact. She approached, and he clasped her hand, leading her and his men along the road till they came to the first open field.

"I will lay one end of it on the earth," he told Damina in a gentle voice. His bride looked at him with concern, and he knew her thought. "It will be unharmed. Besides, I can buy you another, or ask the Mavoldian ruler to send one as a joining present." He unwound the fabric from her shoulders and placed one short end on the ground. "Stay here."

"But your mother gave it to me for my sixteenth Naming Day," she countered, watching him pull the length of the linen away as he walked into the darkened field.

"Damina, the cloth will be fine. Watch." He stood at the far end of the scarf, facing her. The fabric stretched the distance between them and seemed to elongate, as though they were quite far away from one another. Damina gulped.

"It is fine, you will see," Dalich encouraged. He lowered the scarf to the damp grass, and again Damina hesitated, but then followed. The new husband released his hold of the soft fabric and stepped away.

"Set a torch at each corner," the King bade his men as he walked around the fabric toward his bride. They complied, though their faces betrayed their confusion. Taking his Queen's hand, Dalich said, "And we bid you all good night." Leading Damina, he stepped onto the fabric. The men, torches, and field vanished from their view.

"Where are we?" she asked, gripping his hand, her voice a shocked whisper.

"Where no one else may be." The newly joined couple looked about at the strange, directionless light that seemed to come from everywhere. At their feet, an expansive violet surface rippled, as though made of water, yet their feet touched solid ground.

"Oh! It looks as if it goes on forever." She turned to him. "How did you …."

The Strange King smiled. "I just knew. As I knew when I saw you that you were my Queen." He bent to kiss her smooth forehead, inhaled her rosy citrus scent, took her into his arms, and again felt the comfort long denied him melt into his bones.

How long they stayed there is not known, for time is not measured in that place. To the men standing guard, they saw their Lord and his Lady quietly conversing, but to the reunited pair, conversation melted into kisses followed by languid moments, days, hours, years nestled in each other's arms, a complete and whole communion, encompassing all their thoughts and passions in a perfect union, a Gift from The Powers.

"Well," said the King rather wearily when at last they emerged and stepped onto the torchlit grass. "A proper bed shall be novel. Shall we?"

Damina Queen arrived at King's Halls for the first time later the next day, and to the astonishment of all gathered to greet her on the terrace, she dashed to King's Mother first for a tight embrace, as though she were a long absented daughter.

Marna, for her part, found tears standing, then falling, from her eyes at such a loving and exuberant greeting. It was a moment once beyond hope, the conclusion of long years of preparation. Seeing her son gaze upon the pair of them with quiet warmth and affection, a steady maturity in his posture and benevolence in his eyes, completed the circle of joy and brought words of gratitude to her lips. "Thank The Powers, you are here at last, my daighter."

The new Queen's bright eyes, truly as violet as the portraitist had rendered them years before, shone fondly. "Thank you, I thank you, dear Maither."

They clasped hands, and Marna led her across the flagstones to the receiving line to introduce her to the courtiers, beginning with Lord Saril, King's Second, his mother, Lady Saralya, and her daughter.

"Lord Saril! My husband described you perfectly. I would recognize you anywhere." She laughed and hugged him tight, as though this were a moment of reunion rather than acquaintance.

The former Ambassador said smoothly, "I might inquire later as to which words he used, my Lady."

"They were favorable. Mostly." She giggled. "I am teasing! And Lady Saralya, Dalich tells me you are a second mother to him." She embraced the Lady Reader tightly, as if she had known her for years.

Saralya stiffened slightly, unaccustomed to such shows of affection from an unfamiliar person, but she said graciously, "Thank you, my Lady. It is a privilege to serve your family."

"And this must be little Lady Jinilya." Damina placed a pale hand on the child's shoulder. The girl was no longer little; she was tall for seven, and did not need to raise her green eyes much to meet the Queen's. "You will be a heartbreaker when you come of age, pretty one."

Jinilya's bottom lip dropped. "I, I do not want to hurt anyone."

Damina laughed and patted the child's shoulder. "Oh, where are Marnil and Athla and their wee babe? I was truly hoping to hold the little one."

Jinilya looked to her mother, who said, "My Lady, my son Marnil has returned to his army regiment, and my daighter, Athla, brought their son to her parents' estate."

The new Queen looked cross and turned toward her husband, who shrugged apologetically. She stared at him hard, and he looked even more sheepish. Neither said a word, but their expressions denoted a conversation, bordering on an argument, passing between them. She sighed, turning to Saralya again. "My husband says he forgot to tell me. We spoke for so long, I'm not even certain how long it was, but he forgot *that*. I thought we had talked about everything, and he described you all so well, I feel I already know all of you!" Damina sighed again. "Dalich is forgetful sometimes." She seemed an old wife weary of her mate's foibles, but raised her head to the next person in line, beaming. "You must be Lady Dara, the excellent embroiderer."

"Yes, my Lady Queen, I am!"

"Dalich told me you have stitched his Naming Day clothes for him since he was born. I cannot wait to discuss my ideas for gowns with you."

Dara looked to weep from joy. "Oh, I thank you, I thank you, my Lady! You were truly sent to us by The Powers!"

———

At the Joining feast, Marna sat at the head of the nobles' table and watched the admiring stares of their guests as they surveyed the King's beautiful bride, who rose to play her part in the toasting ceremony.

"Her education pays off," murmured King's Mother low, as Damina thanked the men of King's Halls for their honors. "Or is it that Dalich tells her in her thoughts?" She watched them with a keen eye. "Already I sense a distraction in their faces when they speak silently to one another. See how confident she is. That is from her training, not his helping." Marna patted the linen table covering. "Thank The Powers my son finally went to her. Now I will know some measure of peace. Or at least more time to work with my Scholars to stem whatever ill plans The Powers have for us. Though I do worry," and she glanced at the new Queen with a midwife's eye, "if a woman that slim hipped can birth a child safely . . ."

Her gaze wandered to the entertainment below: a scene of two men in single combat whilst a few ragged farmers watched, leaning on hoes with exaggerated aplomb. Marna wondered what Legend it was; it seemed familiar, but she could not place it. One of the combatants wore painted gold armor and a forked blond beard, made of hay.

"More wine, my Lady?" Lady Saralya asked from her seat next to King's Mother.

Marna turned. "Yes, dear friend." Saralya filled her goblet. "How glad I am you were at King's Halls this day."

"I thank you, my Lady. I wish Marnil and his family were here too."

"Mother!" the bridegroom called. She turned to see him leaning across Damina as his bride laughed. "Are you watching?" He pointed at the players.

Marna followed his finger toward a lone actor, the same man who a moment ago was fighting the hay-bearded man. He held a painted wood sword in one hand and turned about, searching for something. Suddenly, a woman dressed in a silver cloth ran toward him, knocking him over, and ran away.

"This is indeed odd," muttered Marna as she glanced at her Reader, who shared her puzzled look.

"Keep watching!" her son commanded, voice quavering with held-back laughter.

A young woman in plain dress walked toward the prone man. She carried a small bowl and helped him drink from it. The man opened his eyes and gazed at her with an expression of recognition and tenderness. The woman helped him to his feet and they shared a warm kiss.

"Mother, it is when you met Father!" Dalich declared with a boyish grin.

"By The Powers!" Marna whispered. She was uncertain how to react. *So we become Legend.* To quell the sadness rising in her chest, she replied sharply, "That is not quite how it happened."

"A dramatic rendering, Mother." The young King flicked the edge of his onyx plate.

From his slightly wounded countenance, she ascertained that he meant well. Inflating her cheeks, she groused affably, "I ask you, who would ever believe a girl that thin could cook?"

Damina giggled, bringing her delicate fingers to her mouth so quickly she nearly knocked over a carved amethyst chalice. Dalich smiled at his mother's jest, gray eyes mirthful above his bride's black hair.

Marna laughed, and in her ease, her gaze wandered to the candles before her, bright in their polished holders. A feeling of foreboding crept into her awareness. Her eyes drifted to her daighter's thin hips and slight frame, and cold fear rose in her chest that the young woman would not survive childbed, leaving Dalich to fall into misery and sorrow. She must do something.

Her son placed a hand around his bride's slim waist as she bent toward him for a kiss. "So wonderful to see them happy," Marna breathed, hoping to dispel her worry that The Powers would not protect her daighter. The candles flickered, as though someone passed by in haste, and the voice of the woman who had appeared to her long ago in Dalock's chamber said in her mind:

> *Doubt will come by flame*
> *By candlelight*

King's Mother inhaled slowly, studying the room, spying Favik on the opposite end. He was just raising a finger to his cheek in the manner of the Havadrans as he gazed intently at her. She met her man's gray eyes. Favik lowered his hand, cutting his eyes to her side. Marna turned slightly to find Saralya speaking with Palika, Chief Scriptor. Saralya's back was to her young daughter sitting beside her. And there, in the air, floating before Jinilya, was a small flame, like a lit candlewick independent of its wax shaft. The girl's green eyes glimmered with intense curiosity; she brought her face closer to the flame as though it beckoned to her. Then Jinilya backed away, a look of angry determination crossing her face. Reaching with her fingers, she pinched the flame dark, and Marna knew.

Jinilya. She is key to our protection.

1 **Heedlich King**   *Queen*: **Said to be a Power**
Colors: Red and White

2 **Heedlock King**   *Queen*: **Maarva**
Colors: Red And Yellow

3 **Heedalich King**
Colors: Gray and Red

4 **Haadlock King**
Colors: Brown and Red

5 **Haadlich King**   *Queen*: **Braanya**
Colors: Blue and Red

6 **Heenlich King**
Colors: Green and Red

7 **Heenlock King**
Colors: Black and Red

8 **Breenlock King**
Colors: Black and Silver

9 **Breenlich King**
Colors: Gold and Silver

10 **Baanlich King**
Colors: Purple and Silver

11 **Baanlock King**
Colors: Green and White

12 **Taanlock King**
Colors: Blue and Yellow

13 **Taanlich King**
Colors: Green and Yellow

14 **Praanlich King**
Colors: Green and White

15 **Praanlock King**
Colors: Gold and Orange

16 **Daavlock King**
Colors: Blue and Gold

17 **Daavlich King**
Colors: Green and Silver

18 **Saavlich King**
Colors: Green and Orange

19 **Saavlock King**
Colors: Yellow and Black

20 **Taamlock King**
Colors: Gold and Gray

21 **Taamlich King**
Colors: Blue and Gray

22 **Taaylich King**
Colors: Blue and White

23 **Taaylock King**
Colors: Brown and Green

24 **Steevlock King**
Colors: Purple and Green

25 **Steevlich King**
Colors: Orange and Red

26 **Keelich King**
Colors: Black and Yellow

27 **Keelock King**
Colors: Gold and Brown

28 **Kaanlock King**
Colors: Silver and Orange

29 **Kaanlich King**
Colors: Red and Silver

30 **Raamlich King**
Colors: Blue and Black

31 **Raamlock King**
Colors: Red and Yellow

32 **Aarklock King**
Colors: Blue and Gold

33 **Aarlich King**
Colors: Black and Blue

34 **Aavlich King**
Colors: Green and Yellow

35 **Aavlock King**
Colors: Green and Red

36 **Maamlock King**
Colors: Black and Red

37 **Maamlich King**
Colors: Blue and Gray

38 **Paarlich King**
Colors: Blue and White

39 **Paarlock King**
Colors: Orange and Red

40 **Aamlock King**
Colors: Green and Purple

41 **Aamlich King**
Colors: Silver and Green

42 **Plaanlich King**
Colors: Yellow and Gray

43 **Plaanlock King**
Colors: Black and Yellow

44 **Maarlock King**
Colors: Red and Silver

45 **Maarlich King**
Colors: Yellow and White

46 **Faanlich King**
Colors: Blue and Brown

47 **Faanlock King**
Colors: Brown and Red

48 **Kaarlich King**
Colors: Black and White

49 **Kaarlock King**
Colors: Blue and Orange

50 **Hoolock King**
Colors: Green and White

51 **Hoolich King**
Colors: Blue and Purple

52 **Taablich King**
Colors: Green and Red

53 **Taablock King**
Colors: Gold and Red

54 **Slaalock King**
Colors: Orange and Red

55 **Slaalich King**
Colors: Black and Green

56 **Aaplich King**
Colors: Brown and White

57 **Aaplock King**
Colors: Purple and Red

58 **Haanlock King**
Colors: Red and Rose

59 **Haanlich King**
Colors: Brown and Orange

60 **Kaastlich King**
Colors: Silver and White

61 **Kaastlock King**
Colors: Blue and Orange

62 **Keernlock King**
Colors: Black and Silver

63 **Keernlich King**
Colors: Red and Yellow

64 **Kaarnlich King**
Colors: Blue and Red

65 **Kaarnlock King**
Colors: Orange and White

66 **Haaydlock King**
Colors: Black and Orange

67 **Haaydlich King**
Colors: Blue and violet

68 **Meedlich King**
Colors: Blue and Orange

69 **Meedlock King**
Colors: Gray and Orange

70 **Aablock King**
Colors: Black and White

71 **Aablich King**
Colors: Yellow and Green

72 **Laaylich King**
Colors: Blue and Brown

73 **Laaylock King**
Colors: Black and Silver

74 **Vaalock King**
Colors: Purple and Red

75 **Vaalich King** *Queen*: **Anya**
Colors: Brown and Red

76 **Aadlich King**
Colors: Green and Orange

77 **Aadlock King**
Colors: Green and Red

78 **Seerlock King**
Colors: Gray and Red

79 **Seerlich King** *Queen*: **Maayla**
Colors: Brown and Blue

80 **Saanlich King**
Colors: Blue and Red

81 **Saanlock King**
Colors: Green and Gray

82 **Maavlock King**
Colors: Blue and White

83 **Maavlich King**
Colors: Gray and Red

84 **Daylich King**
Colors: Brown and Gray

85 **Daylock King**
Colors: Blue and Black

86 **Kraalock King**
Colors: Green and White

87 **Kraalich King**
Colors: Brown and White

88 **Maaylock King**
Colors: Black and Silver

89 **Maaylich King**
Colors: Blue and Red

90 **Stelich King**
Colors: Blue and Brown

91 **Stelock King**
Colors: Blue and Brown

92 **Husklock King**
Colors: Blue and Gold

93 **Husklich King**
Colors: Purple and Gold

94 **Haavlich King**
Colors: Black and Orange

95 Haavlock King   *Queen*: **Dayna**
Colors: Brown and Red

96 Kilock King
Colors: Black and Brown

97 Kilich King
Colors: Silver and Gold

98 Kerlich King
Colors: Blue and White

99 Kerlock King
Colors: Red and Yellow

100 Kamlock King
Colors: Brown and Green

101 Kamlich King
Colors: Blue and Orange

102 Karlich King   *Queen*: **Treeva**
Colors: Green and Yellow

103 Karlock King   *Queen*: **Faya**
Colors: Purple and Blue

104 Kalock King   *Queen*: **Tiya**
Colors: Green and Yellow

105 Kalich King   *Queen*: **Kayna**
Colors: Green and Red

106 Salich King
Colors: Blue and Red

107 Salock King
Colors: Green and White

108 Mavlock King
Colors: Blue and Orange

109 Mavlich King
Colors: Blue and Gold

110 Trelich King   *Queen*: **Deke of
Guerland**
Colors: Orange and Red
Emblem: Tree and two conjoined
leaves

111 Trelock King   *Queen*: **Karel of
Salmand**
Colors: Gold and Red

112 Tremlock King
Colors: Black and Red

113 Tremlich King
Colors: Green and White

114 Narmlich King
Colors: Green and Purple

115 Narmlock King
Colors: Brown and Yellow

116 Palock King   *Queen*: **Bravna**
Colors: Green and Orange

117 Palich King
Colors: Red and Yellow

118 Narlich King
Colors: Black and Green

119 Narlock King
Colors: Blue and Red

120 Merlock King
Colors: Blue and Red

121 Merlich King
Colors: Green and Purple

122 Farlich King   *Queen*: **Merva**
Colors: Gold and Green
Emblem: Gold beaker on green field

123 Farlock King   *Queen*: **Treya**
Colors: Black and Gold
Emblem: Black horse on gold field

Note: Eskalinders preceded by 🖋

Aknil, *a Goldsmith's son and lover of Lady Ala*

Ala, *Lady of the House of Wenil, Farlich King's Friend, daughter of Yadla*

Athla, *Lady of the House of Buloft, Mavlock King's Friend*

Avnil, *Page to Marna*

Baavnif, *born of Thislin, famous Eskalind Loremaster*

Bafnil, *Page to Dalock*

Benasa, *scroll merchant from Ghemif*

Dalich, *King's Son of Eskalind, sole child of Dalock and Marna*

Dalock, *King of Eskalind, husband of Marna, father of Dalich*

Damina, *daughter of Gamin*

Dara, *Lady of the House of Naymil, Merlich King's Friend*

Deenofts, *dye merchant of Havadra*

Durmil, *Wheelwright, lover of Pamina*

Edlaych, *a lord of Eastlant*

Edvain, *born of Mavold, Swordmaster in Eskalind*

Falya, *a Scribe-for-Hire*

Favik, *born of Hudiksland, Ambassador of Eskalind*

Fornil, *Page to Marna*

Gamin, *born of Eastlant, Innkeeper of the Lamorda Meadows Inn*

Grufmit, *king of Ghemif, brother of Mostaza*

Haril, *son of Gamin*

Havnil, *Ambassador of Eskalind*

Hornil, *Ambassador of Eskalind*

Humik, *king of Humiksland*

Jinil, *King's Second, husband of Saralya, father of Saril, Marnil, and Jinilya*

Jinilya, *daughter of Jinil and Saralya*

Kamkai, *soldier of Kaymif, formerly guard to the Kaymif king*

Kaya, *wife to Gamin, mother to Haril, Pamina, Yamina,, and Damina*

Kermon, *Merchant Master of Guerland, cousin of Saralya*

Kinakil, *Ambassador of Eskalind*

Kostaza, *princess of Kaymif, daughter of Mostaza and Koulai*

Koulai, *king of Kaymif*

Kursak, *king of Kursak*

Maknil, *Chief Scriptor of the Scriptorium at King's Halls*

Marna, *born of Hudiksland, Queen of Eskalind, wife of Dalock, mother of Dalich*

Marnil, *son of Jinil and Saralya*

Melande of Havadra, *daughter of Yirlofts*

Melkain, *healer of Mavold*

Moril, *Ambassador of Eskalind*

Mostaza, *born of Ghemif, queen of Kaymif, wife of Koulai, mother of Kostaza and Moulai*

Moulai, *prince of Kaymif, son of Mostaza and Koulai*

Nalya, *Lady and Acta Sua* of the House of Adril, Narlock King's Friend*

Narnik, *born of Hudiksland, First Sergeant of Eskalind, nephew of Marna, cousin of Dalich*

Onath, *scholar of Thislin*

Palika, *born of Hudiksland, Scriptor of Eskalind, niece of Marna, cousin of Dalich*

Pamina, *daughter of Gamin*

Planil, *Chief Records Keeper of King's Market*

Radil, *Lord and Acta Sua* of the House of Valip, Palich King's Friend*

Saralya, *Queen's Reader, wife of Jinil, mother of Saril, Marnil, and Jinilya*

Saril, *son of Jinil and Saralya*

Savsa, *Ambassador of Eskalind*

Sirish, *a colonel of Havadra*

Symeea, *maidservant to Nalya*

Synya, *Apprentice Librarian*

Trevil, *Dalock King's Guard, formerly Page to Dalock*

Varmil, *Soldier of Eskalind*

Voukai, *soldier serving Kostaza of Kaymif*

Werna, *midwife of Humiksland, sister of Marna, mother of Narnik and Palika*

Yadla, *Lady of the House of Wenil, Farlich King's Friend, mother of Ala*

Yamina, *daughter of Gamin*

Yirlofts, *general of Havadra, father of Melande*

***Acta Sua,** *title given to the eldest member of a noble house of Eskalind*

www.ingramcontent.com/pod-product-compliance
Lightning Source LLC
Chambersburg PA
CBHW071551110726
47908CB00007B/2066